PURPLE REIGN

Hanging Chads Book IV

Evan Clouse

Contents

This book is dedicated to every person who cares about our personal freedom. To every person who cares about our democracy. To every person who shuns the politics of hate and division. To every person who accepts and embraces others for who they are. Thank you for your voices. Thank you for your caring. Thank you for your kind hearts. I love you all.

Acknowledgments

I would like to thank every person who has supported me and understands just how important this work is to me. Thank you for reading. Thank you for your input. Thank you for caring. You know who you are.

PREFACE

It entered our world with a high-pitched demonic shriek on Christmas Day, 1963. Its anger was on full display as its tiny, emaciated looking and nearly translucent body writhed underneath the grotesque coating of red blood and puke green afterbirth. Its presence on this most majestic globe was blasphemous enough, but for It to have been born on the day of celebration of the birth of Jesus Christ was additional salt in the now wounded universe.

As Its high-pitched shrieks continued, a young nurse took It to another room to be cleansed. The nurse looked down and gave the vile infant a knowing smirk as she whisked it into the other room, Its mother lying on her blood-soaked sheets clinging to life after the thirteen hour laborious torture that resulted in its birth.

The nurse cleaned the gelatinous goo from the child, then immediately surveyed its scalp. Feverishly parting the brittle copper strands upon Its head, the nurse finally smiled, then cackled with glee. As a single tear fell upon the black birthmark in the shape of the sign of Vetis, the nurse spoke in a hushed yet rapturous voice.

"I have found her my lord, just as you had prognosticated. A new soldier for your army. A new soldier who will trick others into your ranks. The righteous. The holy. So many of them will fall under her spell and the spells of all the others that you are placing upon this earth. The weak-minded and naive will march for you, kill for you, and lift you to your glorious ascension to this world's most powerful throne. Only to find that they have been tricked and oppressed once again. And this time, their oppression will be much more cruel and will be at the hands of their perceived savior. And she shall give birth to another. Another who shall transcend mere sadistic trickery and use her powers to vanquish the holy upon her blood-soaked blades. She shall be your true champion on this earth, my lord. And I accept this most glorious responsibility of grooming both the mother and the daughter until you call for them.

"Oh, most glorious Vetis, The Tempter of the Holy, she will be one of your most loved and special ones. And I shall protect her so that she and her most powerful daughter will one day sit at your side in the glow of absolute victory over the virtuous." The nurse cackled one final time as the squirming, unholy form in her arms finally settled.

It was placed into the arms of her waiting mother. The mother's sweat covered face looked down upon the dark eyes of her daughter and a deep chill ran up her spine as It grimaced up at her then plunged itself into her engorged bosom, gluttonously feeding upon its mother's milk.

It was taken home and raised by doting parents who attempted to be as patient as they could with their temperamental and emotionally distant daughter. As It grew, It rarely played with other children unless there was something that It wanted. It delighted in manipulating other children and sometimes Its teachers into doing Its bidding whether that was taking another child's toy, milk carton or crayons. It especially enjoyed manipulating the boys in Its class into performing outrageously dangerous stunts on the playground equipment. It would watch in silence with a dry smile as an ambulance would take the suffering boy away with a broken arm, broken leg, or severe head injury. It would go over to the spot on the playground that the boy had been taken from, place Its bony fingers in the blood that lay on the ground and then lasciviously lick the blood from itself while cackling. This was Its amusement through the first grade until It began being homeschooled.

Its parents were quite aware that their daughter was not at all like other children. It was selfish. It was arrogant. It was controlling. It would admonish adults in a dry, nasally condescending tone that led its parents to lose a number of friends and become largely isolated from their family. The parents realized that It was their responsibility. But they had no true love for It for they knew in their souls that *It* was incapable of love for *them*.

Shortly after Its sixth birthday, Its mother gave birth once again, this time to a son. The parents were delighted as their newborn infant would coo and beam a smile up to them. By the age of four months, the ever-engaging child had learned to illicit laughter from the adults in the room by sticking his tongue out from the corner of his mouth while crossing his brilliant green eyes. It did not care for this. It did not care for Its brother's spirit. It did not care for how he monopolized Its parents' attention. It did not care for this interloper.

The parents were mindful to not leave It alone with their baby. It would look through Its blackened pupils at the perpetually happy and spirited newborn with its curly copper locks bouncing. It would ask to hold the child. It would always be rebuffed by Its parents. It was always denied the opportunity to mold Its younger brother. It was always denied the opportunity to injure Its younger brother. It needed to do something about this.

In late May 1970, It was invited to a first grade graduation party that was being hosted by the school nurse. Its parents beamed with joy as their daughter was expressing interest in going outside of the house and socializing for the first time. As It embarked upon Its three-block trek to the party, It looked back and waved Its skeletal fingers while giving a wry smile. As the parents watched the tight copper-bunned adorned head of their daughter retreating down the street, they thought that this may be the turning point for their daughter. This may be the turning point for their family. Their family could now come together and live as one. They were correct. Up to a point. Their true family had indeed come together. They re-entered their cozy home and took their places upon the sofa as their bubbly infant fed. They felt drowsy. They fell asleep. They had not detected the faint smell of natural gas that was emanating from the kitchen. The true family had indeed come together, but not in life. They had come together in unceremonious death.

It returned home to the brilliant strobes of emergency vehicles. It glared with anticipation as each body bag was retrieved from the home and placed into an awaiting hearse. It experienced a shiver of delight as a two-foot-long grey body bag was placed alongside that of his parents. It gave a dry smile and returned to the house that had hosted the graduation party.

It knocked on the door. The door was answered by the school nurse who was wearing a flowing, hooded crimson robe. Neither of them said a word as It entered Its new home with the sounds of ominous chanting coming from the basement. It was sat at the dining room table. It was handed a book. The cover of the book said, "Holy Bible". The opening page of the book said, "The Munich Manual of Demonic Magic."

Adoption papers would soon be signed. There would be no family custody battles over It. Nobody in Its family wanted anything to do with It. It would leave public school and become immersed in Its home-schooled studies. Of particular interest to It were studies in manipulation, coercion, and oppression of others' emotions. It excelled in its studies.

In 1984, It met a man. A man that was perfect for It. He was weak-minded, weak spirited and completely subservient to anyone that held the slightest indication of a spine. He was known as "Freddie the Fool." It and Its congregation would call him "Frederick". They began dating and he catered to Its every whim. He attended Its evangelical church. It would frequently speak privately to the pastor following services. The congregation vehemently preached their interpretation of the teachings of Jesus Christ. But the teachings were twisted and bastardized into vile testaments of hatred towards anyone who was different from themselves. Those that looked different, prayed differently, believed different or loved differently. The congregation was being groomed. Groomed into a false belief system that they were being oppressed. That *they* were the downtrodden. That they had divine dominion over the earth and all its creatures, including their fellow citizens. The congregation would swoon during every church service and swoon once again as they listened to more prominent servants of Vetis being broadcast through their radios and later through their televisions, computers, and phones. During each service, It would sit in between Frederick and Its adopted mother and smile wryly at the fire and brimstone pastor. The pastor and It would frequently lick their respective serpentine lips lasciviously.

It was introduced to Frederick's family. It did not care for them. It did not care for their care-free nature. Their unconditional love for one another. Their sense of fairness and justice. Their unwavering support for those that they loved. Their love and support of their community. Their fortitude. They were the antithesis to It. And they needed to be destroyed. But It inherently knew that It was incapable of their destruction by itself. It would need to bide Its time and await the great ascension of Vetis before she had the necessary forces to assure their destruction. It had to wait until the ascension of Its preordained daughter, for it would be one from their own family that would strike them down. It was assured of this by Its pastor and adopted mother.

Upon holding Its daughter for the first time, It knew instinctively that Its daughter was going to need her undying and brutal tutelage in order to fulfill her destiny. The daughter looked up into the cold, dead eyes of her mother and let out an anguished wail while refusing to feed from the mother's bosom.

It was faced with yet another barrier when Its husband told It that their daughter's extended family were planning on taking her away. He wasn't sure when or how, but he knew it. He impressed upon It the danger that his sisters and brother-in-law posed to them. He impressed upon her the advantages of using their lifestyle as an example to their daughter of everything that was wrong in the world. He impressed upon It the need to share custody in order to hold some sway over their daughter's development. The insipid fool was never aware of the demonic intentions that It had for Its daughter, but he instinctively knew that if they did not strike a deal then they would never see their daughter again. It reluctantly agreed to the conditions.

The nurse who was also Its adopted mother and the child's adopted grandmother entered the waiting room to survey the situation with the interloping family members. What she witnessed sent a sharp chill down her spine. As she stood there with a look of frozen horror, she peered into the determined eyes of the infant's uncle. He was holding the content, cooing, and blue blanketed infant in his massive arms. Their eyes locked in an intense stare. And he smiled at her. It was a twisted, maniacal smile that said, "Don't fuck with me". The nurse composed herself and quickly retreated to Its hospital room. What the nurse and It did not realize was that the infant's raven-haired aunt was standing outside of the door, listening. And she heard everything. And she conveyed that discussion to her adored husband who was continuing to bounce his most cherished bundle in his arms. There was a knowing glance between the husband and the wife.

Three evenings later, Frederick answered the door of their modest home. There was an eighteen inch by eighteen-inch package lying on the porch. The package was addressed to It. It opened the package with Its three-day-old's effervescent eyes looking up at her with infantile dread. It opened the note that said, "just in case you're thinking of backing out of our deal." She removed the crumpled newspaper at the top of the box to reveal the severed head of Its adopted mother which was frozen in an expression of pure terror. It stood silently for a moment, told the husband that It was a prank and took the box outside to the burn barrel. It lit a match. It now fully understood the forces that It was going up against. This was a battle that would wage past Its lifetime. This was a battle that would wage for eternity. It also knew that it either had to recruit Its daughter into Its abhorrent cause or...It had to destroy her.

Purple Reign

Hanging Chads Book IV

Evan Clouse

PROLOGUE

As her body convulsed and desperately gasped for life affirming oxygen, her soul was being encased. Her fading emerald eyes peered into those of a kind stranger who was clutching her hand, and she could feel the pools of blood enveloping her very essence. But not just the blood. The bone fragments. The cartilage. The intestines. The fallen appendages. And yes, the blood.

The blood of every 'Chad' that she had ever sent to hell. The blood of the murderers, rapists, wife beaters, gay bashers, pedophiles, tyrants, terrorists, and traitors. It was all slowly oozing and congealing around her soul.

She tried to remain there. She tried to focus on the earthly here and now. She heard the anguished cries of her beloved daughter. She heard the cackling of her former friend as she gloated about her murder. She then heard the dry, condescending and nasal voice of her despised mother, mimicking the outrageous glee of her former friend. She tried to find her ember. She dug as deeply into her soul as she could to tap into her rage. Her fury. Her sense of justice.

But she was too weak. Blood was pouring out of the fourteen bullet holes that had cut her down. Her heart was slowing. The weight of her past murderous acts was encasing her soul with their remains until it was entrapped by an unholy cocoon of gore. She stared blankly upward. Her brilliant effervescent eyes faded into a dull grey as she exhaled one final time and thought to herself *Erick, I'm coming home.*

She was lifted several feet into the air. She looked down upon her stiff body being held by the stranger and her adored Josie. She wept as she witnessed her sixteen-year-old daughter plead for her to stay. She briefly allowed herself a sly grin as she watched The Twins approach their maniacally insane mother, say something to her and unceremoniously snap her neck.

Then, a dark purple cloud emerged from her fallen former friend's body. It had deep red eyes that penetrated her very being. The cloud smiled then cackled insidiously just before it rushed her. Just before the evil apparition could reach her trembling form, a brilliant white and blue light cut it off and engaged it in a fierce battle. *My hero, my prince,* she thought to herself as the swirling manifestations collided with one another repeatedly until finally…they were both gone. They simply disappeared.

"Noooooo!" she cried out. "Erick! Come back! She isn't worth it! Come back to me!" She was lifted higher. Beyond the clouds. As she gazed at the brilliance of the universe, her mind raced with thoughts of betrayal and feelings of anguish, loss, and fear.

Her ascension stopped. She was enveloped in a bright, white light. She saw dark silhouettes coming toward her. She prepared herself for battle, *whatever the hell that looks like in* this *form,* she thought to herself. A hulking dark figure approached. His majestic white wings extended as his golden halo began glowing. He continued his lumbering approach as he said, "Well hello there Buttacup! Damn, I've missed you! Wanna go get some fuckin' ice cream?"

Chapter 70

Hello There

"Please, please stop…please…stop," Rosa Alvarez was saying over and over for the third night in a row as her convulsing, sleeping body lay on her sweat-soaked sheets. "Rosa…Rosa, wake up!" Gregory Davenport pleaded repeatedly as he gently shook his beloved wife's body. Rosa let in a deep gasp of oxygen. She opened her eyes and saw her love's panicked face. She wiped the sweat from her brow with the delicate palm of her hand and smiled up at him.

Gregory had seen his love smile at him many times in the years that they had been together. But never a smile like this. This was a smile of confidence. It was a smile of fortitude. It was a smile that conveyed a deep understanding. A deep knowledge.

"Baby," Rosa stated through her knowing grin, "call Josie. Tell her that I now know what we're going up against. Tell her that I know everything. And tell her to get out of her damned bed! The time for mourning and feeling sorry for ourselves is over. We must prepare for battle. Tell her that it's time to get the band back together again."

"Yes, you are quite accurate," Adam Peterson stated flatly as he and his twin brother peered into the bedroom. "Yes, quite accurate indeed. It is time for Josie to play some games. Oh, how we love to play games with Josie," his brother Aaron added. "Yes… quite accurate my dears," came Vai Denhart's chilled voice as she entered the room with her newly dyed jet-black hair with a single silver streak down one side cascading around her shoulders. "It is time. Thank you, Rosa. I know that this has been painful for you for the past three nights, but I just knew that if you focused on the evil energy that spewed out of Kristy's dead body that you could figure this out. We must know *exactly* what we're going up against in order to prepare ourselves for the battle. We know that it is bigger…*much* bigger…than just the evil spirit of Josie's grandmother seeking revenge. There's way more to it than that. And you have tapped into that energy and unlocked the puzzle. You guys make the call. We'll go get Lionnel and Josie and we'll meet at the Brooklyn house."

"What about the new ones, Vai?" Adam asked. "Yes, Vai," Aaron added. "What about the new ones? The one that held Aunt Maddy's hand as she was passing from us. And her friends. They were quite helpful in keeping others safe that day, Vai. I believe that they too can help us. We have seen it."

"I'll go get them," the twenty-year-old Alexa enthusiastically stated as she came bounding into the room wearing her pink footie pajamas and plopped upon the bed. "I know where they're staying. And they're connected to that Kaneko woman somehow. You know, that rich old Japanese lady that hangs around some-times? She took me shopping once for art supplies. She's *really* cool."

"Ok, great. We have a plan," Gregory agreed. "Now, would you people *please* get the fuck out of our bedroom so we can get ready? And stop lurking outside of our door! It's creepy as hell!"

Everyone in the room rose in reverence as the sixteen-year-old Josie entered. She was flanked by her closest confidants, Lionnel and Rod. The nineteen-year-old Lionnel was her true love. Her soulmate. She looked upon his handsome dark ebony face as they entered. And Rod was not only their resident introverted tech wizard but had been her frequent babysitter since her infancy. She chuckled to herself briefly as she recalled making him laugh as she would wear his pop-bottle glasses, stick her tongue out from one side of her mouth and cross her eyes while smiling.

Her bodyguards, Vai and The Twins entered immediately behind her. Vai had become the reserved and calculating embodiment of her Great-Aunt Blair. And The Twins were…the Twins. Their tall, pale twenty-four-year-old bodies covered, as always, by matching all-white suits. Their love for games, both the customary kind and the deadly kind had become addictive to her. She loved them as brothers, although she was not sure if they were capable of feeling that, or any, emotion themselves.

Josie's five-foot-four-and-a-half-inch petite frame was covered in a skintight faux-leather green catsuit of her own design. Her eyes were shielded by the curly copper strands that bowed down over her lowered youthful face. Her size six feet were adorned by green boots that had three-inch metal arrows protruding from them from every angle. The deadly heads of the projectiles created a strobe effect on the walls and ceiling as she entered the room.

This congregation was not sure whether this young woman was prepared for this challenge. Despite her brilliance, they were unsure that she possessed the same fortitude, tenacity, and killer instinct of their previous leader. Their leader who had just been gunned down three days prior. They just were not sure that Josie could fill her mother's figurative shoes.

There was an audible gasp from everyone in the room as their worries were alleviated. They saw Josie lift her head. They saw the same burning ember in her emerald green eyes that her mother had possessed. They saw compassion for the innocent mixed with a deadly determination against the bullying oppressors. In her eyes, the members of Vendetta Degli Oppressi, better known as Murder, Inc., saw their new leader. And they were immediately comforted by her presence.

Josie looked around the room that was now her domain. The room that she had been told had not changed in generations. The walls were papered in red velour, with gold accents. Multiple priceless paintings from some of the world's artistic masters adorned the walls. The furniture was all deep brown heavy oak with cushions that matched the walls. And there were portraits of all the previous leaders of this deadly organization. Despite his betrayals, the portrait of Detective Edmund Simmons was still in place, only now was being used as a dart board. She looked to the portrait immediately to its right and saw the ornery and beaming face of her mother. Her mischievous smile nearly outshining her penetrating green eyes. She then looked at the latest portrait which had just been hung. It was nearly identical to the previous portrait except the pretty face was several years younger and had curly hair. She wiped a slight tear from her eye as she looked upon her congregation.

There were all the members of the elite hit-man task force along with the various department heads of the organization. There was Sam sitting in her customized lethal wheelchair next to her beloved husband and dangerous sniper, Henri. His brawny dark brown arm was wrapped around her delicate caramel shoulders. A disinterested Jules was looking up at the ceiling next to her tattoo-adorned husband Jerry. Josie knew that her seeming disinterest was no more than an act to keep her from crying as her long, curly brown hair covered her eyes. Lucy's pretty, Laotian eyes were staring at Josie with intense anticipation as though she were a cobra ready to strike. *I really gotta keep a watch on her,* Josie thought to herself. *She can be so sweet. And she's so effective with her lethal potions and bombs, but man can she be unpredictable.* Josie looked at Lucy's girlfriend, Jennifer sitting at her side. Her blonde hair glistened as she whispered something to Lucy in her sweet British accent. *I gotta work with her girlfriend, Jennifer, on helping me with that. She can help me stabilize her.*

Josie forced a smile to ty to appear confident and said, "Thank you everyone. Thank you for your sentiments. Thank you for your love for my mother and my father. And thank you for your confidence in me. I know that I'm young, but I've been learning from my parents and from all of you for some time now. And, I have the greatest team assembled in the history of the world." She looked around the room once again at the reverentially mournful faces and let out a slight chuckle as she said, "man, would mom eat this shit up. She always loved attention. And she always found a way to get it. Of all the lethal characters in this room, she was the deadliest. But, together, we will succeed. We have every lethal character that we need right here. Thank you for embarking on this odyssey with me."

"Ummm…Josie," the ever-diplomatic Gregory interrupted. "We have a few others who wish to join us. We think that they can help. Alexa…Rosa…would you please show our new friends and allies in?"

"Sure!" the bubbly Alexa squealed as she bounced to the door with Rosa. The door opened and there was another gasp as Kaneko Kiaria came marching into the room with several people behind her. "Hiya, folks!" Kaneko exclaimed. "I'm so sorry that this isn't under better circumstances. I think I know several of you. I've been associated with this group for a number of years now, but for those of you who don't know me, well, I'm Kaneko Kiaria. My name in Japanese means Golden Child of Fortune and I'm…well…I'm just damned lucky. I never lose at anything. And I've been helping to bankroll this group for some time now. And these are my friends from New Orleans."

Kaneko grabbed a twenty-nine-year-old married couple by the shoulders and pushed them to the front. "This is Cliff West and his lovely wife Jessie. As many of you know, there are many women in the world who have evolved into having special powers. Special gifts. Mine is that I'm lucky. Your Rosa can connect with and manipulate any kind of energy. This young lady *here* is a Beholder. She can sense pure good. Or she can sense pure evil. Now, that pure evil makes her experience excruciating pain. But there is an incantation that she can recite that turns her intense pain into incredible physical strength. And, once she has used her strength to vanquish the evil, she returns to normal.

Cliff is…well…not really *special*, like all men. Sorry gents. It's just how we're evolving as a species. You might wanna get used to it if you wanna keep getting laid. Anyhow, Cliff is very athletic and strong and can be a formidable opponent in his own right. And he loves his Jessie. Whipped? Sure. But he loves her."

"Which brings me to *these* two lovely ladies," Kaneko stated as she thrust two twenty-five-year-old African American identical twins in front of the group. "This one is Rachel and this one is Kayla…or maybe…this one's Kayla and this one's…oh who cares. They used to be triplets, but they lost their sister Gwen in a battle. Anyway, they are trackers. If there's a dark soul out there that you're looking for, then these two can find them. Then you all can gang up on them and take their asses out. Oh, and they're pretty good with knives too, aren'tcha sweethearts?"

Kayla and Rachel looked at the pair of tall, pale twins standing behind Josie, licked their lips seductively and then squealed "Woooooooo!" at an impossibly high decibel.

"Ok, ok," Kaneko continued. "I don't know what *that* was all about, but whatever. Now, this next lady is Jamie." Kaneko wrapped her arms around the waste of a tall, slender ebony woman who was dressed in a form-fitting pants suit. "Now Jamie here was born James, but then blossomed into who she was *truly* born to be. A kick-ass broad! Although she *does* still have a little James…uh…hanging around, if you know what I mean and I think that you do."

"Now, this rather…um…largish black god here is Marcus. He's really good at…well…he's really good at supply acquisition. Yeah, *that's* it! He's really good at getting stuff that we need. Plus, he keeps *this one* here happy."

The final person stepped forward. The twenty-nine-year-old had a five-foot seven-inch full-figured caramel skinned body that was wrapped in a deep purple dress with hibiscus flowers adorning it. Her tight Rastafarian shoulder length braids tumbled on either side of her pretty face. She giggled slightly and gazed at the group through her bloodshot eyes before introducing herself.

"Hey, all. I'm Arima. Arima Azar. Nice to meet you. Say, do

any of you have any brownies? Y'know. The good kind? And how 'bout some 'tato chips? Man, I could go for a bag of those right now."

Kaneko gave Arima a slight pinch on her triceps and loudly cleared her throat before beginning once again. "Yes, this is our Arima. She's married to Marcus, and they came here on the invitation of Stellan and Paciano to celebrate their one-year anniversary. Since your horrible tragedy, I understand that Stellan and Paciano have been deployed back to the country estate to fortify it in case we need a refuge. But I digress. Marcus and Arima were married last Valentine's Day. Isn't that sweet? Anyway, she is *very* special. Well…when she's not baked. Arima can sense souls who have not been allowed to enter Enlightenment for one reason or another. And she can take those souls into her and help them finish their business so that they can move on. Or, for those who are undeserving, she can banish those evil souls into inanimate objects, then vanquish them forever by destroying the objects. Pretty cool, huh?"

Josie looked upon this new friend and felt a strange connection with her before saying pleadingly, "You can sense *souls*? You *can*? Is my *mother* here? Has she moved on? And my *father*? Can you find them? *Please*. I just need to know if they are okay. I just need to know if they are here with me. *Please!*"

Rosa stared at Arima suspiciously before Arima began stammering, "Ummm….well…you see…um…I think that I…" Arima ended her sentence as she heard a demanding voice from within her soul say, *not one fuckin' word Arima. Don't say a fuckin' thing. Not until I have found her father. Then, she can know. Hey! Can I take control over your body for a bit so I can have some 'tato chips too, hmmmmm?*

Chapter 71

Sabotage

"Um…ok Josie," Arima answered meekly. "I promise. I'll see what I can do. I'll…um…I promise that I'll find your mom, okay?"

"Yeah, thanks," Josie replied as she wiped a tear from her green eye and smiled. "I'm sorry to lay that shit on you. But thanks for any help you can give me. That you can give *us*. And welcome all of you. It's so weird that you guys met Stellan and Paciano and that they brought you to us. It's almost as though…as though…" Josie's thought trailed off for a moment as she shot a quick knowing glance over to a smirking Rosa. "It's almost as though they were used to summon you or something. But it doesn't matter. You're here now and we welcome you into our family. But we must make it official. Mom was a real stickler on making things official, so if you all would please join me at the desk."

Fuck yeah, I was, Arima heard an arrogant voice say in her soul. *She'd better not fuck this up, either.* Arima bellowed back internally, *Will you please be quiet? This shit's weird enough without you constantly interrupting. I'm trying to concentrate!* She was greeted with a snide response. *Yeah, yeah, yeah. What fuckin' ever. Just go sign the fuckin' book and let's move this shit along.*

Each member of the self-proclaimed *Seven Saints* approached the desk. Cliff was the first to be given the pen to sign his name in the register. Upon picking up the ink pen he inquired, "Um…do we need to sign in blood or something?" No," came Josie's bored response, "We're not a satanic cult. Just sign it in pen please." "Okay," Cliff responded, "But is there going to be some sort of an initiation or something?" "No," an increasingly annoyed Josie replied. "We're not a fraternity. Just your signature will do." "Okay…just askin'" Cliff replied as he grinned and signed the book emphatically large as though he were John Hancock signing the *Declaration of Independence*.

Kayla was next to sign the book followed in turn by Rachel, Jamie, Marcus, Arima and finally Jessie. The seven best friends and warriors were then ushered to a small table where Rod was sitting. Displayed in front of him were needles, syringes, and test tubes.

He took Cliff's arm and rubbed alcohol over a vein. His pasty face was inches away from Cliff's arm as he squinted through his pop bottle lenses and said in a dry staccato voice, "Um, this will just pinch a bit."

"Wait a minute!" Cliff yelled out. "What are you *doing*? Why do you need to take our blood? And are you even capable of doing this? Can you see?"

"Well," Rod began to answer before being cut off by Josie. "Yes, Rod is fully capable of doing this. He's done it a million times. And the reason that we need your blood is that we collect the DNA of every member of this organization. Just in case of…um… I don't know. Science or something."

"Oh, I know," Rod answered confidently. "This DNA holds a great deal of potential…I think. I have some theories. Now, please be still," Rod concluded before hearing Cliff yell out "Ow!"

As the blood began flowing into the tube, there was violent rustling in Jessie's backpack. She took the pink sequined backpack off, placed it on the floor and unzipped its upper compartment. Out of the opening came a cute little face with long grey fur and whiskers.

"Oh! A kitty!" Josie squealed in delight until the energetic feline jumped out of the bag and onto the table. The medical supplies were destroyed in an instant as the cat ferociously ripped the tube from Cliff's arm and began lapping up the spilled blood.

"Well, now I've got to start over," Rod stated flatly as he began cleaning up the mess.

"Sooooo," a shocked Josie began asking as she watched the cat ravenously licking up the blood, "what's the cat's name?"

"LucyFur," an embarrassed Jessie replied. "No shit, huh?" was all that Josie could utter.

Holy fuck! Arima heard her new soulmate say while laughing. *That cat's fuckin' nuts! Maybe it'll break Josie of her fuckin' stray animal fetish!*

The voice's hopes were immediately dashed as Josie went up the growling animal, gently picked her up and began cradling her in her arms. LucyFur immediately began purring and giving a giggling Josie blood stained "kisses" on her lips.

Once the blood samples were drawn, Josie resumed her place in the front of the room and said, "Okay, Rosa. You're up. What the hell are we dealing with here?"

Rosa stood in front of the group. She took a deep breath, opened her eyes, and began. "Okay everybody. This is going to be *really weird*, but just listen. I'm going to go through this step by step. There's a demon named Vetis. He is known as The Tempter of the Holy and he has a plan for overtaking the Earth and then Enlightenment afterwards. Enlightenment is where the souls of the deceased go after they…y'know…are no longer here. If they can. Good souls who have no further work to do go to Enlightenment and live in bliss for eternity. Good souls who still have work to do on the Earth or are taken before their time remain here and wait for someone like…well…Arima to help them complete their business so that they can then move on. Then, there are the dark souls. Souls that are pure evil and will never get into Enlightenment, so they are trapped here until they are destroyed by someone like…well…Arima again.

"Vetis has a two-stage plan that he has been cultivating for centuries. The first stage is to use inherently evil and usually charismatic dullards on the Earth to convert the holy into the unholy. His minions seek out self-absorbed followers and use their patriotic and religious beliefs against them. They twist their genuine beliefs into hating others that are not like themselves. They use their religious and political sermons to intensify this hate until they do not view the other people as people anymore. They are viewed as less than human and are viewed as a threat. This then causes these followers to become violent. They oppress the others. They beat them. Rape them. Murder them. And, once they have been indoctrinated into this cult to that level, their souls have become dark. Pitch black, in fact. There is no longer any redemption for them. These human dark souls are trying to sabotage the world's great democracies and turn them into brutal dictatorships that would be led by evil-doers that Vetis handpicks himself. This is what has been happening in *our* country for the past twenty-four years. That is who the fascist militias are. They are the brainwashed cult servants of Vetis."

"Uh…we kinda already know all of this," Arima whispered to her Marcus. "I mean, where the hell have *these* guys been? They've been battling these forces and didn't even know who they were *truly* fighting? Really?" "Shhhhh," Marcus whispered back. "This is for people who didn't read the last book. Just be quiet."

"Okay, everybody still with me?" Rosa inquired to the group who silently nodded in a bewildered response. "Good. Okay, so if Vetis is successful, he will then come to Earth and lord over a population of his created dark souls and the people oppressed by the dark souls. Then, once the dark souls pass away here on Earth, they will all congregate. For generations, Vetis has been collecting these dark souls. He is building an army. And once he has amassed enough dark souls, he intends to wage war against Enlightenment. He will wage war against the peaceful, good souls who exist there. His army will destroy them. He will then rule Enlightenment as well and then…well…the game is over. He will control both the Earth and the heavens and there will be no hope for resisting him. Ever. For all of eternity.

"Now, there are two dark souls in particular who are very powerful and in league with one another. One is Josie's grandmother. She is the one who took over the body of Alexa, Adam and Aaron's mother and used her to…um…y'know. She's the one that killed our Maddy. And Erick the year before. We need to find her. The last we saw of her was three days ago at the murder scene. There was a brilliant flash of blue light that seemed to be battling her then they both disappeared. We need to find them. Then, we need to destroy Josie's grandmother."

Yes, we do, the voice said to Arima's soul. *That blue light was my Erick. He fought her to keep her away from our Josie. And then, they just disappeared. We have to find them Arima. If we find my bitch of a mother, we will find Erick.*

"Yes, we do," Adam stated flatly followed by Aaron's, "Yes. We must destroy her. We have seen it, Rosa. We have seen what will happen if we fail. It was so sad that we had to kill our birth mother, but she had become dark. There was no other option. It was the first step toward the destruction of Josie's grandmother. Oh, how I will enjoy playing games with her." "In due time, my friends," came Vai's calm response to her adopted brothers. "In due time. You have seen Josie's ascension to this position. And you have seen the great battle that lies before us. What you have been unable to see is the end result of that battle. That, my brothers, is what we will be writing from this point forward. This is now *our* story to tell. It is now *our* responsibility to protect democracy. To protect humanity. To protect decency. And, at this moment, no one knows how it will turn out."

"Thank you, boys…Vai," Rosa replied. "Now, there is another. As I connected to the energy that was generated by Josie's grandmother, I had a vision of another. He is just as evil. Just as sadistic. And just as powerful. He is known as the Pastor and…"

A giggling Arima then interrupted. "The *Pastor*? Oh, you don't have to worry about him. He's actually…um…ah shit. I hate to say this, but he's my father…y'know…biologically speaking. Anyway,

I killed him and the spirits of my mother and grandmother, who I call "Grams," well…they took his dark soul away and they have him locked up in like spirit prison or something. So, it's cool on that front. That dick's been taken care of and is out of the picture."

"Thank you, Arima," Rosa sincerely replied. "But I fear you may be mistaken. As long as his soul still exists, there is always the risk that he will be reunited with Josie's grandmother. I saw them together when they were living. I have seen them create… well…I think that we don't need to go into *that* now."

Go into what? The voice in Arima's soul screamed out. *Ask her Arima! Ask her what the fuck she is talking about. I know that she's talking about my bitch mother and I'm guessing that your father is also the fuckin' douche preacher of my mother's church who wanted to molest me and shit when I was a teenager! But my Uncle Joe took care of that fucker. Beat him to a fuckin' pulp then snapped all of his fingers, heh, heh, heh. Man, Uncle Joe is so cool.*

Snapped his fingers? Arima silently inquired to her new soul mate. *Huh. I think that maybe I've met your uncle Joe.*

"So, that's it," Rosa began again in conclusion. "The key to winning this war both here and in Enlightenment is to find and destroy both the Pastor and Josie's grandmother. If we can do that, then the rest of Vetis's forces will be easier to eliminate. So, Josie. What's the plan?"

Hey. Watch this shit, the voice said to Arima's soul. *Watch what my little genius comes up with.*

Josie sat in bewilderment as she listened to Rosa's presentation. Once she had accepted that what Rosa was saying was true, her mind went from bewilderment to planning. She sat in silence for a few more moments as her 153 IQ brain absorbed and sorted through all the information. She then sprang to her feet and took her place at the front of the room.

"Okay, gang! First off, if there is anyone here that doesn't want to participate in this, then now is the time to excuse yourself. I understand that this is dangerous, and I understand that you all have loved ones. So, it's alright if you want out. You will not be judged."

The entire room burst into laughter as one of the lead hit-men said, "Aw, shit Josie. We were built for this. You're not gonna keep us from having some more fun against these fascist pricks and evil demons and shit. We're here. We're with you."

"And don't worry about losing any revenue folks!" Kaneko blurted out. "Just focus on *this* shit and I'll bankroll ya. If we run low, just get me to a casino. I'll take care of ya! You bitches are running with Kaneko!"

"Well, alrighty then!" Josie responded cheerfully. "Ok, then here's my plan!"

Josie then began reading from a notebook that she had furiously been scribbling on throughout Rosa's speech.

JOSIE PARKER'S PLAN TO SAVE THE EARTH AND ENLIGHTENMENT

BY JOSIE PARKER

"Numero-Uno: We find my parents. I think that's the key. If we find them, then I think that we will find my bitch grandmother. So, here's the team in charge of that.

"Jessie- You are a Beholder and can sense pure good or evil spirits.

"Rosa- You are able to tap into energy sources.

"Rachel and Kayla- you two are trackers and can home in on them once their general location is found.

"Rod- You are a genius and can find a way to amplify their powers, just as you did when the entire Coven took down the wireless internet."

"Wait! You did *what?*" a furious Jessie exploded. "It was *you* bitches that did that? *You* are responsible for me losing all my followers, all of my likes, all of my..."

Her sentence was cut off as Cliff put his arm around his beloved wife's shoulder and said, "And we have all agreed that the world is a better place for it. Right, honey?"

"Ok, sorry about that," Josie continued. "Kind of a sore subject, I guess."

I'll say it's a fuckin' sore subject! The voice roared in Arima's soul. *Because of these fuckers karaoke sucked! And I couldn't shop online anymore! And I lost all my followers too! Yeah, sure, the radical right-wing propogandists lost an important tool for spreading their cult bullshit and kids' suicide rates went way down because they weren't trying to live up to these fake expectations of them or be bullied on-line. And yeah, there weren't nearly as many online predators or scammers. But still, it fuckin' sucked for me!*

"Would you please just *shut up!*" Arima yelled out.

"Um...excuse me?" Josie inquired as The Twins straightened their spines and glared at Arima.

"Oh...*heh, heh, heh*...not *you*," Arima attempted to backpedal. "No, not *you*. I was talking to...um...Jessie. Yeah, *that's* it! Jessie, please just shut up about it, okay? Sorry for the interruption Josie. Please continue." *Nice fuckin' save. Now don't you ever tell me to shut up again,* the voice stated sternly. *Yeah, whatever,* was Arima's disinterested, silent response.

"Okeedokeethen," Josie began again cautiously. "Now back to my plan. So, we have Jessie, Rosa, Rachel, Kayla, Rod and finally...

Arima- Once the souls are found, you can absorb them. You can help me communicate with my parents. They will help us find my bitch grandmother and The Pastor. Then, you can absorb them, place them into an inanimate object and...destroy them. Once and for all.

Numero-Two-O: We will have teams who will work with our international syndicate of hit men to continue our earthly battle against CHARLIE and the rest of the Underground Autocratic Movement. We will take out their foot soldiers, yes. But the focus needs to be the *truly* evil souls who hold positions of influence in the world and who are in direct line with Vetis. We need to focus on the propogandists. The business leaders. The political leaders. The religious leaders. We chop the head off of each snake then either destroy their minions or watch them go slithering back into their holes. Either way, we win.

Here are the teams. Each of you will be leading a team of ten hitmen. Oh, and women. We *finally* have a few of those. It is 2040, after all:

Lucy and Sam will focus on the political leaders.

Jules and Jerry will focus on the business leaders.

Henri and Jamie will focus on the religious leaders.

And Lionnel, Vai, The Twins, Alexa and I will focus on the propogandists. We won't need any of the hitmen. We can take these bastards out ourselves.

The rest of Rosa's *Coven* will be responsible for holding down the fort here and looking after our pets and loved ones while we're off on missions. And finally, Jennifer. You will be responsible for coordinating transportation and flying everybody around the world.

Numero-Three-O: Gregory, Marcus and Cliff will go around the world and try to convince the good souls who have influence that this shit is real. Convince them that this is about more than democracy versus dictatorial fascism. Convince them that this is a battle that is an existential threat to humanity here and in the heavens for all of eternity. Convince them so that they will join us. Or at least stay out of our way.

Numero-Four-O: We all get back together, and we *all* fuck up these motherfuckin' douchebag evil spirits once and for all and save Enlightenment. Then, we're going to LOHAD and party like the world is going to end. Because it almost did."

Oooooh, this sounds fun, a male soul's voice was heard by Arima. *I will be invited to play as well, won't I, Arima? And the others?*

Who the fuck are you? *Where did* you *come from?* The female spirit's voice shouted out. *Get the fuck out of here! And watch your fuckin' ghostly hands! Arima, get this fuckin' creep out of here!*

Yeah Howard, an embarrassed Arima answered silently. *I'll pray for you and the others when I need you. Just go now, okay?*

The male's soul departed, and the female spirit said angrily, *well,* that *was fuckin' rude! Didn't even knock. And do you know what he whispered to me before he left? He asked if I was into pegging! What...the...fuck, Arima! And I'm a married spirit. But even if I weren't, I still wouldn't be into* that *weird shit...I don't think. I mean, maybe a little bondage and shit but...nope. Too fucked up for me.*

The entire group applauded as Josie finished. They raised their glasses and proclaimed, "Strength in numbers and long live Vendetta Degli Oppressi!"

As hands were being shaken and hugs were being exchanged a giggling Rachel and Kayla came bouncing up to Adam and Aaron and said flirtatiously, "So, do you fellas wanna get a drink or... maybe play a *game* with us?"

"Oh, we love playing games," Adam answered with a stoic enthusiasm. "Oh, my yes," Aaron added. "We love games, in fact. We are always looking for new people to play our games with."

Kayla and Rachel looked at each other, smiled broadly and yelled out "Wooooooo!"

Chapter 72

Let's Get Together

"So, fellas, what's your *favorite* game to play?" Kayla asked flirtatiously as her twin sister Rachel licked her lips.

"Well, we do enjoy operation," came Adam's response followed by Aaron's, "Oh, yes. Operation is perhaps our favorite game to play. In fact, we are in the middle of a game right now. Would you like to play with us?"

"Sure would," a slightly confused but intrigued Rachel purred.

"Josie, Vai," Adam announced to his friends. "May we go and play a game with our new friends?" "Yes, they seem quite nice," Aaron added.

"Uh…yeah…okay," Vai answered with a hint of suspicion. "But just play *normal* games with them, okay? Nothing too…um…just play something *normal*."

As the quartet made their way down the creaking basement stairs of LOHAD, Rachel asked cautiously, "So, hey guys. Where exactly are you taking us?"

"Yeah, that's a good question," Kayla whispered into her sister's ear. "This is getting kinda creepy. Maybe we should rethink this."

"Oh, this is the basement of LOHAD," Adam began explaining.

"Yes," Aaron added. "LOHAD stands for Land of Hope and Dreams, and it was a nightclub that was owned by Josie's Great-Aunt Patty and her wife. It was to be a place for peace. But there was a terrible massacre here and everyone was gunned down by very bad men. Josie has restored it and it is now a…what does she call it again, brother?"

"She calls it a cool hangout for the kids," Adam answered. "It is to be a place where kids can eat dinner and listen to music and talk with one another in peace. There is to be no trouble at LOHAD. We are here to see to it."

"Yes," Aaron began again. "We oversee the security when Josie is here. We have looked over Josie since her birth, along with Vai. And we shall do so for all time. We have seen it."

"Yes," Adam contributed. "And we are allowed to use the basement here to play our games. Just see our latest gameboard!"

Adam turned on the basement light switch and the overhead neon began humming. The lights flickered three times before finally casting an eerie off-white throughout the concrete basement that was adorned with brownish-red stained pictures of peace signs, smiley faces, and various psychedelic prints. Hanging from a bedroom door in the front of the basement, was also the back of a man's torso that had a perfect rendition of the New York skyline painted upon it.

Rachel and Kayla's eyes darted around the room rapidly as they attempted to orient themselves to their morbid surroundings. They then gasped when they saw what was lying on the large metal table. There was a large assortment of blood-soaked hammers, knives, saws, scalpels, and other weaponized medical tools. And there was a gurgling, paralyzed man who looked at them pleadingly through his tear-filled sunken eyes. He was cut open from his chest to his groin and his nazi-inked skin was pulled apart and fastened to the table, leaving his internal organs completely exposed.

What the fuck? Rachel mouthed to her sister whose brown eyes were as wide as saucers. They started to carefully walk backwards towards the stairs when Adam said, "In order to play this game you must wear this." "Yes," Aaron added. "This game tends to be a bit messy, and we wouldn't want to stain our white suits or your pretty black dresses."

Rachel and Kayla took the plastic hazard material suits, looked at them and immediately tossed them onto the red vinyl couch.

"We have a *better* idea," Kayla stated. "How about if we play this game...um...*naked?*"

"Oh! What a marvelous idea!" Adam exclaimed followed by Aaron's, "Yes! We have never played naked before. That way we can keep our suits clean and not have to buy so many plastic suits. We do go through so many plastic suits."

Rachel and Kayla began quivering slightly as they rapidly disrobed. Adam and Aaron removed their white suit coats, ties, and shirts. They then removed their shoes, socks, and slacks. They then removed their underpants.

Rachel and Kayla's eyes widened once again as a slight trail of drool dripped down their chins. They looked at each other, then looked back at the Twins, although *not* in their brilliant blue eyes. They smiled lasciviously before yelling out an unbridled "Wooooooooo!" at an impossibly high decibel.

"Okay, that was really hot," Rachel stated breathily as she leaned her blood-soaked naked body against the metal table that was now adorned with various bodily organs.

"Yeah, that was fun," the quivering Kayla answered softly as she wrapped the man's slimy intestines around her shoulders and neck like a demented boa.

"Okay, boys," Rachel stated tersely as she began regaining her composure. "*You* got to pick a game. Now it's *our* turn."

"Oh joy!" Adam exclaimed. "Yes!" Aaron added. "We are not yet done playing games! Oh, do tell us what game you would like to play next!"

"We want to play something that's called...hide the sausage," Kayla answered with a twisted little smile upon her brown lips.

"Oh, my. That does sound fun!" Adam answered enthusiastically followed by Aaron's, "Yes! Quite fun! We have never played that game before. But, we haven't any sausages."

"Oh, *yeah* you do. You've *definitely* got sausages," Rachel responded as she sauntered over to the corpse and lifted the man's limp phallus. "*This* is the sausage that you will hide. Well, not *this* one, but the one that you have on your…incredibly beautiful, pale, tall, skinny blood-spattered bodies. This is *your* game piece and…well…*this* is mine. Now, this is a game that is played one-on-one…um…*usually* so we need to split up. Kayla, why don't you take Aaron into that back room and teach *him* how to play. And I'll stay in here and play on the couch with Adam."

"Oh, *hell* yes!" Kayla yelled out as she grabbed Aaron's blood covered hand and began hastily leading him to the back room. There was a thick trail of blood and crimson footprints left behind their naked frames as the door was slammed shut.

Following a brief explanation, Adam kneeled in between Rachel's opened legs and said, "So, if I understand the rules correctly, I insert my game piece into your game piece like this, then I move back and forth and then…oh my. I'm sorry. I seem to have made a mess in your game piece. Does that mean I win the game?"

"Nope," a visibly frustrated Rachel stated bluntly. "Nope. You definitely did *not* win the game. The object of the game is to move back and forth for as long as you can *before* you make a mess."

"Oh, I believe I understand now," Adam replied gleefully. "Oh brother! I have lost the game! But we are going to play again!"

"Yes, me too!" Aaron's voice came through the thin drywall. "We are about to play again as well. Oh, this game is such fun. I do hope I win this time!"

Rachel's shaking body lay on the couch. The dried blood had turned into liquid once again as it dripped down her muscular ebony frame along with her sweat. Adam looked down upon her and said, "Did I win the game?"

"Yeah," the nearly hyperventilating Rachel replied. "Yeah…you *definitely* won the game. Yeah. You're *really good* at this game. And your game piece is…perfect. Yeah…you won."

"Oh joy!" Adam yelled out. "I won the game brother!"

"Yes!" Aaron replied with the same enthusiasm. "I did too! This game was such fun. We should play again sometime!"

"Oh…we will," Kayla's exhausted voice was heard from behind the wall. "We're *definitely* playing this game again."

Later that evening, the Twins returned to the Parker-Sommers residence that they shared with Josie, Lionnel, and Vai.

"What the hell are *you two* so happy about?" Josie inquired as she saw the broad smiles on Adam and Aaron's faces.

"Oh, we had such fun playing games with Kayla and Rachel!" Adam declared, followed by Aaron's, "Oh yes! They were such fun to play with."

"Uh, huh," a suspicious Vai interjected. "So…what game did you play with them?"

"Well, we played operation!" Adam stated followed by Aaron's, "Yes! We played operation with them. They are quite good at it."

"*Operation?*" Vai yelled out. "*Operation*? You were *supposed* to play something *normal* like cards or a board game or something. You played *operation* with them? Wait…are they still alive?"

"Well, of course they are alive, Vai," Adam answered followed by Aaron. "Yes, they are quite fun. And since we picked out the first game then they got to pick out the second game."

"Aw, shit. If those chicks were into operation, I can only imagine what the next game might be. What was the second game?" Josie inquired hesitantly as Ziggy and Stardust curled up on her lap and began purring. Lionnel entered the room with a curious look on his face as he took a bite of his hot dog.

"Well," Adam began. "They introduced us to a new game called 'Hide the Sausage.'" Aaron then added, "Yes! It is quite fun. We did not win at first but then we understood the rules better and then we won the second time we played. Kayla and Rachel said that we were very good at playing and that they enjoyed our game pieces."

Lionnel burst out laughing. Partially chewed pieces of hot dog and bun went flying across the room as he fought to clear his throat so that he could breathe.

"Wait!" Josie blurted out. "Did you two *fuck* those girls?"

"We don't believe so," a confused Adam replied followed by Aaron. "No, that is not a word that they used before, during or after the game. I do not believe that we played that game. And perhaps it is that we do not know exactly what that word means. Uncle Erick and Aunt Maddy used to use it quite often and in a variety of ways. And now you are using it much more often as well, Josie."

"Okay," a slightly relieved Josie replied. "Okay, good. If you had…y'know…done that…well… it's just best that you didn't. So, tell me what the rules of 'Hide the Sausage' are."

Lionnel ran up the stairs in a fit of laughter following an unnecessarily vivid description of the rules of the game and a blow by blow, as it were, of how the game had been played. Josie and Vai could only sit together on the couch while holding their shaking heads in their hands.

"And in order to win the game," Adam concluded, "you must do that with your game piece for as long as you can before you make a mess." "Yes!" Aaron added. "That is what we were told. Is that correct, Josie?"

"Yup," Josie answered in a bewildered tone as she stared directly up at the ceiling to avoid eye contact with the Twins. "Yup, they're right. That's how you win the game."

"But listen to me my dears," Vai interjected. "You must *never* play that game against someone's will. Do you understand? You may ask a woman to play that game, but if she says 'no', which is more likely than not, then you *do not* try to play that game with them ever again. That is a very personal game that *both* people must agree to play. And *do not* go showing off your…um…game pieces either! Women hate that! Do you understand?"

"Why, of course, Vai," Adam replied followed by Aaron. "Yes, we understand. We never force anyone to play games with us. Except for the bad men, but you said that we can play any game we like to with them. We would never play hide the sausage with a woman who did not wish to play with us. That would be rude."

"Okay," Josie replied. "They have a bit of a moral compass

when it comes to this. Good. It's a moral compass that's *twisted as fuck,* but still a moral compass. Listen. Let's continue this conversation later. Vai, we've got to get the next year's worth of assignments ready for the assassination groups. By my birthday next year, I want this planet to be *strewn* with the bodies of these evil, fascist fucks. Then Arima can destroy their dark souls for eternity. And I want to know where my parents are and that their souls are alright. C'mon, let's get to work."

CHAPTER 73

─────────

GHOSTS

"C'mon! It'll be funny!" Maddy urged her husband as he stood there looking at her in disbelief. "No…it won't," Erick tersely replied. "Our daughter has been through *enough* this past year and *now* you want to put on *sheets* and walk around making ghost sounds? It's *totally* fucked up! Besides, she's going to end up shooting me with an arrow!"

"Oh, who fucking cares? She can't kill us," Maddy replied dismissively. "Maybe not," Erick countered, "but *that* shit is *still* going to hurt. Let's just find a more…sensitive way to make our appearance to her, ok?" Erick could tell by the ornery look on his beloved wife's face that this was a debate that he had no hope of winning.

Ten minutes later, Josie woke up in her bed and shook Lionnel. "Hey! Baby! Wake up!" she implored as she witnessed two eerie, white shrouded figures at the foot of her bed moaning and saying in ghostly falsetto wails, *"They tooooold us to coooome here!"* *"Yeees, we were toooold to coooome here! We were toooold to coooome for Joooosie Paaaarker!"*

As Lionnel wiped the sleep from his eyes and his mind was

beginning to process the scene he heard his beloved girlfriend say, "Oh, fuck this!"

Josie grabbed her bow from beside the bed and launched an arrow into the taller of the "ghosts". "Ow!" He surprising yelled out. "Goddammit! I fucking *told* you that she'd do that!"

The smaller "ghost" was bent over laughing hysterically. "Oh, my fucking God! That was so fucking *funny*! Okay…I'm sorry. Are you alright baby?"

The taller ghost took off the sheet and Josie shrieked in surprise as she saw the animated body of her deceased father. "Yeah, I'll heal up. But it *hurts* like a motherfucker!"

Maddy took her sheet off and Josie shrieked once again. "What the fuck are you guys *doing* here? You're fucking *dead*!" She cried out in disbelief. "And why are you dressed like ghosts and scaring us?"

"Okay sweetie…a couple of things here," Maddy replied calmly. "Numero-Uno, it's fucking nice to see you too. Numero-Two-o, we thought it would be funny to scare you. And it fucking was. Numero-Three-O, your first question is a really good one and we'll circle back to that in a bit. It's kind of a long story. And, most importantly, Numero-Four-O…what's with the *fucking language*? We raised you *better* than to talk like that!"

"Mom!" Josie barked back. "No, you didn't! Neither *one* of you did! My first words were *fucking fascists*! You both talked like sailors for my entire fucking childhood!"

"Yeah, that's true, I guess," Maddy conceded. "Well, I have a simple explanation for that. I've always been fond of *seamen*. Hey, baby. Get it? I said *seamen* because it sounds like *semen*. You know like cum or jizz. Get it?"

Erick rolled his eyes at his beloved wife and replied in an exasperated tone, "Yeah…I get it. I got it the other *bajillion* times that I've heard that too! You *really* need some original material."

Maddy stood there with her arms folded while tapping her size six left foot and glaring at her husband from under her straight, auburn bangs with an annoyed expression. "Y'know? I *really* thought that you *dying* might lighten you up a little bit. That *maybe*, just *maybe* the universe would finally give you an appreciation for great humor. But nope. I guess I'm going to have to spend eternity with a fucking wet blanket!"

"Well," Erick responded as he looked at his wife from the corner of his eye with a mischievous grin. "Now that we have bodies and…*everything*…I know something that we could do to make *these* sheets wet."

"Oh…my…God…*gross!*" Josie cried out in embarrassment. "It's bad enough thinking about my *parents* having sex! It's even worse thinking of my *dead* parents having sex!"

"Sweetie," Erick began compassionately. "First of all, please don't think of us as dead. Think of us as…oh…I don't know… living impaired."

Maddy burst out laughing and chimed in. "Yeah! We're *living impaired* and we think it's really fucking *not cool* of you to stereotype us because of our non-living status! The living impaired have needs *too* and it's *really* fucked up of you to try to oppress us under your living human fascist regime!"

Lionnel laid in the bed with a bewildered face holding the covers tightly to his chin. He gulped hard as he watched Erick pull the arrow from his heart while staring right at him without blinking.

"So…. Lionnel," Erick began as he glared at the slightly trembling young man. "So, just how old *are* you now?"

"Dad!" Josie yelled out.

"Not right now sweetie," Erick replied with a determined softness in his voice. "I'm getting reacquainted with your Lionnel here. It's been such a long time. Now, Lionnel, please answer my question. How *old* are you?"

"Well, uh, sir," Lionnel answered with a quivering voice, "I-I'm nineteen."

"I see, I see," Erick calmly replied as he pushed the arrow through the palm of his left hand in a display of "manliness." Maddy rolled her eyes and placed her hand over her mouth to try to conceal her laughter at her love's obviously over-the-top display of testosterone.

"Dad! Stop it!" Josie yelled out again.

"Just a moment, sweetie," Erick replied softly to his beloved daughter without dropping his glare from Lionnel's flushed ebony face. "So, you are above the age of consent for certain... um...mature activities then, aren't you?"

"Uh, uh, yeah. Yeah, I am." Lionnel hastily replied.

"Yes, good for you, young man, good for you," Erick continued as he pulled the arrow from his hand and watched the wound heal before his eyes. He gave Lionnel a slight smile as he showed his healed palm to his young adversary. "And you must forgive me. My having been murdered seems to have affected my memory a bit. Please, could you remind me what the age of consent is in this state?"

Beads of sweat began pouring down Lionnel's forehead as he realized where this inquisition was going. "Uh...listen sir...I didn't...I mean...I wouldn't...like *ever*...unless..."

Lionnel was cut off by Erick's cold, calm voice. "Please, please young man. Just answer the question for me. What is the age of consent for such adult activities?"

"Dad, please," Josie began pleading. "C'mon. Just leave him alone."

"Yeah," Maddy interjected. "Leave the fuckin' kid alone. He hasn't done anything wrong."

Erick smiled first at his wife then at his daughter before saying, "Please ladies. This is a talk between Lionnel and me. This is a *man-to-man* talk, isn't it Lionnel? Because you are nineteen, and you are officially an adult. You are *officially* a man. Whereas my *daughter* just turned *seventeen* today. Why, that would make my daughter a child now wouldn't it. And I believe my memory is coming back. Yes. I believe the age of consent is *eighteen*. So, *that* means she has *one year left* before she reaches adulthood and the age of consent. Now, as you were trying to answer me, you said you wouldn't do something. Just what is it that you wouldn't do...Lionnel?"

"I...I would never..," Lionnel blurted out, "never, *ever* do anything like that unless Josie agreed to it. I swear! I wouldn't do *anything* that she didn't want to do!"

"I see," Erick responded coolly. "So, you are saying that my daughter *wants* to do this? Is *that* what you are saying? Are you saying that my daughter is a slut? Well, *are you*, Lionnel?"

"Ok, that's fuckin' it!" Josie yelled out as she bounced upon her knees on her mattress directly in front of her father. Her glaring emerald green eyes burned into the pupils of her father as she shouted, "Lionnel! Go change your shorts! I could tell that you just pissed yourself! And Dad, I may be seventeen, but I am now the head of an international freedom fighting hit man syndicate. Plus, it's not like I've had any parental guidance for the last year, so I think that I'm *completely capable* of making my *own* decisions about my *own* body and that includes when and with whom I have *sex!*"

"Oh my God! Gross!" Erick cried out. "Don't say it like that! Okay, okay. This conversation is over. You're right, of course. You are mature beyond your years. Always have been. I just wanted Lionnel to understand that I've got your back. That your dad is here to protect you, okay? Can we just drop it now and never, ever, *ever* talk about your personal life again, okay?"

Josie looked into the panicked eyes of her father. She looked over at her grinning mother. Tears began flowing from her green eyes as the weight of the moment finally hit her. "Oh…my…*God*! You are both *here*! You are *alive*!"

The entire *Family of Fury* embraced for the first time in two years. Their joyful sobbing was saturating their tops until the group burst into uncontrolled laughter after Maddy exclaimed, "That's right bitches! We're *aliiiiiiiiive*! MWAHAHAHA-HAAAAAAA!"

Lionnel emerged from the bathroom wearing a fresh set of clothes. He sheepishly looked at Erick who said, "Come here Lionnel. I'm sorry. I just tend to be a bit…um…overprotective of my Josie. I know that you love her and that you will treat her right. Please, join us. Please, join our family."

As the foursome descended the metal staircase that led to the living room, Maddy whispered to her husband, "Nice save, mister. I'm very proud of you right now."

They entered the living room and their mouths dropped as they looked upon the carnage that was on their couch.

A giggling Arima Azar and Marcus Jefferson were sitting on the couch passing a joint to each other. There was an empty pizza box on the floor that Ziggy and Stardust were eagerly eating discarded cheese and sausage from. Littering the coffee table were crumpled up cheeseburger wrappers, empty french fry containers and milk shake cups that were melting all over the rich mahogany table. The jovial pair were covered in crumbs, ranch dip, ketchup and what appeared to be the remnants of carrot sticks, for some unexplained reason.

"Arima! Marcus!" Josie yelled out. "What are *you* guys doing here?"

"Oh, yeah, hey Josie," Arima replied as her bloodshot eyes squinted the newly arrived family into focus. "Yeah, wow man, you have some great food places in this neighborhood. Pizza place. Burger place. Mini-mart. You people live like kings. And this pizza is like the best pizza in the history of the world, man."

"Yeah, yeah, yeah," a slightly annoyed Maddy retorted. "That's what you said about the pizza place *last* night. *And* the night before that. Jesus, you guys. You really should start watching your diets."

Marcus looked up at Maddy with a confused expression and said, "Why?" before he and Arima once again burst into laughter. "Yeah, that's a good question, baby," Arima replied through her chuckles. "Hey, pass me that bag of chips. These are the best 'tato chips in the history of the world, man."

"Okay," Josie replied coolly in an attempt to calm herself. "How about we all just have a seat. Lionnel and I have just a *few* little questions at this point. Y'know, questions like, oh I don't know…how is it that my *dead parents* are *alive* and walking around in bodies *younger* than when I knew them? *Where* have my parents *been* for the last year? If they *were* around, why did my parents not try to contact me? Y'know. Just little questions like that. I think that maybe we can discuss Arima and Marcus's diet at some *other* point. That really doesn't seem to be the *most* pressing issue at this moment. Okay?"

Arima then blurted out, "Hey, Josie. You forgot one. You forgot a question."

"Oh yeah?" a suspicious Josie countered as her copper curly locks hung just above her glimmering emerald eyes. "And just what might *that* be, Arima?"

Arima began chuckling as she answered, "Well, you might want to ask how it is that I'm your *aunt*!"

Chapter 74

Feeling Gravity's Pull

"Aw, fuck," Maddy stated under her breath before saying to the group, "okay, let's not lead with that. There's a whole lot of ground to cover before we get to that. Everybody, just take a seat and get comfortable. This is going to take a while and…Arima! Where the fuck are you going?"

"Well," Arima answered as she began floating toward the kitchen area of the home, "I thought I'd heat up some of this left over lasagna that I saw in the fridge. Or maybe I can just eat it cold. And…ooooooh, cold cuts. And cheese."

"Okay, whatevs," Maddy dismissively replied before adding, "but make me a gin and tonic while you're up. I haven't had one of those for over a year!"

"Oh yeah, me too!" Josie added. She then looked over at her father's disapproving face and said meekly, "I mean, maybe just bring me a soda, okay?"

"Yeah, sure man. I'm on it," Arima agreed.

"Okay gang," Maddy began. "This shit all started exactly one year ago on Josie's sixteenth birthday. You all know that I was gunned down by my former friend, Kristy who had been possessed by my evil cunt of a mother. You all saw me die. Josie was holding one hand and Arima, who I did not know at the time, was holding the other as I passed away. Now, for the part that you *don't* know from this past year. Once I died…"

———

As her body convulsed and desperately gasped for life affirming oxygen, her soul was being encased. Her fading emerald eyes peered into those of a kind stranger who was clutching her hand, and she could feel the pools of blood enveloping her very essence. But not just the blood. The bone fragments. The cartilage. The intestines. The fallen appendages. And yes, the blood.

The blood of every 'Chad' that she had ever sent to hell. The blood of the murderers, rapists, wife beaters, gay bashers, pedophiles, tyrants, terrorists, and traitors. It was all slowly oozing and congealing around her soul.

She tried to remain there. She tried to focus on the earthly here and now. She heard the anguished cries of her beloved daughter. She heard the cackling of her former friend as she gloated about her murder. She then heard the dry, condescending, and nasal voice of her despised mother, mimicking the outrageous glee of her former friend. She tried to find her ember. She dug as deeply into her soul as she could to tap into her rage. Her fury. Her sense of justice.

But she was too weak. Blood was pouring out of the fourteen bullet holes that had cut her down. Her heart was slowing. The weight of her past murderous acts was encasing her soul with their remains until it was entrapped by an unholy cocoon of gore. She stared blankly upward. Her brilliant effervescent eyes faded into a dull grey as she exhaled one final time and thought to herself *Erick, I'm coming home.*

She was lifted several feet into the air. She looked down upon her stiff body being held by the stranger and her adored Josie. She wept as she witnessed her sixteen-year-old daughter plead for her to stay. She briefly allowed herself a sly grin as she watched the Twins approach their maniacally insane mother, say something to her and unceremoniously snap her neck.

Then, a dark purple cloud emerged from her fallen former friend's body. It had deep red eyes that penetrated her very being. The cloud smiled then cackled insidiously just before it rushed her. Just before the evil apparition could reach her trembling form, a brilliant white and blue light cut it off and engaged it in a fierce battle. *My hero, my prince,* she thought to herself as the swirling manifestations collided with one another repeatedly until finally…they were both gone. They simply disappeared.

"Noooooo!" she cried out. "Erick! Come back! She isn't worth it! Come back to me!" She was lifted higher. Beyond the clouds. As she gazed at the brilliance of the universe, her mind raced with thoughts of betrayal and feelings of anguish, loss, and fear.

Her ascension stopped. She was enveloped in a bright, white light. She saw dark silhouettes coming toward her. She prepared herself for battle, *whatever the hell that looks like in* this *form*, she thought to herself. A hulking dark figure approached. His majestic white wings extended as his golden halo began glowing. He continued his lumbering approach as he said, "Well hello there Buttacup! Damn, I've missed you! Wanna go get some fuckin' ice cream?"

"U-u-uncle Joe!" Maddy exclaimed as she rushed into her beloved uncle's brawny arms. "Y-you're here! I am s-so happy to see you!"

"Yes, dear. We're all here," came the calm voice of her Aunt Blair. "Yeah, we are!" came the gruff, yet cracking voice of her Aunt Patty. "Now get your fuckin' ass over here and give us a hug!"

"Oh my God!" Maddy cried out as she was enveloped by the love of her spiritual family members. Her tears flowed onto their celestial white gowns and angel's wings as she sobbed uncontrollably. She sobbed out of the joy of being reunited with her beloved family. She sobbed out of the fear of realizing that she was no longer living on Earth. She sobbed out of worry for her adored husband's spirit who she knew was locked in an existential battle with her reviled mother. And she sobbed out of no longer being able to be with her cherished daughter and other earthly friends. She sobbed for what seemed like an eternity before composing herself, wiping her tears from her glowing green eyes and saying, "So, I guess I'm fuckin' dead, huh? I was so stupid. So arrogant. I didn't even check my surroundings. Fuck, man. *Now*, what do I do?"

"Well, dear," Blair's soothing voice surrounded her like a warm baby blanket. "Yes, you have passed away. And yes, you are here with us…for the moment. But it is much more complicated than that. There is a war that is being waged on the Earth. It is the same war that we all were engaged in. The war against the narcissistic fascists who are attempting to overthrow the world's democracies. But what we did not know until our passing was that *that* war was simply a prelude to an even larger battle. That once the Earth has been conquered, the war will come here. It will come to Enlightenment. All the dark souls that remain upon the Earth will be summoned here and they will engage us in battle. They will attempt to conquer us and turn the heavens black. As black as their demonic souls. Our work is far from over, my dear. *Your* work is far from over. Both *here* and upon the Earth."

What is your name spirit? Maddy heard a soft voice within her very essence.

"What? Who the fuck is that"? Maddy asked as she looked around for the source of the question.

"That, my darling," came the reply from Maddy's father, Freddie who had emerged from the white mist to join the reunion. "That, I am both happy and sad to say is the voice of your…half-sister."

"My, *what?*" What the fuck are you talking about Dad? Oh, and great to see you. I've missed you so much too!" Maddy yelled out. "I don't have a half-sister! I mean unless you…oh my God…Dad! Did you fuck some waitress or something? Oh, that would be classic! I mean, I'm not into the whole infidelity thing, but given who you were married to, who could blame you?"

"Yeah, it's not quite *that*, Mads," Patty chimed in as she rolled her spiritual eyes, "I once said that it would be impossible for my brother to jizz into that glacier that was your mother. And sadly, well, I was right."

Freddie began to weep as he continued meekly, "Yes. I would never have had the backbone to ever violate my marriage vows. No matter how justified I might have been. Your mother, on the other hand, did not have such…reservations. I did not know until my passing that your mother was a hand-picked demon upon the Earth. She was a servant of the demon, Vetis. And she was destined to consort with another servant of this demon. He was to sire a daughter. A very powerful daughter who would wage war and rule the Earth at his side. *He* is your true father. Your true, biological father is…the Pastor."

"*Whathefuckyousay!*" Maddy screamed out. Her ember began burning anew as she shrieked, "You mean that motherfuckin' *douchebag* pastor? He is my *father*? I mean…Jesus Christ! He tried to *molest* me! What type of sick fucks are we *dealing* with here?"

"The sickest, buttacup," Uncle Joe answered in a deepened voice. "The absolute worst. These are dark people and dark forces with dark souls, if you can call them that. They want what they want when they want it. And they have no regard for anyone other than themselves. They don't care about *who* they hurt or *how* they hurt them. As long as they achieve ultimate power. And that included you. He was going to *groom* you. He was going to *rape* you into submission. Then, you would battle by his side. But you were too strong for them. That is your special gift. All of the women of the world have a special gift. Rosa, being a prime example. It's just that many women have yet to evolve enough to be able to recognize it. Your special gift is your fortitude. Your special gift is your undying servitude towards justice. That is your…"

Please, spirit, tell me your name, came the voice again.

"Jesus! There she is again! Kind of a persistent bitch, isn't she?" Maddy declared.

Maddy turned back towards her family and said with tears

forming once again in her eyes, "So, this means that you guys... none of you...are my *real* family?"

"Aw fuck, Buttacup," Joe replied as he wiped a tear from his majestic eye. "Yes, we *are* your real family. Family isn't defined by some biological connection. Family is defined by the *love* that we hold for one another in our hearts. They say that blood is thicker than water. But do you know what's thicker than blood? *Ice cream!* C'mon, we still have a little bit of time before...well...we have a little bit of time. Let's go get some fuckin' ice cream!"

"Yeah, time's really fucked up, up here," Patty added. "What seems like a long time up here may be only a few minutes on Earth. And sometimes just a few minutes up here is like a whole year on Earth. It all depends. It all depends on our needs at the moment."

Maddy, Freddie, Blair, Patty, and Joe went into the mist arm in arm. The dense shroud lifted, and they found themselves in a perfect rendition of the Argento home in Madison.

"Oh my God!" Maddy cried out in disbelief. "It's *exactly* the same! The pictures! The furniture! And...and Rascal!" The small dog came running up to Maddy and began yipping and jumping until she picked him up and cradled him like a baby as he licked her overjoyed face.

"Yes," Blair began explaining. "We can create our own paradise up here. And our celestial paradise is the same as our Earthly one. This house. This home. Oh, and we have taken in Erick's cats, Hunky and Dory as well. Although, Rascal's spirit doesn't seem to care for them much."

Maddy burst out laughing as Hunky began waddling in behind his sister Dory. Joe entered the room with five bowls of the greatest butter ripple ice cream in the history of the world... er...universe and they silently began eating while looking reverentially at one another.

Please spirit, tell me your name, came the disembodied voice once again.

"Okay, this is starting to really piss me off," Maddy stated with an annoyed tone. "Hey! Bitch voice! Leave me the fuck alone! I'm trying to have some quality family time here!" She then looked at the smiling faces of her beloved family and said softly, "Yeah, quality time with my family. I don't care who fucked that bitch in order to create me. *This* is my family. You always have been, and you always will be. And Dad. You *are* my father. I know we didn't get much time together when we were…um…alive, I guess. But I am *so proud* to be your daughter."

"Th-thank you Madeline," Freddie replied through his choked-up voice. "A-and I am *most* proud to *have* you as my daughter. Now, and for always".

Maddy gave a slight chuckle as she wiped yet another tear from her shimmering green eye and said, "Okay, c'mon. Enough with the mushy shit. Now, what is this bullshit about a half-sister?"

What is your name spirit?

"Oh, for fuck sakes! Shut the fuck up bitch!" Maddy yelled out once again.

"Well dear," Blair began explaining, "Your demonic mother and father failed with you. So, the Pastor moved on to sire another. He moved to the New Orleans area and impregnated a young woman of Jamaican descent. Three days after the birth of his second daughter, he murdered her mother. He sliced her open on an altar in the swamp and placed her head on a spike. Your half-sister's grandmother is quite powerful in her own right as is the group of women that she belongs to. So, the Pastor decided to bide his time and wait until your half-sister realized her special gift. He then tried to bring her under his spell. There was a fierce battle, and her grandmother perished."

"Yeah," Joe added while chuckling deeply. "And I went back and snapped that motherfucker's fingers again. In fact, I do that *every fucking day*. Your half-sister's mother and grandmother have imprisoned him up here. We all take turns watching over him. He can only be released by his soul mate. And that, unfortunately is your cold-ass bitch of a mother. We don't know where she is. All we know is that she was locked in a battle with your Erick and then they disappeared. That's why you need to go back, Buttacup.

You have to use your friends on Earth to help you find Erick. Help him win that battle. Help him destroy her and the Pastor. They are the key to this whole thing. If they can be destroyed, then the Earth will be free to fight for their *own* freedom without the influence of demonic powers. And then Enlightenment will be safe once again as well. You have to go back now. You have work to do on the Earth before you join us. But you *will* join us."

"Yeah!" Patty yelled out excitedly. "And then we are gonna have a *fuckin' party*! Oh Mads! Just wait until you see the lineup that I'm putting together! It's gonna be a concert for the ages! We're talkin' Hendrix, Lennon, Holly, Prince, Joplin both Scott *and* Janis, Benny Goodman, Bon Scott, Lux Interior, Lou Reed oh…and Bowie! I got fuckin' *Bowie* to do "Life on Mars!" With fuckin' *Gershwin* accompanying him on piano! How fuckin' cool is *that* going to be?"

"But first, my dear sister," Blair interrupted. "There is much work to do. Maddy. I'm so sorry dear, but you must go now. You must join your half-sister and all of the others. You must join them in the battle for the Earth. And then, you will join us in the battle for Enlightenment. And then, my dearest Patty…then we can fuckin' party."

Please spirit, tell me your name.

"Ah, fuck. I really don't want to go. Please, can't I stay longer? I've missed you all so much. Please?" Maddy pleaded.

"No dear," Blair answered coolly. "You must go. Go to your daughter. And most importantly, go to your half-sister."

"Fine, fuck it, whatevs!" Maddy replied incredulously. "So, what is this bitches name anyway?"

"Her name, my darling daughter," Freddie answered, "is Arima."

What is your name spirit?

"Just hold the fuck on, *Arima* or *whoever* the fuck you are!" Maddy yelled out once again. "Arima, huh? That's a stupid fuckin' name, but whatevs. Okay, but before I go, I have to ask you guys something. So, you guys *really* have angel wings and halos and white robes and shit?"

Joseph began laughing out loud as he replied, "Nah. We just put this shit on to freak out the newbies. Your Aunt Patty nearly *shit* herself the first time she saw me!"

Maddy's spiritual form began descending. She looked up and saw the smiling faces of her loved ones disappear into the cosmos. She felt the full force of destiny's gravity as she fell through the clouds until she was hovering over a young woman wearing a purple coat. Her Rastafarian braids partially covered her brown pretty face. She wondered for a moment how it was that she was supposed to answer her.

Then, she felt another form of gravity. The young woman's soul was pulling her inside of her. Welcoming her. Maddy's soul became entwined with that of her host. Maddy felt a comforting warmth of familiarity, let out a deep sigh and said forcefully, *My name? My name's Maddy* fuckin' *Sommers! Who the fuck are* you, bitch?

Oh, hey, Arima replied. *Yeah, I'm Arima. It's like, really nice to meet you. Sorry it's not under better circumstances, but, hey, you wanna go with me to get baked? This has been a really screwed up day.*

Oh, you think it's been a screwed up day? Maddy roared back. *Really? Gee, I didn't notice. I've only been gunned down in the fuckin' street, went to something called Enlightenment and chatted with my dead fuckin' relatives and found out that I have a half-sister! Which is* you *by the way! Yeah, I think calling this a screwed-up day is kinda downplaying it a bit there, Arima!*

Yeah, I know. Really screwed up, huh? Arima casually replied. *So, how 'bout we get my husband and friends and get baked, then? Oh, and you're the one that's my half-sister. That's really cool. My Grams told me that I'd meet you someday, so...um...nice to meet you. And feel free to hang out with me as much as you want. I have plenty of room in my soul. Hey, do you want me to tell your daughter that you're...um... y'know...here with me?*

Maddy watched through Arima's eyes as her shocked and grieving daughter was being led away by Lionnel, Vai, and the Twins. She shook her spiritual head vigorously in order to clear it then said softly, *No. Not just yet. Not until I figure some shit out.*

She'll be okay. I need to find her father first. Then, I'll let her know that I'm...um...still around or some shit.

Yeah, ok, cool, totally understand, Arima hazily replied. *So, how 'bout that whole plan of getting baked and then maybe getting a little snack. Y'know, maybe some burgers. And fries. And donuts. And maybe a pizza. I'll even let you take over my body every other bite so you can enjoy it too. What do you say?*

An amazed Maddy replied, *Burgers? Fries? Donuts? Fuckin' pizza? That's your response to this shit? Well, if that's your response then mine is...fuck yeah! This whole dying thing has made me famished. C'mon! I know just the block to go to. Grab your friends and let's get busy! Y'know, maybe being joined with my sister's soul won't be so bad after all.*

Chapter 75

Hey You

Maddy was seated in Arima's body alongside Cliff, Jessie, Jamie, Marcus, Rachel, Kayla, and Kaneko in the furthest pew in Pastor Tim's church observing her own funeral service.

Hey! She screamed out at Arima's soul. *I can't see a fuckin' thing back here! Why don't we move up a few pews, hmmmm? Kick those bastards out five rows ahead of us. I barely even knew those fuckers. It was nice of them to show up though.*

Maddy, Arima responded. *We are pretty much strangers here. They don't know us very well yet. The only reason why we were invited was because we know Stellan and Paciano. Please just be quiet and enjoy, um, I mean, y'know...just watch the service, okay?*

Yeah, fuck whatever, Maddy barked back. Her heart then sank as she watched her beautiful sixteen-year-old daughter climb the steps and take her place behind the pulpit. As her beloved daughter began to speak, Arima could feel the overwhelming anguish that her half-sister was experiencing. She could feel her pain. She could feel her loss. She could feel Maddy's desire to rush to the front of the church and embrace her daughter. She could also feel Maddy realize that that would be an unwise move at this heavily armed gathering.

Just be cool, okay? Arima advised. The only response that she received were the sobs of a grief-stricken spirit.

"Well," Josie began with a forced chuckle, "Mom was the one who was good with a joke, so I'm not even going to try. Oh, who am I kidding? We were both just horrible at jokes, and Dad was always quick to point that out to us. Then Mom would say something like, 'Why aren't you laughing, mister? That was pure gold!' And my dad would just roll his eyes at her. And then they would hug and laugh."

Maddy stopped sobbing for a moment and laughed out loud through her spiritual tears. *Yeah, that motherfucker always loved to roll his eyes at me. He never thought that my jokes were funny. But you know what it was? Jealousy! Pure fuckin' jealousy! His jokes always sucked so he had to make fun of mine. Man, I'm gonna lay into him when I see him again!*

Shhhhhh! Arima scolded. *Please! We'll miss the entire thing!*

They both listened intently as Josie continued while wiping a tear from her youthful eye. "I am here today to lay both of my parents in everlasting peace. I am here to give their souls back to the universe. I am here to remember their spirits. I am here to say goodbye to them.

"And I am here to say hello to the future. I am here to look forward to a future where we are all able to come together as one. A future where we don't hate one another for our petty differences. A future where we love and embrace one another *because* of those differences. A future where we do not have to live in fear of the bullying bastards who oppress us. Abuse us. Rape us. Murder us."

Yeah! You tell them baby! Maddy yelled out as Josie paused.

"That is the world that my parents were trying to build. For me. For you. And they, along with millions of other people throughout the world, took a step toward that. Christ knows they weren't perfect—none of us are. But they tried. They, alongside so many others, fought against the fascist forces of oppression. They fought against the forces of pure evil. And they taught me to do that as well. It's just that—"

Maddy's heart began to wilt once more as she heard Josie's voice begin to crack. "It's just that . . . I don't know if I have the strength to do this anymore. I've lost *so much* in these wars. We have *all* lost so much in these wars. I just don't know if I can—"

Aw shit, she' losing it. Maddy stated to Arima in a mournful voice. *She's losing her mojo. She's losing her will to fight.* She watched as her daughter's curly copper locks descended behind the tall, oak podium. She watched as her daughter tried to conceal her anguish and hide away from her tortured reality.

Maddy noticed a window that had been left cracked open. *I gotta go, Arima! I gotta do something about this. She needs me. She needs my strength. She needs to feel hope. I'll be right back!*

Arima felt her half-sister leave her being. A few moments later, she heard the incessant chirping of a small bird from outside the cracked window. Maddy sat on the branch and looked through the window at her grieving daughter as she sang to her. She watched as her Josie began to rise once again. She watched with pride as her daughter nodded to the musical director with fortitude.

Maddy's soul began laughing and clapping as a thunderous AC/DC song came blasting out of the church's speakers and her daughter strutted down the center aisle as she tore off her conservative black dress to reveal a skintight green faux leather catsuit. She watched as Josie kicked open the church's doors and screamed to the universe, "Here I am, motherfuckers! Time to fuck some shit up!"

Maddy re-entered Arima's soul in a flash and said triumphantly, *Fuck yeah, Boyeeee! That's my fuckin' daughter! She's going to be okay. But Jeezus! That painted on green suit doesn't leave much to the imagination. That's* really *gonna piss Erick off if she ever wears that shit around him!*

———

The teams had been assigned and the missions had been handed out a day earlier by Josie. The team that was responsible for tracking and finding Maddy and Erick's souls began their first meeting. The participants looked at each other with unease and uncertainty about how to proceed, until Rosa began to speak.

"Okay, everybody. I know that what we're trying to do is *really strange*. And I know that none of us have tried this before. What we have to do is track two lost souls throughout the cosmos. We have to track them from another dimension of existence. But we can do this. With Rod's technical expertise I can amplify Jessie's Beholding ability. Once she has sensed the general area where the spirits are, we can then amplify Rachel and Kayla's ability to track them down. Then it will be Arima's turn to call out to them and bring them home. Simple, right?"

The entire group let out a nervous chuckle before they heard a familiar voice bellow from out of Arima's mouth.

"Okay, I can't stand this fuckin' shit anymore!"

"Maddy, um, what are you doin'? I thought that you wanted to stay hidden for right now," Arima's normal voice stated through the same parted lips.

"Yeah, yeah, yeah," Maddy replied dismissively after taking control over Arima's body once again and continuing. "But I can't just sit here and watch these amateurs try to run this fuckin' meeting, so I'm gonna have to take charge. Um, no offense everyone, but…"

Arima's body got up from her chair and began excitedly flailing her arms as Maddy began her declaration. "Here ye! Here ye! Here ye! We are officially calling this spirit location and acquisition meeting to order! That's right bitches, I'm back! I'm kinda in a spirit form hanging out in Arima, but I'm still back! So *obviously* you don't have to waste any time looking for lil' ol' me."

Shocked faces began shedding tears of joy as Maddy continued.

"Okay, okay, enough of the blubbering. Rosa and Rod, it's so nice to see both of you. And it is so nice to meet the friends of Arima, my half-sister. So, Rachel, Kayla, and Jessie, welcome. But Jessie, keep that fuckin' cat away from me! That fuckin' thing is nuts!"

Lucyfur let out a low growl from Jessie's lap as Jessie stated meekly, "Yeah, I know. I'll try to keep her in check."

"And yes, I *did* say half-sister," Maddy continued. "You see, apparently that freak fuck of a Pastor fucked my bitch cunt of a mother and made *me* so that I could battle alongside them and help this fucknut Vetis take over the world and Enlightenment. But I was like, '*fuck that*. I'm going to use my abilities to battle you and your soldiers.' So that pissed them off and the dick Pastor seduced Arima's mother and tried to make her do the same thing. But Arima said, '*fuck that*. I'm going to use *my* abilities to battle you and your soldiers.' So that pissed them off again, so they tried to kill Arima, and they did kill me. But that just brought us together. We are now two souls in one, and once I get my Erick back, we're going to join with Josie and everybody else and fuck them and their douchebag overlord up! Oh, and one more thing. Please. Not a word of this to Josie, okay? I'm not ready to reveal myself to her yet. Not until I have brought her father back to her, all right?"

The shocked group nodded obediently before Maddy yelled out of Arima's mouth, "Now let's say our new cool cheer! *Fuck* Vetis! *Fuck* the oppressors! And long live Vendetta Degli Oppressi!"

Everyone embraced Arima's smiling body as they yelled out at the top of their lungs, "*Fuck* Vetis! *Fuck* the oppressors! And long live Vendetta Degli Oppressi!"

Days passed. Then weeks. Then months. Day after day Rosa sat holding hands with Rachel, Kayla, Arima and Jessie as electronic circuits that they were connected to buzzed. Every day began with hope. Every evening ended with futility.

"Rod," Rosa inquired after month three. "Can we turn up the intensity? Can we turn up the amplification? We aren't getting anywhere with this."

"Yeah," Maddy yelled out of Arima's mouth. "This shit's getting old! I'm fuckin' bored and I need to find my husband. Rod, I love you, but can't we do something more? And stop staring at Arima's chest!"

"Um, I'm sorry Arima, er um, Maddy," Rod replied as he began sweating and adjusting his pop-bottle lensed glasses. "We really can't turn up the amplification anymore. Not without frying everybody. I mean, well perhaps we could for a *short* period of time. Yes, if we turn it up in short thirty second increments every ten minutes or so, then maybe -it *might* just be possible. I'm not sure. Please let me do some calculations and we'll start fresh tomorrow, okay?"

"Sure, sure," Maddy replied. "You go do your fancy math shit. Arima and I have a date with a joint and large pizza tonight, anyway, *don't* we sis?"

Arima replied out loud so that everyone could hear the conversation. "Well, um, Maddy, I was kinda thinkin'."

"Kinda thinkin' *what*, sis?" Maddy inquired in a suspicious tone.

"Well, I mean," Arima replied through forced chuckles. "Y'know, this trip was *supposed* to be a celebration of my one-year wedding anniversary. And, well, *now* we've all moved to New York to help in this battle. And, well, Marcus just got back from one of his missions. And, well, it's been a while since he and I have been able to, y'know, *do* stuff together. So, I was just thinkin' that maybe for tonight I could put you in something that you'd really like, and I could hang with Marcus. Alone."

"Oh, I see," came Maddy's hurt voice from Arima's mouth. "I see. Your newfound sister…your flesh and blood…well, maybe not flesh and blood *anymore* but you know what I mean…is a *third wheel* and I'm not *welcome* with you anymore."

"Maddy, please don't be that way. Just for tonight, okay?" Arima pleaded.

"Sure, sure," Maddy replied again with fake sincerity and more than a hint of martyrdom. "No, it's okay. I understand. You have needs. Man, I sure do envy you. I'm sure it's nice to have an actual *body* and be able to *satisfy* those needs. But that's okay. I can just hang out in a picture or something all night. Don't worry about me. I'm sure that I can find some way to pass the time while you're having your fun. It's okay. I understand…Sis."

Several hours later, Arima and Marcus were lying in their bed that was covered in fast food wrappers, an almost empty pizza box, two empty containers of ice cream and assorted loose candies that kept rolling underneath their asses.

Soooooo, Arima heard a familiar voice in her soul. *Anyone gonna finish that last piece of pizza? Maybe you'd allow your dear ol' sis to have some, hmmmmm?*

"Oh, whatever. Just take it. We're going to sleep anyway," a frustrated Arima replied as her face beamed a wide smile and reached for the pizza.

The following morning, the group was back at work. Rod increased the amplification of Jessie's Beholding abilities every ten minutes for thirty seconds, until all the women cried out for him to turn it down.

Three hours had passed when Rosa suddenly said, "Wait! I sense something. Actually, I sense nothing. There's a dark space that is completely devoid of any form of energy. It is unlike anything that we've explored in this dimension. Rod, try to turn up the amplification as I focus Jessie's powers on that area."

"All right, Rosa," Rod dutifully replied as he turned a dial slightly.

"Oh, Jeezus this hurts." Jessie stated. Then she screamed out, "Don't touch that dial! I feel...I feel...absolute *peace* and absolute *evil* in one form! It's like they are intertwined or something! How can that *be*? How can *both* extremes exist in one form?"

"I'll tell you how!" Maddy yelled out through Arima. "It's *both* of them! My bitch mother *and* my prince! They're entangled or something! Jesus Christ, Jessie! You've *found* them!"

"Okay, okay," Rosa began through her near hyperventilation. "Ok, Rod, leave the amplification up for a bit longer. Maddy, I'm going to connect your energy with Rachel and Kayla's, okay? Girls, just focus! Maddy, do you see it? Do you see the path?"

"Oh, fuck. Yeah, I see it!" Maddy responded with dismay. "It's nothing but black. But he's in there. He *has* to be. Okay, kids, thanks and see ya in the funny pages!"

Arima felt Maddy's soul disconnect from hers and leave in an instant. The group sat there in a sweaty, exhausted dismay while wondering if they would ever be with their friend again.

———

"Oh fuck, it's dark," Maddy's freed spirit stated aloud as she entered the black void. Even in her lifeless state, Maddy could sense the plummeting temperatures as she ventured further into the blackness. She could feel Rachel and Kayla leading her through the void as though they were creating an other-worldly lighthouse through the densest of fog.

Then, she saw something. It was a mass of faint light blue and purple. She floated towards it and looked upon the emaciated forms of Erick and her mother. The mother was completely encased by Erick's spiritual form. Both shrouds' faces were drawn in and looked as though all their spiritual nutrients had been sucked from their being.

"Hey you!" Maddy yelled out.

Erick's beleaguered and withered face looked upon his love for the first time in three months. He managed a slight smile and said in a raspy whisper, "Go away Maddy. Go away, my love. Leave me here."

"Fuck that!" Maddy yelled out. "Just let her go and I'm taking you home, mister! We have shit to do!"

"No, Maddy," Erick responded sadly. "This is my contribution to the battle. I must hold on to this…this…thing. I must hold it for eternity, so it doesn't escape. So it doesn't release the Pastor. So it doesn't come after you. I took it from the Earth and brought it to this remote void so that I could hold it and imprison it for all time. I must hold onto this for all of eternity so that you and our loved ones throughout the Earth and Enlightenment can remain out of their grasp. Please, just go now. I do not want you to see me like this. Please tell Josie that I think of her every moment of my existence. I love you both so. Please, baby. Just go now."

"Fuck this!" Maddy yelled out as she rushed the entangled

form and began furiously pulling Erick's essence from that of her reviled mother.

The mother began cackling with glee as she said through her weakened nasally voice, "Yes, take this bastard away from me, you little whore. Take him away you foolish little tramp. Release me so that I can once again regain my strength. Release me so that I can find your father and we can *both* finish your little ass off once and for all. Release me so that the wars against the Earth and Enlightenment can start anew. That's right, you selfish little bitch. Don't think of anyone else. Just think about your own needs. Make your bastard of a husband release me."

Erick was clinging to the mother's demonic essence as hard as he could, but he no longer had nearly the strength of his wife's spirit as she tore him from her mother's vile essence. "No, Maddy. Please just let us be. Let me protect you and Josie and everyone else. Please," Erick stated through pleading tears.

"Fuck that baby," Maddy responded through her own tears. "Fuck *that* and fuck *her*. We'll find her again and we'll *destroy* her fucking ass!" Maddy gave one final vicious pull and the cackling mother's purplish smog of a form went flying away into the black abyss.

Maddy's spirit was holding that of her existentially wounded husband. "I, I can't go back like this Maddy. I need to stay here. I need to…"

Erick's soul faded into unconsciousness as he and his beloved wife were suddenly wrapped up in delicate leaves, stems and blossoms of a giant purple iris. They were being gently taken towards a bright, white light.

Maddy heard a booming voice say from within the brilliance, "Thanks Herbert! I owe ya one! Helluva job Buttacup! It'll all be okay! We'll get him fixed up as good as new!" Maddy wept as she realized that they were being gently taken back to Enlightenment. They were being taken back into the bosom of her family. They were being taken home.

"What the *fuck* do you *mean* we've been here for almost *nine months*, Earth time?" Maddy screamed out at her beloved Uncle Joe and Aunt Blair. "We just got here like, *yesterday!*"

"We told you dear," Blair responded through her chuckles. "We told you that time works differently up here. What seemed like just a day or two to us was nearly nine months upon the Earth. But in that time, your Erick has been nurtured back to health. It is time for you to go back now. It is time for you to call out to Arima and for you both to re-enter her soul and re-enter the battle upon the Earth."

"Well, *that* fuckin' sucks," an incredulous Maddy retorted. "I mean, I want to get back to see Josie and everything, but fuck! We hardly had any time together and she's now nearly seventeen! I've missed so much!"

"Yeah, yeah, yeah," Maddy's Aunt Patty stated gruffly as she entered the room in a huff. "Yeah, you think *you've* got problems? Do you know how hard it is to get a *whole fucking concert* organized with a bunch of prima donna spirits? I mean, who *knows* how much time that we have to get this shit together. Jacklyn and I have been working our *asses* off in getting these fuckers rounded up, just in case this war comes to an abrupt end. This is going to be the concert of all fucking time! And it has to start as soon as victory is achieved! And we don't even have an *opener* yet! Why? Because Prince is being a *fucking tool*, that's why! He's insisting on opening the show, but I already promised Jerry Lee that he could open with "Great Balls of Fire." I mean, what's a better opener than *that* after an epic war? So now, he's all pissed off and won't come out of his corner of paradise! Yeah, cry me a fuckin' river sister! Just take your husband and his pussy music back to Earth and get this shit straightened out. I've got larger problems to fix up here!"

Erick and Maddy embraced Joe, Blair, and Patty for what seemed like an eternity. Joe turned to Erick and said, "Hey buddy. It was nice to finally meet you. It was nice to meet the man that is deserving of my niece. It was nice to meet the man who would do anything to protect her and your lovely daughter. And it will be nice to get to know you more once this shit's all over."

"The pleasure sir," Erick replied as he was failing to match the firmness of Joe's handshake, "Is all mine. We'll see you all soon. And we're going to have that bitch's head on a fucking platter."

"Okay, well here we go," Maddy stated with a mixture of remorse and hopefulness. "I'm going to call out to Arima now and have her lead us back into her soul. Erick, just stay next to me. And don't go *wandering off* and getting your ass lost again! Okay, let's just see what she's up to."

Maddy peered down upon the Earth and found her half-sister. She shook her head and said, "Yeah, we're going to have to wait for just a bit."

"Why, dear," Aunt Blair inquired.

Maddy replied in an exasperated tone, "Well, she's *kinda* fucking her husband right now. How the fuck do they do that on top of all of those *crumbs*? Don't they get shit in their um, crevasses and shit? *Jeezus*!"

CHAPTER 76

SO ALIVE

"So that's where we've been for the last year," Maddy stated matter-of-factly as she munched on a ham and cheese sandwich that was drenched in mustard. "Y'know. The same old, same old. What's new with you?"

"Well," Josie answered as she looked at Lionnel's bewildered face then back to those of her parents. "That's all very *interesting*, but aren't you leaving out one small detail?"

"Uh, I don't think so, sweetie," Maddy replied with a confused expression as she looked at her beloved Erick. "Baby, do you know anything that we left out?"

"Nope," Erick replied as his eyelids were beginning to droop. "I think that pretty much covers it. At least for tonight. How about we just get a good night's rest, and we can answer any questions you might have tomorrow, okay?"

"Uh, no. Not okay." Josie replied sternly. "You ended the story with the two of you about to re-enter Arima's, well I guess, *Aunt* Arima's soul, right?"

"Yeah, what's your fucking point?" Maddy asked in an annoyed tone.

"Well," Josie answered as she attempted to maintain her

composure. "Do you want to *maybe* explain *how the fuck* you are sitting here in human form and looking younger than I can remember? Do you think that maybe *that* would be a little detail to share with your fucking daughter?"

"Oh yeah," Erick replied with a chuckle. "We probably should explain that. But sweetie, I have to say that I really don't care for your newfound use of profanity. It just isn't ladylike."

"Yeah, act like a fuckin' lady, wouldja?" Maddy exclaimed in agreement before catching herself and saying, "Hey! Wait a minute! Are you saying that *I'm* not a lady?"

Erick felt sweat upon his brow for the first time in two years and looked down at his twiddling fingers as he began stammering, "Um, no. Of course not, dear. I was just *saying* that, um, well, I was just *saying* that…"

Erick was granted a reprieve by his daughter's booming voice shouting, "Oh my *GAAAAAWD*! Would you two *please* stop bickering and just tell me *how the fuck* it is that you're alive?"

"Well, it is a good question," Maddy playfully responded as she tussled Josie's curly locks. "Look at you. Just look at our little genius asking brilliant questions."

"Mother," Josie replied through gritted teeth. "It is very late. This has been quite a shock. It is an incredibly *pleasant* shock, but it is still a shock, nonetheless. So please. Please just explain this to me. Okay?"

"Wow, man, I mean, like, um, Niece Josie," Arima chimed in. "You seem pretty uptight. You maybe wanna take a hit off this and, y'know, chill out a bit? It's really good stuff. My own harvest. Well, I can't take *all* the credit. You see, there was this spirit named Herbert, but he liked to be called the Botanist. So, he helped me off some murdering fascists and I helped him get into Enlightenment. Anyway, he was a wiz at anything with plants and before he left the Earth, he gave me his secret to growing *killer* dope. Anyway, where was I? Oh yeah! Do you want some?"

Josie looked at her aunt, cocked her head, and gave Arima a patient smile beneath her burning green eyes before saying in an annoyed, lilted voice, "No thank you, Auntie Arima. I think that I would like to be in complete control of my faculties as my parents explain their reanimation to me. I think that this is a conversation that I would like to be *completely* alert for. But thank you very much for your offer. Perhaps *Marcus* would like to have another hit."

"Oh, hell yeah, gimme that spliff baby," Marcus replied with the enthusiasm and energy of a sloth.

Josie turned her glowering emerald green eyes to her parents and said with a determined softness, "Okay Mother. Father. Would you *please* begin?"

"Yeah, yeah, yeah," Maddy began as she rolled her eyes at her daughter and wiped mustard from her chin. "Y'know you're getting a little overbearing."

"Mother, *please!*" Josie shouted back causing her copper curls to bounce above her reddening face.

"Okay, okay," Maddy replied in an exasperated tone. "I *kinda* wanted to finish my sammich first, but whatevs. So, we were watching Marcus and Arima fucking and…"

———

"Finally! They're done! C'mon, let's go!" Maddy stated to her apprehensive husband's spirit.

"Um, can we wait for them to, um, cleanup a bit first? I mean, it just seems rude to enter her soul as they're, um, wiping themselves down."

Thirty-seven Earth minutes later, Arima jumped up out of bed and yelled, "Jesus Christ! Could you *at least* give me a bit of warning? I know I told you that that my soul was open to you whenever you need it, but a little heads-up would have been nice!"

Happy to see you too, Sis! Maddy's soul said to her half-sister. *Surprise! We're back! And by 'we' I mean me and my prince of a husband Erick! Erick, this is Arima. Arima this is Erick."*

Hello Arima," Erick's soul stated. *It's so nice to meet you. It's much roomier here than I thought. Thanks so much for letting us…*

Erick's voice was cut off by his yelling wife. *Yeah, it's roomy* now, *but this bitch has* all kinds *of fuckin' spirits invading our territory! There's this one dick named Howard. Do you know what he asked me? He asked me if I was into pegging! Are you fucking kidding me? Who the fuck says that to a spirit that you've just met? Or anyone, for that matter! So, if that motherfuckin' douchebag shows up again uninvited, I want you to kick his ass, okay?*

Well, maybe. Erick cautiously stated. *I mean, like, how big is he?*

A frustrated Maddy replied, *You know what? Don't worry about it. I'll take care of him, you big pussy.*

Pussy? Erick roared back. *Where the fuck do you think that I've been for the last year? Sacrificing myself by holding onto your bitch demonic mother, that's where! Pussy? Are you fucking kidding me?*

Okay, okay, I'm sorry baby, Maddy responded contritely. *Now Arima, what's the fuckin' plan? We want to go see Josie now.*

"Um, not quite yet," Arima stated out loud so that Marcus could hear her side of the conversation. "A couple months ago, I was told to bring you two to Rosa and Rod as soon as you returned. They have something to tell you. They've kept whatever it is from the rest of our team. Y'know. Jess, Rachel, and Kayla. But we'll all find out tomorrow. I'm too messed up to drive tonight."

Tomorrow? Maddy yelled back. *Fuck that! Let me take over your body. I'll drive.*

Why do you get to drive? Erick inquired. *Why can't I take over her body and drive?*

Because, Maddy replied in a condescending voice. *You, my dear, are directionally impaired and will get us fucking lost. I want to hear what the fuck these people have planned. And I want to hear it now.*

*Yeah, but...*Erick tried to interject before looking at the glowing green eyes of his beloved wife's spirit. Realizing the futility of the situation, he concluded with, *Yeah, all right. You can drive.*

I know I fucking can, Maddy stated arrogantly as she took control over Arima's body and made her way to the white telephone that was hanging from the kitchen wall.

"They are here!" Jessie, Kayla, and Rachel said in unison as

Arima and Marcus entered the room.

"Both of them," Jessie continued. "I can feel them inside of Arima."

"Yeah, yeah, yeah, we're fuckin' here!" Maddy said through Arima's mouth. "Hello everybody. Um, Erick. These are Jessie, Rachel, and Kayla. You know Rod and Rosa, of course. He says it's nice to meet you. What's that baby? What's that growl?" Maddy inquired before LucyFur made her way from under a table, jumped into Arima's arms and stared at her intensely.

"Just chill the fuck out, cat," Maddy stated through Arima's trembling voice. "It's me. It's Maddy. Remember? We met. Don't worry. Your friend is in here too and she's safe. You can retract your claws now, okay?"

LucyFur took one last deep look into Arima's eyes, let out a mew, jumped down and went to her food dish.

"That cat's fuckin' nuts," Maddy said under Arima's breath before saying to Rod and Rosa, "Okay troops. Boy, do we have a story to tell you! But first, what's the plan? Why can't we go see Josie yet? It's her seventeenth birthday in four days and I want her to be able to actually celebrate this year. So, tick-tock moth-erfuckers. What's the plan?"

"Well," Rod replied in his nasal voice and staccato cadence. "How would you like to present yourself in your original human form? Or would you prefer to be ghosts?"

Whatthefuckyousay? Maddy yelled out. "Yeah, that's a good question baby. How is that possible?"

"Well," Rod replied through a rare chuckle. "First, we need to obtain two bodies. Two bodies that are still alive. Gender doesn't really matter, but the transformation will be easier if they are, um, hormonally similar to you both. So, we need one male and one female. And we have several candidates. This isn't necessary for what we're going to do, but from an ethical point of view, they need to be people who won't be missed and preferably at the end of their life. Now, there is an elderly husband and wife who are both on life support. They don't have any other family. No one will miss them. All we have to do is go to the hospice where they are living their final moments and retrieve them. But they do not have long. A day or two at the most before the decision is made to let them pass. Time is of the essence."

"Well," Kayla chimed in with a playfulness in her voice. "*We* know a couple of pale studs who are pretty good with, *tee hee*, *everything* to do with bodies."

"Yeah," Rachel added. "Let's send in the Twins.

"Yeah," Maddy stated with a deep determination in Arima's voice. "I don't know what all of your fucking tittering is about but go get the Twins."

Fuck. That shit's gonna get old, Maddy stated internally to Arima's soul as she heard Rachel and Kayla yell out, "Woooooooo!"

———

What the fuck is this? Erick said internally to his wife as he looked down upon the pair of barely alive octogenarians.

"Yeah, you're right baby," Maddy replied through Arima. "Nope. Not gonna happen. Find another pair. Listen, we don't mean to be ageist and shit, but *how the fuck* are we supposed to battle demonic forces of evil in *these* fuckin' prunes? Oh, yeah, that's a good point too, baby. And *how the fuck* are we supposed to *fuck?* We'll break our fuckin' *hips* just getting out of our pajamas!"

"Maddy, Erick," Rosa's calm voice responded. "Please just be patient for a moment and allow us to explain. You will not be in these bodies. I mean, well, they will start out as these bodies, but they will be transformed into your own bodies. And your bodies will be, um, what age will their bodies be, Rod?"

"Well, let me just look at the date on this vile," Rod responded as he lifted two glass tubes from a tray. Yes, Erick's age when we extracted his DNA in 2023 was, let me see here. Oh yes, his body will be forty-seven! And Maddy's DNA was extracted the same year which would make the age of her body thirty-five!"

"Oh yeah *boyeeeee!*" Maddy yelled out through Arima. "I'm *still* fuckin' younger than you! I don't know. I'll ask. Erick would like to know if he could be closer to my age. Even though I never considered it a problem, he always felt a little creepy about being twelve-years older than me. So whaddayasay Rod? How about making him around forty? That way, he's happy but I'm *still* younger than him and can give him shit about it. Okay? Cool. I'm glad that's settled."

"Yeah, that's not quite how this works," Rosa began again. "Just bear with me here and I'll try to explain. As you know, I am able to control and enhance energy. All forms of energy including energy from souls. Arima can bring souls into her essence or place them in inanimate objects, but she can't place a soul into another living being. But I can. Arima will release your souls. I will capture their energy and place each of your souls into these respective bodies. Rod will then inject their brains with your DNA from 2023. Then, the magic happens.

"With Rod amplifying your DNA through electricity and my amplifying the energy generated by your souls, the combination will overtake that of the original hosts. Their souls will be released and yours will take over. Then your DNA will begin to dominate theirs and the bodies will begin to transform at the molecular level. The central nervous system will be transformed first. Then the bones, tissues, cartilage, and muscles. Then the organs. Then the blood-type, and so on until your exact body from 2023 exists once again."

"How about my tits?" Maddy blurted out. "I mean, I'm sure she was probably a looker in her day, but this is some saggy shit right here."

"*Everything* will transform," Rosa replied following an eye roll and deep sigh. "After three days of intense, non-stop concentration by me, your souls will be in your bodies from 2023. And they will remain that way. Your DNA from 2023 will not allow you to age. It will kill off any disease or virus. It will regenerate wounded body parts. The only way that you will be able to die is if the body's nervous system is detached. So, um, don't get decapitated."

"Well, that's not *entirely* true," Marcus added. "My Moms and

Pops came to me one night in a dream and told me the rest of it. I mean, it's true that your bodies will live forever but only as long as your souls are in them. Once your work is done on Earth, then your souls will be recalled to Enlightenment. When that happens, your bodies will turn to dust. You will be purely in spirit form from that point on and will only be able to visit Earth through someone like Arima. Or birds. Or something. I actually don't know. It feels like I'm just making this shit up as I go along."

"Well, let's get this shit over with then," Maddy stated excitedly. "What's that baby? Yeah, I know. I tried. But it doesn't really matter now. As long as we're in human form we're, like, immortal or something, so our age doesn't matter. And it sure as hell won't matter once we're spirits again. Oh, just quit your whining and get your misty ass into this old coot you big baby! Jesus fucking Christ!"

———

"Jesus fucking Christ!" Maddy yelled out as her born-again bare torso rose from the cold metal table following her three-day transformation. "And what the fuck am I *covered* in?" she exclaimed as her astonished green eyes looked at her thirty-five-year-old body that was encased in an oozing greenish, reddish, whitish, brownish, gelatinous goo.

"Wassupbuttacup?" Erick stated as he entered the room wearing a plush, white robe and carrying a steaming cup of coffee.

"Hey you!" Maddy yelled out. "Oh my God! It's *you*! It's really *you*! Like, your *face*! Your *body*! Your – hey open your robe really quick."

Erick turned his back to the observation window and did as he was instructed.

"Yep! It's totally *you*!" Maddy cried out as she began clapping which sent streams of the thick goo flying across the room. "When did you wake up?"

"Oh, just about a half hour ago. And to answer your question, you are covered in all the remnants of the poor soul whose body you took over. It's like their leftovers get put into a blender and kinda ooze out of the skin. It does not look…or *smell* very pleasant. So, you might want to take a shower. And Arima said that she saw the smiling faces of the elderly couple moving on toward Enlightenment. So, all's well that ends well, I guess. So, are you gonna take that shower or what? I mean, it's great to see you but you're *really* fucking ripe and gross right now. But before you jump in the shower, go ahead, and say it."

"Uh, say what?" a confused Maddy asked.

"You know. Just say it. It'll be *really* funny this time," Erick answered as he flashed his beloved wife his mischievous grin.

An understanding Maddy mirrored his grin, lifted her head, and screamed out, *"I'm Aliiiiiiiiive! MWAHAHAHAHAAAA!"*

She then jumped off the table and began approaching her Erick. She made sloshing sounds with each step as the thick ooze from her size six feet met the concrete floor.

"What the fuck are you doing," Erick asked with trepidation as he began slowly walking backwards away from his approaching, well marinated wife.

"Oh, I'm *ripe* and *gross* now, am I?" Maddy stated through an evil little chuckle while wearing a playfully demented expression on her thirty-five-year-old face. "Well baby. We took a vow to share everything. And I mean *everything*. Through sickness and health. Through good times and bad times. 'Til death do us part. And since *that* shit's not happening, like ever, I have something to share with *you*."

"You wouldn't," Erick responded in a pitifully pleading tone. "C'mon. I just got that shit off of me. Maddy, I'm serious. Maddy, I'm *warning* you!"

"Noooooo!" Erick cried out as his mischievous wife leapt upon him, covering him in her afterlife, after-birth. "This is fucking gross!" He kept crying out as his wife covered his face with gooey, smelly kisses.

"Oh, fuck it," he finally said with loving resignation. He took his disgustingly slimy wife into his arms, looked deeply into her emerald green eyes, wiped some thick mucus from her auburn bangs and gave her the most tender kiss in the history of the world.

Maddy and Erick emerged from their unnecessarily long shower wearing beaming smiles and white bath robes. As they entered the room, they heard applause from Rod, an exhausted Rosa, Arima, Marcus and Jessie. They then heard two familiar, yet creepy voices.

"Oh my, Uncle Erick and Aunt Maddy are back!" Adam stated with a giggling Rachel draped around him. "Yes, indeed!" Aaron added as Kayla tittered next to him. "Oh, how joyous! Now we will be able to play more games. Games that are even more fun than we have ever played before. Uncle Erick and Aunt Maddy are indeed back. Everything is coming to fruition just as we have seen, brother."

"Well," the snickering Kayla added. That's not the *only* thing that's *cumming* to fruition. Get it, boys?"

"No," is all that Adam said as he looked at his brother. "No, we do not get it," Aaron added. "Perhaps you will need to explain that to us."

"What the fuck is going on?" Maddy yelled out. "Did we fuck up the space-time continuum or some shit? How the *fuck* did *those two* ever get laid? Oh, fuck it. I'll deal with that shit later. C'mon, baby. There are only a few hours left of Josie's birthday and I want us to surprise her. I've got an idea that'll be *really* funny. Hey, are there any white sheets around here?"

———

"And that's where we've been for the last few days. We went through all kinds of shit just to surprise you before your birthday ended. Happy now, little miss thing? Now, I heard you give out assignments to the various teams. So, I'll ask again. What the fuck has been happening with you guys this past year?"

"And, *more* importantly," Erick added in a deep growl as his face began to twist into a sadistic glee. "When do *we* get to play?"

C HAPTER 77

L IVING D EAD G IRL

"Well Dad," Josie began with a sly grin upon her slightly befreckled seventeen-year-old face. "We've actually made a lot of progress this past year. Mom probably heard me hand out the assignments a year ago and heard me say that I wanted the world to be strewn with the bodies of these demonic fucks. And that is *just* what we've done. Each group is led by members of our inner circle, including one of our primary hit men. And the primary hit men lead a *group* of hit men...oh and women...we really need to change that title. Anyway, there are fifteen hit...um...*persons* in each group and there are seven primary hit men. Fuck. They really *are* all men. Another little tweak that I've gotta make. Anyway, that means we have one hundred and twelve hit...um... experts. No wait. *Assassination* experts. No wait. Assassination *technicians*! Yep, that's the term.

"So, each group had their assignments, and they went after the top people...well...they're not so much *people* as they are *demonic servants* of Vetis. Anyway, they went after some of the top ones that held influence over the weak-minded and the weak-willed. We really didn't go after any of the layperson members of their flock. They aren't demonic. They're just self-centered and stupid and self-serving. Most of them piss their pants, drop their stupid guns, and go running for the hills as soon as we or any type of resistance shows up.

"And it has been working. With each high-profile assassination, their ranks become increasingly splintered and have less conviction in their endeavors. We have assassinated hundreds of these motherfuckers and their followers are beginning to go back into their little racist, sexist, homophobic, transphobic closets. They're still little pricks. But they aren't *nearly* as dangerous as they were because they are fragmented and lack leadership. And since they have no original thoughts of their own, they are practically immobilized without some higher power telling them what to think and what to do.

"And we think that the higher power that was ultimately mobilizing these forces on the Earth were none other than the Pastor and my...*yech*! Grandmother. They seem to be the hand-picked servants of Vetis who have been charged with influencing and leading Vetis's puppets. They are the ones who have been whispering in their ears and giving them instructions."

"Wait just a fuckin' minute!" Maddy exclaimed. "Now it all makes sense! I remember the *one time* that I was in that dick Pastor's office. The time he was going to begin grooming me by raping me and shit. Before he came in, I was looking at his wall of pictures. Hundreds of pictures with him and some of the most influential business leaders, politicians, religious leaders, and radical right-wing media types. All smiling and shaking hands. And I remember thinking to myself, 'how is it that this fuckin' podunk preacher knows all these high-profile douchebags?' Then I felt his slithery fucking hands on my shoulders and all I could think about was getting the fuck out of there. And how much I hated my bitch mother. I haven't thought about that moment for years. It was just too creepy and painful. I had shut it out. Until now."

"Yes, Mom," Josie began again. "We think that you're right. And since those two haven't been around for some time, these *other* demonic servants have been pretty easy to pick off. One by one. A bomb here. A bullet through the brain there. Hundreds of them left lying in their own blood. Hundreds of shredded corpses to send a message. Hundreds of pretty pink roses left on their lifeless frames to send the message that Murder, Inc. is *not fucking around!*"

"Whoa!" Maddy yelled out. "You're still using your cool calling card? That's so cool sweetie."

"Yeah, it is pretty cool, I guess," Josie replied as her face slightly blushed, and she let out a light chuckle. "You can take the girl out of her hippie utopia, but you just can't take the hippie utopia completely out of the girl, I guess, *tee hee.*"

"Well," Erick chimed in with a sarcastic tone as he stared at Lionnel. "At least there's still *some* innocence left in our daughter."

Josie and Maddy stared at him silently and slowly shook their heads. Josie then let out a deep sigh and rolled her eyes before continuing.

"So, you can read all the reports of everybody our *Assassination Technicians*, heh, heh, heh-have taken out if you want. But let me just tell you about a few of the highlights."

"Okay, but before you do," Erick interjected. "Does that mean that we don't have anything to do? That it's all been taken care of? That we don't get to have any fun? Well fuck this! I didn't *die* then hold onto your bitch grandmother for a *fucking year* which nearly extinguished my soul then get *re-animated* just to hang out and twiddle my thumbs! I want some action *goddammit* and I want it *now!*"

"Jeezus," Maddy replied condescendingly while shaking her head at her beloved husband. "You are such a fucking baby sometimes. *Of course*, there's more to do, otherwise we wouldn't even *be* here. We'd be in Enlightenment hanging at one of Aunt Patty's cool parties. Remember what we were told? That we'd be called back to Earth when we were needed. It seemed to us that we were in Enlightenment for only a few days. But we were up there for nearly a year, Earth time. We've been called back at this point in time for a reason. Isn't that right, sweetie?"

"Yes, Mom. You are correct." Josie answered as Maddy looked

at her husband with a haughty expression. "You *are* needed. What we have been told is that Vetis must conquer the Earth before he can engage in battle with Enlightenment. That his demonic anti-democracy forces will take over the Earth. They will then collect all their fallen dark souls and wage war against Enlightenment. That is what we have been told. But we have been wondering. What if that isn't *necessarily* the case? What if this Earthly war is nothing more than a ruse? What if conquering the Earth is nothing more than icing on the cake? That it isn't really that important? What if this Earthly battle is being waged not for domination of the Earth but to simply collect more and more dark souls for the *ultimate* goal of conquering Enlightenment? That his followers aren't the only ones that are pawns here. Maybe we are too. We have sent a lot of evil fucks to their Earthly grave. And we have created a helluva lot of dark souls who are just hanging around waiting for their final marching orders. We now believe that is why you are here. We need to focus not just on getting rid of the Earthly threat but the threat in the afterlife as well. And we believe that the key to that is your union with Aunt Arima. That the two of you will be able to lead our forces against both the *living* and the *dead*. That the two of you can lead our forces to protect both the *Earth* and *Enlightenment*. From this point on, we need to focus on continuing to rid the Earth of the demonic pawns and then rid the cosmos of their dark souls for all eternity. Make sense?"

"Fuck, my heads hurts," Erick replied as he held his newly generated face in his hands. "I'm really sorry I asked. So, we kill their bodies then Maddy and Arima destroy their souls? Is that basically it?"

"Uh, yeah," Josie answered. "That's much more – um- simple. Yeah, that's basically it."

Arima's mellow voice then entered the conversation. "So, hey- um – like Niece Josie. So how is it that we're supposed to destroy all these dark souls? I mean, I can only do, like, one at a time. There's gotta be thousands of them."

"Yeah, there's the rub," Josie sheepishly responded. "We're not sure yet. We're working on it. It's like we need to create a huge dark soul vacuum or something that you can suck them into. Then we need something *really big* that you can send their souls into for their final destruction. We have Rod, Rosa and Lucy working on it. Oh. And speaking of Lucy, let me start telling you about the exploits of each group. Mom, as you may remember, Lucy and Sam were put in charge of taking out some of the top political leaders who were actually demonic pawns throughout the world. There have been so many at all levels of government. Local. State or Province or whatever. Federal. Most taken out by the Assassination Technicians under the leadership of Sam and Lucy. But there was *one* hit that stood out from the rest. Mom, you may want to put down that second sandwich. This is some twisted shit."

———

"This isn't just a hit," Sam lamented as Lucy assisted her in placing her fifty-two-year-old paralyzed legs into a pair of black faux leather slacks. "This is primarily a rescue mission."

"Yeah," Lucy replied, echoing Sam's subdued tone. "This is going to complicate things. It's so much easier to find out where a bunch of them are going to be congregating and plant a bomb or unleash one of my toxins. Just hit a button and watch their organs spill out. It's just so...hot. We don't have to worry about innocent bystanders in those situations. But this one is different. There are so many innocent people in this complex. And we're so isolated in this remote part of this Eastern European country. It won't be easy to get them out. And it won't be easy to get them two hundred miles to the airport where Jennifer is waiting with the plane. The hit men can take out the outside security. But how in the hell are we going to get in there? And how much security is on the inside? We need a better way to get in. We need someone on the inside. Any thoughts?"

"Yeah," Sam answered reservedly. "But I really don't like it.

Here's my plan. And Lucy, just in case I don't make it, well, I love you."

The beautiful African American woman rolled her wheelchair into a neighborhood pub on the outskirts of the remote village. She feigned not understanding the language that was being spoken. She also feigned not understanding the meaning behind the guttural laughter of a small group of filthy men at a corner table.

The men approached her wearing broad smiles. Everyone in the bar looked away or down at their respective drinks. A rag was placed over her mouth. She breathed in deeply and allowed herself to succumb to the blackness.

Sam woke up and began coughing as a thick plume of smoke rolled from a large man's cigar and into her lungs. She lifted her head slightly to take note of her surroundings. She was in a small concrete cell with iron bars and still in her wheelchair. Most importantly, she was not bound. She looked up at the broad man who was wearing a devilish grin as he puffed away. He was well over six feet tall and nearly four feet wide. His thinning black hair was trimmed short, and he had stubble on his upper lip and chin. He was dressed in an all-black double-breasted suit. Sam looked down at her still legs and smiled. He was their primary target. He and the skinny white man who was standing next to him wearing a white coat.

He was an influential member of this country's Parliament. He was being groomed to be its next President. He was being groomed by Vetis.

To demonstrate his loyalty, ingenuity, and worthiness of being one of Vetis's hand-picked pawns he had begun experiments. Experiments to build the ultimate human fighting machines. To literally piece together an army made up of human parts of the highest quality. This had been done in fiction. It had never been accomplished in reality. Until now.

This wretched man and his more than willing scientist brother had succeeded in harvesting parts from multiple people and combining them to build the perfect fighting machine. They were so close to its completion. A fighting machine that could not feel pain. One with no feelings. One that was completely obedient to its overlord.

A fighting machine that was large. And fast. And strong. And…intelligent. A fighting machine that could process information. That could plan attacks. And counterattacks. A fighting machine that could travel with their orders and complete their mission anywhere in the world without being supervised. A fighting machine that, when completed, would be assigned to complete its first experimental mission in Brooklyn. Sam was aware of this. Rod had shown her the plans.

"Wh-what happened?" Sam asked as she tried to appear confused. "Where am I? I just got lost and was looking for directions to my hostel. What am I doing here?"

The large man laughed deeply then said in English with a thick accent, "You my dear are the final piece. The final piece of my most glorious puzzle. Do not fret, my dear. You won't be harmed…much. You will actually come to thank me as *you* are going to make history. You will be the first of your kind. The first of our super-soldiers.

"We have constructed the perfect fighting specimen. The heart and lungs of a former swimmer. The arms of a former weightlifter. The legs of a former gymnast. And so on. Why former, you might ask? Well, we take the parts from those who have been met with some… misfortune. Usually because of some accident. Usually, heh, heh, heh. They have become disabled. They are of no use to our world any longer. So, we have given them purpose. We have taken their beaten bodies and transformed them into something magnificent. Something that will aid our glorious Vetis in taking over this world. We have many of them here just waiting for their blessed transformation. Their blessed destiny.

"Yes, we have now created one. Our first. All that we need is… the right brain." The large man then looked at his quivering brother who stated, "I-I'm sorry. The jar just slipped, and I didn't think that the brain was damaged."

"Well, it was!" the large man roared back. "It *was* damaged! It too would have been the perfect brain. But now it is too damaged. Too unpredictable. Too emotional. But it has at least given us an opportunity to test some of our indoctrination techniques until we could find the right one. And you, my dear, are perfect. My men took you from the bar when they saw your damaged legs. They are to take anyone that we might be able to… harvest. But imagine our surprise and glee when we ran a scan of your brain. Your beautiful brain. So analytical. So unemotional. So compliant with rules. So transactional. It is perfect. *You* are perfect. So, let us celebrate! What would you like to dine on tonight, my special pet? You may have anything. For tomorrow, you will be dining in the greatest body that has ever been created. Then, we will begin your…conditioning, heh, heh, heh."

Sam looked up at the pompous man and said with a condescending arrogance, "Very well then. I will have vegetable lasagna. Not too much sauce and not runny. And *do not* use frozen vegetables. A small side salad with no cheese. Just greens and vegetables with a light vinaigrette dressing. And two slices of garlic toast. Lightly toasted. If they are too hard, then I'm sending the whole meal back and you can start over."

The large man stared at Sam's stoic face and burst into laughter. "Why yes indeed, princess! Coming right up! It's the least that we can do for our most honored guest!"

The pair left as Sam thought, *Well, that should keep them busy for a while. Let's start with the cameras.*

Sam reached under the right arm of her wheelchair, dislodged a small cover, and pressed a button. All the security cameras were still completely operational except that they were now frozen on a static image. Anyone who was not paying close attention would never notice the lack of movement from behind the multiple iron-barred doors. Or on the outside of the complex.

Lucy's transmitter began flashing green and she flashed a devilish smile to the nearest hitman. There was a nod of understanding followed by sixteen soft pops from the surrounding forest. Lucy and her sixteen partners exited the brush and quickly traversed the perimeter of the small concrete complex to ensure there were no survivors. There were none. Just ten men lying in their own blood and brains with bullet holes displayed perfectly between their eyes.

Sam took three small metal picks from inside of the left arm of the wheelchair. Reaching between the bars and with a slight flick of her wrist, her door swung open with a rusty creak.

She wheeled herself into the aisle with her toned and powerful arms. She looked around at the other nine cages with desperate eyes peering back at her. She looked to the back of the room and saw metal tables that were covered in bloody surgical tools. Beneath the tables were rusty metal bins that contained various body parts from the innocent victims. Sam wheeled her chair in a full circle and took in the entirety of this travesty. Her mind was immediately triggered back to her time, not so long ago, when she was brutally beaten and raped by men exactly like these. She looked down upon her shapely but immovable legs. And she wept.

Her tears of rage flowed down her caramel cheeks as she began barking orders. "Okay everybody. Listen up! If you want to get out of here alive, just listen to me. If you are able to fight, then join me in getting some weapons. If you aren't able to fight for any reason, just stay in your cell until I come and get you. And I would appreciate it if you would keep the profanity to a mini-mum. Everybody understand?"

"Oh, we understand," a middle eastern man with removed arms answered from a dark corner of his cell. "We understand *completely*. And we most *definitely* are going to fight."

As each metal door swung open, its occupant walked, limped, or wheeled themselves to the back table where they retrieved any weapon they could find. Three of the downtrodden had no arms. They were placed upon the lap of three people in wheelchairs and held long knives between their feet. The other three had disfig-ured features but full bodies. They picked up saws and cleavers and waited anxiously beside the heavy metal door.

Sam approached the door with a mixture of trepidation and

fury. She placed the picks into the locks and turned her wrist. There was a slight *click*.

The red lights and sirens that began blaring upon the door being swung open were quickly joined by screams of anguish as Sam launched four-inch metal projectiles from the arms of her wheelchair into the reacting guards. The three full-bodied persons launched themselves into the hallway and began hacking and slicing at anything that was approximately their height. The other three wheelchairs shot themselves down the hallway where their passengers planted the long knives into fleshy abdomens.

From behind the carnage there were light 'popping' sounds and little red dots. One of the red dots rested upon Sam's forehead.

"The Calvary's here," Lucy stated flatly as she surveyed the bloodbath that laid beneath their feet. Twelve sadistic men were lying on the concrete floor. Their blood was oozing from their skewered bodies. Only three had been killed by a gunshot. The rest had been disposed of in a gloriously messy fashion by those who had been called 'worthless.'

"Wow," Lucy stated with admiration. "Nice work. Remind me to never park in a handicapped spot again."

"Yeah, that's not really the term anymore," Sam admonished just before there was the booming sound of repeated banging from behind a large metal door to their left.

As Sam approached the door and took out her picks, a female in a wheelchair said, "Um. I don't know if you want to open that. She's…um…she's not very friendly."

The warning had come too late. The lock clicked open, and Sam was knocked backwards by the force of the swinging metal door.

"Who or *what* is that?" one of the hitmen yelled out.

Standing in the doorway was a six-foot-seven-inch behemoth. Her muscular arms clung to her toned torso that presented large perfectly shaped bosoms. Her front presented an equally impressive male member that dangled between a pair of impossibly muscled legs. Her stitched frame slowly approached, and the entire group was greeted by a beautiful, feminine face that was encased in platinum blonde shoulder-length hair. She smiled with a demure rage and said in a soft, childlike voice, "So where are they? You know. That politician and his twisted fucking brother. Where are they?"

"You mean these two?" One of the hitmen answered as he led the large man and his scientist brother into the hallway.

"Hey, hey, now," the large man began stammering. "P-please. You want money? I have lots of money. Jewels? Anything that you want. A-and, oh! Your lasagna is just about done miss! Just how you ordered it!"

The powerful transexual stood menacingly over the quivering pair. She flashed a devilish grin and said in a breathy, Monroe-esque voice, "No. We don't need anything from you. We are just going to take your lives. Just like you took ours. The torture you put us all through. And we're the lucky ones. So many didn't make it. So many who didn't live to see our revenge against you. You called us worthless. Because we didn't look like you. We didn't have the same body parts as you. You thought us to be weak. But we're not. We are strong. Stronger than you, in fact. We have been made strong because we have had to put up with the painful glances in our direction and the discrimination. The pitiful looks on others' faces as they look at our missing limbs. We are just people. We are not experiments. We are not objects of ridicule. And we are *not* objects of pity. We are just people. *You* are the ones that are worthless. *You* are the ones that oppress us. Belittle us. Use us. We are *not* freaks. *You* are the freaks. Anyone who abuses others for their own gain is a freak. A completely worthless freak. But maybe I can do you both a favor. Let me show you how it feels to be us. Let me free you from your freakishness."

The giant transexual reached down and grasped the large man's arms. He screamed in agony as she strained and pulled at the immobilized appendages. There was a loud 'pop' followed by two geysers of blood as the man's arms were ripped from his body. He collapsed upon the floor whimpering as he bled out.

She then picked up the skinny scientist and cracked his back over her steely knee. She tossed him onto the concrete floor with a thud. She smiled at him as though she were posing on a red carpet. She watched his lips tremble as he tried to move his paralyzed appendages with futility. She blew him a kiss then crushed his face and skull with her size sixteen foot.

"Ew," she said softly as she tried to shake the blood, skull fragments and brain matter from her right foot. "So. Does anyone have a cigarette? And maybe some tequila? I'm just *dying* for a drink right now. Oh, and you can call me...*Dragenstein*. And I am the transphobes *worst fucking nightmare.*"

———

"What the fuck!" Maddy cried out in dismay as Arima and Marcus sat on the couch giggling at the scene. "Are you telling me that we have a fucking Amazonian *Drag Queen* on our team? Really? Where the fuck is she? I gotta meet this bitch!"

"Uh, yeah," Josie replied nonchalantly. "She's on our team. I don't know where she's at tonight. She might be performing. She's really popular at this little place in Soho. Anywhooo, so that's *that* story. Now Jerry and Jules and *their* team had quite a different experience."

CHAPTER 78

MONEYTALKS

"Lucyfur! There you are!" Jessie exclaimed as she entered Rod's electronic lair. "C'mon, baby. It's time for your nummy-num-nums. I have fresh blood from a fascist for you!"

Lucyfur looked up from her comfortable perch on Jules's lap and looked up at her with slight confusion in her green eyes.

"Yeah, it's okay," Jules responded dryly to her feline companion. "Go get your nummy-oh Jesus Christ I can't say that. Go get your meal."

Lucyfur got up, stretched, and let out a soft mew of understanding before jumping from Jules's lap and making her way over to the welcoming Jessie.

Jessie picked the grey and white furball up and flashed her a broad smile. She then turned around and glared at Jules. "Hey! Bitch! Don't be stealing my cat!"

Jerry and Rod immediately looked away from the scene and toward the computer screen that was between the trio. This was not a confrontation that either of them had a desire to participate in.

"Yeah," Jules replied in a dismissive tone. "A couple of things here. For starters, LucyFur isn't *your* cat. She isn't *anybody's* cat.

Cats aren't owned by *anybody*. They exist for their own pleasure and are dismissive of anyone and anything that does not bring them that pleasure. Or entertainment. Or food. When they want to eat, they'll find someone to feed them. When they want to fuck, then they'll find a temporary mate. There are no feelings. No emotional connection. Unless it serves their purpose. They love those that *they* choose, and they love them on their *own* terms. LucyFur loves you. And she loves Arima. And she loves me. You don't have anything to worry about. Well, from her. But if you ever call me a 'bitch' again, I will rip out your fucking throat with a fork. Or have you *not* heard the story about Maddy's hand? And just like LucyFur and all other cats, I won't feel a fucking thing for you. You got that…bitch?"

Jessie stared into Jules's eyes, which glowed with a detached intensity. Realizing that this was a battle that was best left alone, she gulped and said meekly, "Okay. Listen. I'm sorry. I shouldn't have said that. We're all on the same team, right? Friends?"

Jules gazed at her with disinterest and replied, "Yeah, whatever. I forgive you, I guess. Now leave us alone. We've got work to do. Okay Rod, what have you found for us?"

"Well," Rod began in his staccato, nasal voice as he began typing on his keyboard. "You wanted to find a gathering of multiple influential business leaders that are, in fact, earthly servants of Vetis. You wanted the worst of the worst. I believe that I may have found them."

He clicked his mouse and the image of two brothers popped up on the screen. They displayed broad, arrogant smiles and were wearing generic hunting garb, complete with matching cute little gun and ammo purses. They were two of the children of Vetis's failed hope to overthrow America's democracy. But although their father turned out to be a failure at everything that he touched, the brothers were still able to indoctrinate his gullible followers into believing that he was a prophet sent directly from God. And that they, in turn, were conceived to continue their dullard father's work to rid the world of the "unholy" democracies and replace them with "holy" and "patriotic" dictatorial autocracies that placed White Christians in dominion. All for a price, of course.

"I found this on the darkest site on the web. It is quite hard to find and quite expensive to join," Rod began explaining as he peered at the brothers' image through his pop-bottle lenses. "Only the wealthiest can join this site that peddles the most horrific lies and propaganda. And, of course, only the wealthiest would even have access to it since there is no wireless internet. Most people are still blocked from the web and only a few have the equipment to access it. It costs $50,000 a month to belong. It costs even more for what these two are offering."

Rod clicked 'play' and the image began to move. The brothers' sleezy smiles became broader before the dark haired one said gleefully, "Greetings fellow patriots! As you know, our great father was on a lifelong mission to rid the world of the scum of this Earth. The Non-believers. The N*****s. The K**kes. The Sp***s. The G**ks. The Fa*s. His glorious policies were working until the damned libs intervened and *sacrificed* our father at their unholy altar of 'wokeness.' They say that what they want is to promote understanding and acceptance. But that is a socialist lie. What they *actually* are doing is denying *you* your rightful place of dominion over our Earth. Denying *you* your God-given *right* to harvest Earth's bounty without government intervention. Denying *you* your God-given *right* to use the scum as your laborers. Denying *you* your God-given *right* to reap your entitled rewards of money and fame and women as has been pre-ordained. *They* have denied *you* your God-given right to own whatever it is that you want to own whether that's jewels or property or...people."

The lighter-haired brother then spoke with a noticeable slur of intoxication. "That's right brother! And now we are offering *you* the chance to join our battle to reclaim this Earth in a more exciting way than your corporate influence. You can now own a part of this movement! For the low, low price of *One-hundred-million-dollars* you have the opportunity to join us on a once in a lifetime experience. You have the opportunity to join us at our undisclosed private big game hunting grounds. We have rounded up some of the most prominent libs from around the country. We have stripped them naked and sent them out into the woods. The entire complex is surrounded by armed guards and electric fencing. They cannot escape. They cannot escape being hunted. They cannot escape being hunted by *you*. That's right fellow patriots! Join us on July 4! Join us so that you can now literally *Own the Libs!*"

The beaming dark-haired brother then concluded with, "Yes! You can now own your *very own* lib trophy. You think your friends are impressed by that elephant tusk or lion's head hanging from the wall of your den? Just imagine how impressed they will be when they see the head of a lib politician or clergy or industry leader hanging prominently in the middle of your showcase. And, as an added bonus, we will include a complete mounting and lighting kit that will allow your servant to hang your prized trophy upon your wall with ease! So, join us for this once in a lifetime event, won't you? Join us in *Owning the Libs!*"

Jerry wiped a tear from his eye with his tattooed and brawny right hand before saying, "Yeah. This is perfect. But how the hell are we supposed to get in there? I'm sure our hit-squad can take out the guards around the complex, but we still need to get inside. How the hell are we gonna break in? How the hell are we gonna do *that?*

"Oh, that is quite easy," Rod answered as his gaze rested unfortunately upon Jerry's chest. "You won't be breaking in. You both will be participants in the hunting party."

"C'mon, Rod," Jules dismissively countered. "I know Murder, Inc. is rich as fuck but we're talking two-hundred-million-dollars! Plus, the fee to join this twisted website. It won't work. We need to find another way."

Rod let out a slight and uncharacteristic snort before answering. "You have already joined the website. For the past two months, both of you have paid your dues. And I have constructed the perfect identities for you both so that you will be above suspicion. And, as far as the two-hundred-million-dollars goes…"

A delighted cackle came from a dark corner of the room before an enthusiastic voice proclaimed, "That's where *I* come in bitches! *I'm* going to bankroll this little adventure and *I'm* going to join you. I think that you will need all the luck you can get. Oh sure, they don't like my kind *either*, but money talks! I'm a member of this site too already. So, strap yourself in because on July 4 you're going hunting with Kaneko!"

"And one other thing," Rod added. "Once you have…um… eliminated the businessmen, you will need to be careful to navigate around the big cats that they have there. They have two lions, two tigers, two panthers and two cougars that they keep as living trophies. They have been hardly feeding them so that they are quite hungry and can be released if there is any trouble. You need to be mindful of that."

"Big *cats*, you say?" Jules replied with a sly smile. "Well, let's get the hit squad together then and start making our plans. And Rod, I think you miscounted."

"What is it that you mean, Jules?" a perplexed Rod inquired.

"There's about to be *three* cougars in that fucking place," Jules answered through a malicious grin.

———

"I look fucking ridiculous," Jerry whispered to his wife as he looked at himself in the mirror wearing his khaki hunting outfit.

Jules rolled her mahogany eyes and shook her brown curly mop as she slid her taught middle-aged frame out of her jeans. As the seven other male hunters ogled her female form, they did not notice the ignored figure of Kaneko floating around the room and dropping small acid pellets into the barrels of their guns, rendering them useless.

Jules tersely replied to her husband, "Just be cool. It'll look much better once it's covered with the blood of these rich fucks and…oh! Hey! Nice to meet you!"

"Yeah, nice to meet you too!" the bulbous gun manufacturer stated through an enthusiastic grin. "I'm just going around introducing myself and inviting everyone to a little post-hunt party I'm throwing at my resort. It's just twenty miles away outside of Little Rock. We're going to have some great laughs talking about our hunt today. A few drinks. A few jokes. Maybe a little...strip poker?"

Jules fought the urge to rip the lascivious man's throat out as she watched his eyes traverse her body and wipe drool from his mouth. Luckily, she was saved from another voice.

"Poker, you say? Well, I'm a bit of a novice, but what the hell? If I can afford to own a lib, I sure as hell can afford a new pair of panties!" Kaneko stated as she slapped the man's back-fat then fat ass.

"Uh, sure, maybe," the man replied as he calculated his next move to get into Jules's pants. "Hey, listen you three. There's a little catch to all of this. There's ten of us on this hunting trip but only nine libs. One of us is going home empty-handed. So, just stick with me, alright sweetheart? I've paid extra to find out where the libs have been hiding in the trees. Don't worry about it. Just stick with me and I'll get you your head. And that way, I'm pretty sure to get a little head *too*, huh sweetie?"

As luck would have it, a voice came over the intercom before an enraged Jerry could react. "Welcome everybody! My brother and I hope that you all have a wonderfully patriotic time today! Now, we put some tampered food out last night, so if your prey ate it, they should be really slow and easy to sneak up on. Hey! We're sportsmen after all, right? Some of you more than others. I see that some of you are choosing to use knives and swords and shit instead of guns. Cool with us. Whatever gets you off. It's your money. And there are nine of those lib assholes lurking some- where in the woods. So just one head per hunter, understand? Don't be greedy. Or do! That's what this shit is all about! And if you do *not* get a trophy today, don't worry about it. You will be comped to an hour with one of our slave concubines. Believe me, these women will *not* disappoint you. And if they do, well, then just kill them and take *her* head home. No extra charge! Alright everybody. Get ready! Get Set! Go own those fucking libs!"

A large metal garage door on the side of the dressing room lifted to reveal a small pasture that was surrounded by dense forest. The brothers sat on golden thrones on a golden stage as gold-bikini clad young women brought them drinks and fed them grapes. They laughed with sadistic glee as they watched one-billion dollars' worth of "hunters" fan out with their guns and ridiculous matching costumes.

"This way!" the bulbous man yelled out to Jules and her companions. They entered the dense forest and cautiously walked twenty yards before the man held his hand up signaling them to stop. "There's one now. Up in that tree. Now everybody just be quiet. We wouldn't want our little snowflake to melt away now." He lifted his gun and put his right eye up to the telescopic gunsight.

He then silently fell into the brush. His gun was attached to his face by a metal rod that had been thrust through the sight, into his right eye and out the back of his head.

"That wasn't enough," Jules dryly stated.

"Enough for what," the slightly calming Jerry asked.

"Enough blood to make that silly fucking outfit look cool." Jules answered. "C'mon. One down, eight to go. You know what to do."

Kaneko looked up at the shivering figure hiding in the tree and said, "Go to the west gate. Tell any of the others to do the same. The outside guards and electric fence have been taken care of. There will be men and women in black suits waiting behind a hole in the fence. They will take you to safety. Now go."

Jerry ran frantically back into the pasture, flailing his arms. "What the hell are you two pulling here?" he screamed at the two confused brothers. "The quarry! They're fucking armed! Call the hunters back now! We have to get out of here!"

The shocked dark-haired brother held the microphone up to his mouth and announced, "Uh, listen up everybody! There's some sort of an…um…issue. Just come back to the pasture so that we can work it out. We'll get this shit straight then continue the hunt."

From inside the dense woods Jules could hear voices exclaiming, "Goddamit!"

"I knew that this was too good to be true!"

"Fuckups, just like their father!"

"Hey! My gun's jammed!"

"What should we have expected from a couple of con men?"

"Those bitch slave girls *better* be real!"

"I'm gonna have *someone's* head on my wall tonight! And I don't care whose!"

Jules could also hear scurrying feet from behind her heading towards the west gate. As soon as she heard a voice, Jules crept toward that area of the woods and hid behind a tree. She heard a "hunter" approach. As the disappointed body passed by her with his gun slumping at his side, she wrapped serrated razor wire around his throat and began sawing. She was showered with the blood that was spewing from the gurgling man's throat as she continued her frantic motion. She grunted one last time until the severed head dropped pathetically into the lush shrubbery.

The next one received a hatchet to the forehead the moment she jumped out in front of him. Then a knife to a man's temple. Then a machete was buried in the back of another man's head. Ten people went into the woods. Only five re-entered the pasture.

A blood-soaked Jules strode into the pasture and joined Jerry, Kaneko and the final two hunters.

"How do I look?" Jules asked her husband as blood dripped off her petite nose.

"You never looked better, baby. Damn, I love you," Jerry replied reverentially.

"Don't get all mushy and shit," Jules answered as her blushing face was concealed under coagulating blood. "Take care of these other two. My arms are tired."

As the brothers descended their golden staircase they were yelling, "Okay. What the hell is going on? What do you mean they're armed? That's impossible! Why is she covered with blood? Where are the rest of the hunters?"

"The same place as these two," Jerry replied sinisterly as he stood behind the confused final two "sportsmen." "In fucking hell!" Jerry unsheathed his broadsword and decapitated the two men with one furious swing. He continued to stand directly behind the men's torsos that were spraying blood into the air and upon his strapping frame. He smiled contently as he realized that his khaki hunting costume finally looked cool.

The brothers let out a panicked squeal and turned to make their retreat. They were blocked by twelve scantily clad young women. They grabbed the shrieking brothers by their arms and forced them to their knees.

"Thanks for the assist, ladies," Jules stated as she looked at the caged pairs of majestic cats looking at her with pleading eyes. She walked up to the large confinement and said something quietly to them before turning the lock.

The noble creatures sprang from their cage and immediately pounced upon the cowardly, piss-stained brothers. Their legs, arms and torsos were being ripped apart by gnashing teeth and flying claws as the brothers begged for their daddy. Their pathetic whimpering finally ceased while the mammoth cats continued to chew upon their intestines.

"What did you say to them?" an intrigued Jerry asked of his beloved wife.

Jules responded coldly, "I told them to leave their heads for me."

———

"Okay, a few questions here sweetie," Erick asked his daughter once she had concluded her tale. "Firstly, did Jules and Jerry keep their outfits? If so, did they launder them? And if so, how did they get the blood stains out? I have always had a helluva time getting blood stains out of my clothes, so if they've stumbled on a good detergent, I'd really like to know."

Maddy looked at her husband in shocked disbelief before roaring, "*That's* your brilliant fucking question? *That's* the first thing that popped into your head? *That's* what you took from this story? Seriously, man. What the fuck is *wrong* with you?"

"Yes," a defiant Erick yelled back. "That is *exactly* what popped into my head. You know that I'm the one who does *all* of the laundry around here and if we're going to war then there's going to be a lot of it! So, yes! I am looking for a detergent that is *really good* with blood stains! What's wrong with *that*? What brilliant question do *you* have?"

A dismayed Maddy responded as she tried to calm herself, "Well. How about if we ask about Jules who can now *apparently* talk to animals or some shit. Might *that* be of interest to you?"

"Yeah, I guess," Erick replied with a hint of an attitude. "But it doesn't do anything to help me with my laundry problem."

An unblinking Maddy could only stare at her husband with a look of dismay as Josie re-entered the discussion.

"Wow. You guys really haven't changed a bit, have you? And to answer your questions, I do not know Dad about the status of their outfits. And I do not know of any better detergents. And Mom, Jules can't talk to just any animal. She can only communicate with cats. She has the same detached 'fuck you' attitude that they do, I guess. Oh, but she brought them all back and they are now living on our estate with Stellan and Paciano. And we have built a climate-controlled barn that they can go into if they get too hot or cold. And my other cats and dogs just adore them, because no predator, human or otherwise, *dares* to set foot on our land with *them* lurking about. We now call the estate the Cool Cat Club. Isn't that great?"

"Uh, no," Maddy answered. "That *isn't* fucking great. How the fuck are we supposed to visit our own home with giant fucking cats waiting to eat us?"

"That's not a problem, Mom," Josie replied through her light chuckles. "Lucy has developed a perfume that is made of Jules's scent. Just a spritz behind the ears and those lovely animals will leave you alone."

"No, they don't!" Lionnel bellowed out. "They *do not* leave you alone! They jump on you and lick you all over your face! Or rub up against you and knock you over! Those cats are a *real* pain in the ass!"

"Yeah?" Josie replied to her boyfriend with a cocked head. "Well, they weren't so much of a pain in the ass when we fed those radical religious fucks to them now were they? Oh! That reminds me of my next story. So, Henri and Jamie were tasked to head up a group to take down demonic religious leaders. Little did we know that we'd need to get Pastor Tim involved in this one. But before I tell that one, come to the basement. I have something to show you."

Josie led her family down the basement stairs and flicked on the light. The jaws of Maddy, Erick, Lionnel, Arima, and Marcus dropped as they saw the severed heads of the traitorous brothers mounted on the wall, bathing in a white-hot spotlight.

Josie stood triumphantly in front of the pitiable faces that were frozen in the moment that they had let out their final high-pitched squeal. She firmly placed her hands on her pajama-adorned hips, flashed a devilish grin and shouted out, "As the saying goes, two heads are better than one! Hey, get it? Why isn't anybody laughing?"

"Shit, that really *isn't* very funny, is it?" Maddy whispered to her exasperated husband who was holding his head in his hands.

CHAPTER 79

DEAR GOD

"Henri, do you think that there is a God?" Jamie inquired of her friend and teammate as she applied dark blue eyeshadow on her eyelids. She looked at herself in the mirror as she awaited his answer. It had been many years since her reflection cast the image of James Johnson. In his place was now Jamie Johnson, an attractive African American transexual whose full afro was reminiscent of female activists from the Black Panther movement in the 1970's. Her full bosom was draped in a black and blue flowered gown that rested just above her knees to conceal the one remaining part of the time when she was known as 'James.' She gazed upon the colors in her gown and was briefly transported back to the evening when her father made her skin as black and blue as her elegant gown. Ever since that brutally tragic night, she had wondered why a benevolent God would make her the way that she was. Why would a benevolent God trap her feminine spirit in the prison of a male's body. Why would this God make someone in a way that made them the subject of harassment, ridicule, discrimination, and merciless beatings. Beatings from classmates, hooligans, and her very own father. Was this truly some form of spiritual or intelligent design? Or was it simply biological happenstance.

"Well, I honestly don't know," Henri replied in his thick Cameroonian accent. "I would like to think that there is a God. I have seen so much pure evil in this world. The beatings. The rapes. The oppression. The murders, including that of my beautiful first wife, Abana."

Henri wiped a tear away with the rag that he was using to clean his sniper's rifle before continuing. "But I have also seen absolute goodness as well. I have witnessed miracles. I truly have. My Sam's being able to survive the brutality that she was subjected to. I believe that to be a miracle. My son, Lionnel. To me, he is *my* miracle. The powers that so many women possess and are beginning to tap into. Your best friend Arima. Rosa. Now Jules. Those, to me, are miracles. And the way that people have banded together over these past two decades to beat back these forces of evil. That, too, I believe to be a miracle. I think that there is a never-ending battle between pure good and pure evil. We understand that better than ever now. We now know that there are demons in our midst. We are battling the forces of one right now. And if there are demons, there must be a Satan, right? And if there are demons, then there must be angels to serve as a counterbalance. And if there are angels, then there must be a God, right?

"That is what I think, anyway. I do not know if God and Satan are individual beings that hold dominion over their respective planes of existence or whether they are the combination of souls that creates a good or evil movement and leads each of us on our respective paths. Every time that we make the decision to act in a way that is purely self-serving, are we feeding into the entity commonly known as Satan? And every time that we act in a way that is selfless, are we not contributing to the power of God?

"That is *my* faith, anyway. We know there is pure evil, so therefore there must be *something* that is Satanic. And if there is pure evil, then I believe that there must be pure good as well. And that pure good is God-like. But what I pray that I am wrong about today is how the demons project their own greedy and sometimes sadistic deeds upon those that are unlike them. They have been doing that for decades. If there is something that they, themselves, are guilty of, then they project those sins upon others in order to further divide people and stoke hatred. There are many examples of this.

"They rail against the "socialist takers" and "welfare queens" while taking government money for themselves. But when the government gives *them* money, they are entitled to it. When it is given to someone else, they are accused of being takers. They yell about us 'cancelling' things that we disapprove of. They then 'cancel' everything from movies to candy to cereal to amusement parks. Hell, they even cancel types of beer. They have spoken for decades about being the victims of the liberal "deep state," when it was in fact *their* leader who tried to install subservient dullards into positions of power at all levels of government in order to turn our country into a dictatorship. They were correct. There *was* the beginning of a deep state. But it was a deep state that *they themselves* were creating. And are still trying to.

"But this is one projection that I pray is not happening. All of their other projections carry at least some truth to them. There *are* people who take advantage of government programs. There *are* people who overreact to a joke or use of the wrong pronoun and try to 'cancel' the offender. To humiliate them. To shame them. To ruin their careers and livelihoods. All for a joke that was not intended to harm and did not age well. But there is *nobody* that we would embrace who are doing what the most extreme of their voices say that we are doing. There is *nobody* that is sacrificing infants and drinking their blood. And I pray that *they* aren't either. But I won't be surprised. They are pure evil, after all."

The pair left their room and strode down the hallway of their Boston hotel. They knocked upon the door. They waited a few moments then saw the door open slightly to reveal a mahogany eye peering out from behind the security chain. The chain was unlocked, and the door was opened.

"Hello, my friends," Jeremy stated as he welcomed Henri and Jamie into the room. "He is almost ready."

Sitting cross-legged on the king-sized bed wearing a black suit was Pastor Tim. He was in a trance-like state and chanting something in Latin while clutching onto children's squirt guns. He was surrounded on the bed by various Holy texts of every major religion. His chanting stopped and he opened his blue eyes. He smiled upon his friends and said, "Well, I've done what I can do. I've never blessed this much before. Nor have I done it in so many languages and using so many religious philosophies. If this works, then we may have found a way to rid both the Earth and Enlightenment of these dark souls for all of eternity. And, if not, well- then I guess it's back to the drawing board."

Henri and Jamie wore long overcoats that swayed with each step as they entered the grand marble church. They looked up in awe at the prism of color that was being generated by the sunlight beaming through the priceless stained-glass windows. A member of the clergy entered the room and dark clouds immediately blotted out the sun. The room's vibrant colors were replaced by somber, grey shadows.

"Huh," Jamie whispered into Henri's ear. "Well, I don't know if that's a *good* sign or a *bad* sign."

Henri replied, "It is a *very* bad sign. And it is a sign that we are in the right place."

"Hello, my children," the clergyman began with an assumed kindness. "How may we be of service to you today?"

The pair looked upon the man's serpentine smile and knew that they had found their target. Ever since this clergyman's arrival, multiple infants had been reported taken from hospitals and from their warm cribs in their homes. Anguished parents feverishly made pleas to the local authorities and to the public for assistance in finding their precious children. Flyers were posted and phone banks were created. None of their efforts were fruitful in stopping the frantic parents' endless tears.

Rod had done an analysis comparing the arrival of new residents to the Boston neighborhood to the times and proximity of the disappearances. Once he had identified a prime suspect, Jessie was brought in to look at his image. Jessie did not even have to be in the vile man's presence to use her Beholding ability. "Yeah, that's him. I can feel his evil just by looking at his picture. Tell Jamie and Henri that we've found him. And tell them to be careful. He's powerful. I pray that I'm wrong about what the source of his power might be."

Jamie smiled demurely at the clergyman and said, "Yes, hello. I am Jamie and this is my handsome fiancé Henri. We are looking for the *perfect* church to hold our ceremony and the *perfect* clergyman to help us prepare for the day that we take our vows. Would you be interested?"

The pale clergyman licked his lips slightly as he looked upon the dark complexions of his guests. He was also momentarily fixated by the size of Jamie's adam's apple before he responded. "Why yes, we would *love* to serve as your gateway to eternal happiness. And I would be *honored* to be your personal spiritual guide as you walk together into heavenly marital bliss. Please, come to my office, won't you?"

The three entered the clergyman's plush office. Jamie looked around the room at the various pictures on the wall. One in particular sent a chill down her spine.

"That picture, there," she whispered to Henri. "That is the Pastor. That is Arima's demonic father."

Henri gave her a nod of understanding before being struck on the back of the head. When Henri and Jamie woke up in their chairs, they saw two men standing over their bound bodies with the smiling clergyman between them.

"Well, *that* wasn't so bad, now, was it?" the clergyman began arrogantly. "You've only been out for about ten minutes. And I am *so sorry* to inform you that you *will not* be able to be married in this church, or *anywhere*, for that matter. You see, we do not perform services for...*your* kind. You are both *definitely* the wrong color and *you*," his voice trailed off as he glared at Jamie.

"Well, I'm not really sure *what* you are. So, we will be unable to perform your blasphemous ceremony. Oh, but we *can* perform experiments upon you. Yes, yes. That is something that we are *quite* fond of."

He then took two items from behind his back and said, "I really don't understand why you were concealing these toys under your coats. I shot them both onto a chair. It is nothing but water. Perhaps you were trying to intimidate me in some way, hmmmm? Regardless, let me tell you about my experiments. I think that you both will find it fascinating.

"The Pastor told me long ago that in order to get into the good graces of our glorious Vetis, that I must find ways to enhance myself. To enhance my influence over others. To enhance my power. And I believe that I may have found the perfect thing. And it is so wonderfully simple. Blood. Human blood. There is a vibrancy to human blood that, once ingested can enhance our-let's just say *darker* side, shall we? Yes, by drinking the blood of innocents I have been able to be more powerful. More convincing. My flock has grown tremendously since I began this practice. Some of the blood, as you will both soon find out, comes from relatively innocent adults. That is how it began a few months ago. But then I started wondering. What blood would be the *most* innocent? What blood would be the *most* powerful? What blood would offer me the best opportunity to sit at the side of the Pastor and of our glorious Vetis? Yes, you may have already guessed. The blood of infants. They are so unsullied by the world. Unjaded. Innocent. Pure. And, I might add, *quite* delicious, heh, heh, heh. Since I have been consuming the blood of infants, I have felt my power grow exponentially! They are now my main source of nutrition! But that doesn't mean that I can't be a bit *naughty* and have a little snack between meals, now does it?" he concluded as a slight trail of drool leaked from between his slithery lips.

"That's it! I've heard enough!" Henri yelled out as two thin, red laser beams came from outside of the office window. They rested upon the foreheads of the two guards. Then, the guards' brains rested upon the face and suit of the clergyman.

The office door opened, and two more Assassination Technicians entered the room with their guns drawn and pointed directly at the clergyman. Henri and Jamie were unbound, and they retrieved their squirt guns from off the desk.

"Take us to where you do your "experiments," Jamie commanded to the shivering clergyman. He stood there staring at the foursome in disbelief as blood, brain and skull fragments dripped slovenly off his face.

"Take us now, you sick fuck!" Henri ordered before grabbing the clergyman by the arm and marching him out of the room.

They went toward the back of the bastardized church. The pleading clergyman pulled a secret lever on a mantle. A door ominously creaked open. Henri roughly shoved the clergyman in front of him and commanded that he lead the way. Halfway down the ancient, winding stone staircase, Henri and Jamie could hear the sounds of men and women gagging and vomiting. They knew that it was the sounds of their associates who had used another secret entrance that Rod had located by analyzing blueprints that were centuries old. And they knew that any remaining guards had been taken care of.

Another of the Assassination Technicians came running up the staircase to greet Jamie and Henri. "Stop," the black-clad ninja-esque woman stated pleadingly through her black mask. "Please, just stop. We are highly trained. We are highly trained and have been desensitized to be able to confront *anything*. But *nothing* that we have encountered could have prepared us for… for…" The assassin's sentence was cut off as she lifted her black mask and vomited all over the face of the clergyman.

"No, we must see," Henri responded with pain and trepidation as they continued to descend the staircase. "We must confront this evil before we pass judgment onto…" Henri would never be able to cleanse his memory of the image that he had allowed himself just a glimpse of before the entire party turned their backs in disgust on the grisly scene.

"Back upstairs, now!" Jamie commanded. Henri shoved the clergyman repeatedly up the stairs and down the hall until they were once again in his office.

"Strap this motherfucker down!" Henri ordered as he began circling the pathetic clergyman. "Yes, you are correct. Blood is our lifeforce. And your demonic kind are correct when you preach about protecting innocent children. They deserve to live a childhood that is safe and innocent. But you are *wrong* about what they need to be protected *from*! They do *not* need to be protected from understanding who they truly are! They do *not* need to be protected from age-appropriate books! They do *not* need to be protected from beautiful drag queens who read to them! They do *not* need to be protected from learning their actual history and actual heritage!

"No! They *don't* need protection from *any* of that! What they *do* need to be protected from is being indoctrinated into hating others that don't look or love or worship like them! What they *do* need to be protected from is *bigots* who try to whitewash their education! What they *do* need to be protected from is the scourge of gun violence! What they *do* need to be protected from is autocratic tyrants who will strip away their rights! And what they *do* need protection from are monsters like you! Oh, you may take this shit to a *whole new*, twisted level, but there are *so* many more of you out there. Pathetic little worms who have no self esteem who abuse and rape and murder children just for their own feelings of power. It is pathetic. *You* are pathetic. I cannot give those poor babies their blood or lives back, but I sure as hell can take it from *you*!"

Jamie then twisted two knobs on an electric pump that began humming slightly. The bound clergyman was frantically trying to free himself from his bindings as he watched his crimson life force move down the four plastic tubes that had been inserted into veins in his arms and legs. He screamed in agony as he could feel himself weakening from the loss of blood. Once the blood reached the end of the plastic tubing it was sprayed throughout the room by attached lawn sprinklers.

Jamie and Henri's blood-soaked faces looked on with maniacal glee as the repugnant man began meekly gasping for air. Just before he exhaled for the final time, Jamie and Henri pointed their squirt guns at the emaciated near-corpse and began firing the blessed holy water. There was a dark purple smog that billowed from the perverted man's mouth with a high-pitched squeal. Henri and Jamie continued to spray the holy water at the floundering apparition until its shrieks ended in one final brilliant flash of dark purple light.

Henri and Jamie looked at one another with tearful eyes before falling into each other's arms in a release of pent-up anger, grief, and revulsion.

An assassin came up from the morbid basement and entered the room with a small bundle. "We-we're so sorry. We should have been earlier. Maybe we could have…could have saved more. But there is one. He is alive and unharmed."

Henri took the bundle and opened the blanket. Inside was a lightly cooing six-week-old infant of Persian descent. Henri enveloped the child in his hulking frame and re-entered the chapel. He looked down again and the infant flashed a slight smile of contentment. Henri laughed through his tears and declared, "He is a miracle!"

The dark shadows receded from the chapel as Jamie, Henri and the assassins all looked up once again in awe at the prism of color that was being generated by the sunlight beaming through the priceless stained-glass windows.

———

Maddy, Erick, Arima and Marcus sat expressionless in a stunned silence before Maddy yelled out, "Oh fuck! I shouldn't have eaten that second sammich!" She then ran to the kitchen and vomited in the sink.

"Yep, that's what we're dealing with," Josie said in a remorsefully controlled tone as she was being lovingly held by her Lionnel. "There is no bottom to this. There are no limits to their depravity. There is *nothing* that they won't do to assume power. Just like the Nazis. They were an earlier form of this evil. And now, we have *these* heartless, morbid fuckers. The cycle just continues.

"There are a lot of families in Boston who will never be able to have a restful night ever again. But that little boy survived. And maybe Henri was right. Maybe his still being with us *is* a miracle. His dead parents were found in the basement of that church too by the police after we tipped them off. A number of the cops that responded to the scene are still receiving some pretty heavy therapy. No one should ever witness something so horrid, let alone experience it."

Josie wiped tears from her remorseful green eyes and looked up while forcing a smile. "But, by the grace of God, or whatever, we have that child. He is about one year old now. We took him to the estate, and he was adopted by Stellan and Paciano. They break down crying every time they lift him from his crib. They love him so much and the baby loves them. The baby also loves to smile and laugh and play. He loves to play with toy trains and loves to play with the big cats. They just adore him. Stellan and Paciano will lay him down on a blanket near the apiary and play a Cat Stevens CD. The pairs of big cats then come from the surrounding woods and lay around the blanket forming a formidable feline shield. It is as if they sense that this child is special and needs to be protected."

Josie let out a slight chuckle of emotional release as she concluded in a cracking voice, "They named him Zihad. It is Muslim for 'fighting for peace.'

"Okay gang," Josie segued as she let out a deep exhale and returned to her normal lilted tone. "There's only so long that I can dwell on that shit before I feel like it's dragging me down permanently. Jesus, the Twins had to be pretty much locked up for a week after they heard about that. Fortunately, Rachel and Kayla agreed to spend several days just playing 'Hide the Sausage' with them, so they were able to kinda fuck out their aggression.

And once we got them past *that,* it was then time for them to join Vai, Alexa, Lionnel, and myself for one of *our* little missions against the on-air demonic propogandists that are spreading the gospel of Vetis. So, lets lighten the mood up and have a little fun, shall we?"

CHAPTER 80

LIAR

"I'm telling you Josie; I just don't like it!" Lionnel yelled out as Josie was applying a generous amount of makeup to her befreckled face. "I didn't like watching you kiss your first boyfriend, or whatever that dick was to you. I don't like it when you use yourself as bait to lure creeps to the basement of LOHAD for one of your slash dances. And I *sure as hell* do not like what you, Vai and Alexa are planning for tonight!"

Josie placed a pink rose over her left ear in her curly auburn locks, got up from her vanity and strode toward her love. Her black mini-dress clung to her seventeen-year-old, five-foot-four-and-a-half-inch frame as she sauntered closer to him wearing a broad smile on her face and black pumps on her size-six feet. She opened her arms and embraced him tenderly. She could feel his heart beating rapidly over concern for her well-being. She opened her petite, mauve lips and whispered into his ear, "I understand my love. And I truly appreciate your concern for me. I love you for wanting to protect me. To protect my safety and my innocence. You are much like my father in that respect. But what you don't understand is…"

Her voice trailed off as she pulled back from him revealing an even broader smile. She tussled her fingers through his black, curly hair and exclaimed playfully, "That this is gonna be *fuckin' funny*! Are you *kidding* me? We get these perverted propogandists all heated up and then…and then…Oh my *God*! It's going to be *so cool*! So just *lighten the fuck up* wouldja? You and the Twins will be around if we need you. But we won't. Tonight, my darling, the sisters are doing it for themselves. MWAHAHAHAHAAA! Now just chill out. I've gotta go see if the other two are ready. But first, we really need to play some appropriate prep music."

Josie strode over to the forty-year-old portable CD player and mused to herself as she began surveying her musical choices, "Let's see here. What would be a good song to get ready to? Something that *really* captures the moment. Oh! I know!" She took a CD out of its case and placed it into the player. She pushed 'play' and gave Lionnel a not-so-subtle wink as she strutted out of the room.

Lionnel settled into his oversized chair in the corner of his hotel suite as Bob Dylan's "The Times They are A-Changin'" came floating from the speakers. He shook his head and chuckled as he picked up a printout of the invitation that Rod had sent the three propogandist servants of Vetis on the darkest corner of the dark web. All three had replied immediately and enthusiastically. *Wow*, Lionnel thought to himself as he began reading the invitation. *This shit is really going down tonight. And she's becoming more like her mother every day.*

Greetings friends and fellow servants of Vetis,

As a small token of our undying gratitude for your decades-long service to our Glorious Vetis, you are hereby invited to join us for a private party where you will partake in any and all of the mortal pleasures that you desire. We will be providing you with the most exotic drinks ever created. We will be providing you with the most succulent cuisine that will be freshly prepared by the world's greatest chefs. And we will provide you with three of the most delectable virgins for you to play with, keep and mold as you see fit. Please RSVP to this private channel upon your receipt. This is a one-time opportunity to celebrate your undying loyalty to our cause.

Date: August 28, 2040

Time: 8:00PM SHARP!

Location: Upstage International Hotel, Penthouse Suite, Las Vegas

Weaponry: But of course! Feel free! We want you to feel safe and comfortable.

Security: Provided by us. No one besides your driver is allowed to know your location on this evening and the driver must remain with his vehicle. The event will be immediately cancelled upon detection of any person that was not personally invited. This is for both your safety and ours.

Lionnel's anger began to swell as he thought about what he was about to witness his love and the other two women on their team do this evening. He took out another piece of paper and began reading. His anger swelled further as he read a small sample of the hate-filled, treasonous lies that this trio had been spreading for decades through personal appearances, print, web, radio, and television. His eyes skimmed the headlines of the conspiratorial garbage that were intended to stoke fear in the White population. Then stoke hatred. Then stoke violence. Until the nation would be submerged in a cataclysmic race and culture war that would ultimately upend America's great Constitutional democracy and all the others throughout the world. Then, the dark souls would be summoned to Enlightenment for the ultimate battle for the control of people's souls throughout the cosmos.

Lib Demons Feast on Blood of Infants in Basement of D.C. Pizza Parlor!

Patriotic Freedom Fighters Incarcerated for Defending America's Only True President!

Twenty-three Adult Actors and Seventeen Child Actors Fake Own Deaths! Stage False-Flag Mass Shooting at Amusement Park for Gay Pedophiles!

Jews Control Everything! Even Space! Secret Jew Space Lasers Discovered!

Lib Books Teach Our Children to Hate Themselves! Suicide Rates Among White Children Explodes!

Fact! The End of Our Democracy Started When Women Got the Vote!

Freak Teachers Allowed Employment! They are Turning our Children Gay!

Innocent White Teen Defends Himself Against BLM Terrorists!

Gun Advocates Rejoice as Madison Man Protects Girlfriend!

Patriotic Motorist is Forced to Drive Through Violent Antifa Crowd in Self-Defense!

Kung-Flu Alert! Avoid All Asians!

Government Microchips Found in Vaccines! Deep State Using AI to Control Your Thoughts!

And so on and so on and so on, Lionnel somberly thought to himself. *How is it that so many people are susceptible to this indoctrination? This is shit that a five-year-old would laugh at. How can millions of people fall for this? Some are just stupid, I guess. But that can't be the whole thing. There were plenty of highly intelligent, accomplished people who knowingly gave their children poison at Jonestown. So, it isn't intelligence. It is personality. Anyone who gets indoctrinated into a cult of any type seems to share many of the same personality traits. Eccentricity. Narcissism. Paranoia of anything that is different from them. Grandiosity. A belief in self-entitlement. Distrustful. All of this adds up to an inability to process information and draw reasonable conclusions. They believe what they want to believe, despite actual facts that are staring them in the face.*

And it is these types of people that these three servants of Vetis, and thousands of others, prey upon. They use their additional personality trait of charismatic manipulation to draw these people in and brainwash them. The foot-soldiers aren't the ones who are evil. If anything, they are pitiful. But those that wield influence over them are truly evil. Like these three that have been knowingly spreading outrageous lies for their own personal benefit and power. They know what they are saying. They know what they are doing. They know that they are creating millions of violent people. And they do it while sipping their wine and getting a blowjob from their mistress. They love it. They love the power that they wield over the feeble-minded. And that is pure evil. I may not like how Josie is going to do this tonight, but there is a part of me that is going to enjoy watching this.

Josie bounced into the room and yelled out, "Hey! I've been trying to get your attention for like five minutes! What the fuck are you thinking about? Never mind. We're ready. Let's go take these traitorous fucks off the air!"

"Good evening gentlemen," the tall, thin pale man with long, light blond hair stated before his identical twin immediately added, "Yes. Good evening. We are so pleased that you have joined us."

"Yes, quite pleased," the original twin agreed. "We are so

pleased that you have agreed to play games with us this evening. We do enjoy games. Please, won't you come in?"

The Twins opened the door of the suite, and the three men were greeted by the sight of a long dark oak table that was covered in bottles of libations and a vast array of finely presented culinary delights.

"Please, have a seat, won't you?" Adam said followed by Aaron's, "Yes. Please make yourselves comfortable. You may place your guns over there if you wish. I believe that you will find that they may get in the way of some of the games you will be playing tonight. Especially 'Hide the Sausage.' Your guns will most definitely be in the way should you choose to play that game. But you must have someone to play with. It is time for you to select your dinner companions. We believe you will enjoy dining and playing with them. They enjoy playing games as well."

The three men sat in large red velour chairs that could easily seat two people. Aaron presented the first man with a purple bowl and said, "Won't you please select a key from the bowl? That will tell us which room to unlock in order to bring in your new playmate."

The obese man who was slovenly dressed looked up from under his long, feathered silver hair. He wore a misogynistic grin upon his stubbled face as he reached into the bowl and withdrew a key.

"Oh, Number three!" Adam exclaimed. "That is a very fine choice." "Yes, very fine indeed," Aaron echoed. "She is quite fond of games. Our houseboy Lionnel will now go and retrieve her. Lionnel! Please come in here!"

Lionnel entered the room wearing a sharp black suit on his body and an annoyed expression on his face.

"Please bring the occupant of Door Number Three to this fine man," Adam ordered.

Houseboy! An infuriated Lionnel thought to himself as he approached the door. *I'll show them fuckin' houseboy. Those two are enjoying this too much.* The door opened and Lionnel said in a flat tone, "Okay, you're up. You got one of the fat ones."

"Cool," the room's occupant replied casually as she sauntered past Lionnel and entered the main room of the suite.

The man's blood rushed from his head to his much, much, much smaller head as he witnessed the twenty-eight-year-old Vai Denhart come strutting in wearing six-inch pumps and black stockings over her toned legs. Her long, black hair contained a two-inch-wide silver streak down one side which cascaded down upon her shoulders, just above the bustline of her black-sequined mini-dress.

"W-well," the disgusting man began stammering. "Yeah, you'll do. But you look a bit too old to be a virgin."

"Well," Vai responded breathily. "I was raised by a *very* strict father, and I was never allowed to play with *boys*. But *men* are a different story. I *do so want* you to teach me games to play. And to spank me if I don't play them right. You'll teach me…won't you?" She concluded with a slight pout of her ruby lips.

"Very nice, Vai. Welcome to the party," Adam stated before Aaron took the purple bowl and presented it to the second man. His bulbous belly was covered in an ill-fitting blue striped oxford that did little to hide a pair of fleshy breasts. There was noticeable drool on his manicured black beard as he reached into the bowl greedily and pulled out a key.

"Room number One," Adam stated. "Another very fine selection. Lionnel, if you would please retrieve the occupant from Room One?"

"Of course, 'master,' Lionnel replied bitterly as he took the key and went to Room One. "Okay, your turn. You got the other fat one."

"Oh, how fun!" the young lady squealed out as she bounced past Lionnel and into the main room.

The twenty-two-year-old Alexa came bounding into the room wearing the identical black sequined dress, only her blonde hair did not reach her dress. She had placed her hair in pigtails to accentuate her seeming innocence.

"Oh, well, you look fun!" the man boomed in his deep, boisterous voice.

"Well, I certainly *hope* so," Alexa replied with a youthful exhuberance. "I will do *anything* that I can to help *you* have fun. I think that you'll find me to be a *very good* student. And *very* enthusiastic."

"That only leaves Door Number Two," Adam stated followed by Aaron's, "Yes. Lionnel would you please retrieve the occupant from Door Number Two?"

Lionnel said nothing as he took the key from Aaron's pale hand and trudged his way to Door Two. He opened the door and said, "You got the one that wears bow ties."

"That's perfect. That reminds me of a story Mom told me one time about this insurance company fuck that she strangled with his own ties, heh, heh, heh." Josie then kissed her love passionately, gave him a slight wink and strutted into the main room.

"Fuck, this sucks," Lionnel said to himself under his breath as he watched his lover seductively saunter over to the man, smile and sensually undo his bowtie. She then let out a light giggle and said, "Okay boys. Here we are. We are all so ready to play games with you. Would you like to eat your main course first, or..." Her voice trailed off suggestively before staring at the third man with a devious little smile upon her mauve lips. "Or should we start with a little dessert?"

"Dessert! Dessert! Dessert!" the overstimulated pigs yelled out as their members stood as upright as they could manage.

"Very well, then," Josie said through a playful giggle as Lionnel's ebony face darkened with rage. "But we have something *very special* planned for you boys tonight. We thought it might be fun to start with a game that *we* picked. We just need to go back to our rooms for a moment and put on something a bit more...*revealing* as to who we truly are. Something that we don't mind getting a bit...*sticky*. Strap yourselves in boys, we're going to take you all for a fun ride."

The three tittering women left the room arm in arm. The three men sat there chortling with lustful, sexist anticipation. Lionnel re-entered the room and begrudgingly nodded at the Twins.

"Oh my, the games are about to begin!" Adam stated, followed by Aaron's, "Yes! This game will be quite fun. Let us begin!"

Aaron pressed a button, and the lights began to dim. The synth-heavy industrial beat of "Sex on Wheelz" by My Life With the Thrill Kill Kult began pulsing through a set of speakers and bright multi-colored strobe lights began illuminating the enraptured men's faces. Their expressions of delight immediately changed to confusion as thick, metal belts came from the sides of their chairs and began constricting their bloated abdomens.

"Wh-what the hell is going on?" One of the men cried out as three distinctly feminine forms emerged into the frenzied kaleidoscope of colors. They all wore skintight black vinyl body suits that were adorned with two-inch golden spikes, placed every inch around the entire garment. The only part of their actual bodies that were visible were their smiling, lush lips, and penetrating eyes. Two pairs of eyes gleamed in an electric blue. The third pair glowed in an intense emerald green.

Vai strutted up to the first bound man. His long, silver hair was now a mop of sweat as she said to him sternly, "I see you like looking at my tits. Here. Have a closer look." With that she grabbed the struggling man by the back of his head and plunged the two spikes that were directly over her nipples into his eyes. The man screamed in agony as blood from his eye sockets flowed down the spikes and onto the black vinyl. Vai laughed maniacally as she ground the man's face deeper onto the spikes until his pathetic gasps ceased.

Alexa then bounced to the second quivering man and enthusiastically yelled out, "Hey! You wanna lap dance? And believe me, this is *really* happening! This isn't some sort of false-flag!" She then straddled the man's lap and began bouncing up and down like a child playing on a trampoline. She squealed in delight as she plunged the golden spikes into his groin, legs, and thighs repeatedly in a fit of pure pleasure. She launched her torso upon his and began writhing up and down on his chest and abdomen. The sadistic man mercifully stopped his wails of angst and Alexa looked down upon her new piece of art. Her gyrations had slashed his flesh into a nearly perfect rendition of a Jackson Pollock painting.

"Your turn, baby," Josie stated menacingly as she approached the final traitorous provocateur.

"P-please. N-n-no. P-please. Stop," he pleaded as his face appeared as wilted as his now flaccid penis.

Josie stood over him and flashed her wicked little smile before saying softly, "Hey, hey. It's all going to be okay. It's all going to be okay because we are ridding the world of scum like *you*. Scum who twists people's devotion to their God and their country into something sinister. Scum who preys upon those who *you know* are vulnerable to your lies and manipulations. Scum who preaches hate over peace. Fiction over fact. Violence over love. We are sending a message. We are sending the message that you cannot hide behind the First Amendment any longer to spew your radical ideologies. You can't yell 'fire' in a movie theatre and incite panic, right? Well, our message is that if you incite a violent uprising, then that is *exactly* what you will get. A violent uprising. Against *you,* motherfucker. Now, how about a little kiss?"

The man shrieked with morbid torment as Josie straddled his lap and tightly hugged his torso. The golden spikes planted themselves effortlessly into his quivering flesh. Josie could feel the free flow of his blood dripping down her vinyl clad body. And she liked it. Her vibrant green eyes looked deeply into his. They were eyes that were filled with fearful tears and were pleading for mercy. She smiled demurely, slowly moved her spiked, vinyl face towards his and tenderly kissed his lips. His head struggled for release as the golden spikes slid into his face and eyes. He squealed in torturous muffled wails as his lips were encased in a death grip with hers. And then, he was still.

Josie began grunting as she tried to remove herself from the impaled traitor. She heard chuckling from behind her before yelling out from the side of her mouth, "Hey! Fuckers! I'm stuck on this little prick! How about a little help here!"

The next morning, the entertainment coordinator for the hotel turned on the stage lights in the auditorium to begin preparations for that evening's musical act. She shrieked, then fainted as she found three bloody heads covered in small craters planted upon microphone stands. The polished wooden stage was awash in a demented dark crimson. Each of the faces had a pink rose sticking out of one of the many holes. There was a note nailed to the head of the silver-haired man that read, *You've Just Been Upstaged, Fuckers*!

————

Erick and Lionnel shook their heads disapprovingly while Arima and Marcus giggled with delight.

"Well, that *was* more fun!" Maddy yelled out. "Way to take the 'Slashdance' thing to a whole new level! And I'm still lovin' the calling card, sweetie." She then beamed at her husband and exclaimed, "Hey, baby! We need one of those! We can't have our daughter being all cooler and shit than us!"

Erick looked into the green eyes of his beloved wife and said with a slight tone of exasperation, "Haven't you learned *anything*? Not *everything* is a competition. It is *okay* for other people to have things that we don't. It is *okay* for other people to have successes that are uniquely theirs. Let other people have their victories. In fact, *celebrate* their victories *with* them. It causes you *no harm* for others to have something that you don't. It costs you *nothing* to be genuinely happy for someone else. Celebrate the unique gifts that *you* bring to the world and be thankful for the unique contributions that *others* bring to this world. That is what makes this world an interesting place to live in. And it is what makes us humane. Don't you understand, dear?"

Maddy stared at her husband with a perplexed expression upon her slightly befreckled face before roaring back, "Well, I don't know what *that* fucking diatribe was all about, but it did *nothing* to help me think up a cool calling card! Whatevs. I'll think of it later by myself, *like always*. Okay sweetie, so how about Gregory, Marcus, and Cliff. Did they convince the world leaders to join us or stay the fuck out of our way, or what?"

CHAPTER 81

I THINK I SMELL A RAT

Cliff bowed his head and clutched onto Marcus's sweaty hand as they both said a silent prayer together before the international dignitaries were shown into the conference room in one of the New York buildings owned by Murder, Inc.

Seven Assassination Technicians dressed in their customary all-black suits entered the room silently as they ushered in fourteen diplomats from countries representing every region of the world. The diplomats took their place in plush white swivel chairs surrounding a large, black marble, oval meeting room table while looking at each other wearing confused expressions.

"Why the hell are *we* here?" the twenty-nine-year-old Cliff whispered to his thirty-one-year-old dear friend, Marcus. "We don't know *anything* about diplomacy. That's Gregory's deal, I guess. What are *we* supposed to do? What if we blow it?"

Marcus gave his friend a nod of understanding before replying in a hushed voice, "Because Josie wants only those within her inner circle to lead these efforts. She trusts us, man. We may not have all the skills needed, but those can be taught. You can't learn to be trustworthy. You must *earn* people's trust through your deeds. And that is what we have done. We have earned her trust and everyone else in Murder, Inc. So, we'll just stand here, and we'll take Gregory's lead. And we will not blow it or do *anything* to violate her trust. And, I don't know about you, but then I've got a date with a huge spliff and an even larger pizza."

Cliff let out a nervous chuckle, before a dignitary from a Central African nation broke the room's silence by saying, "Okay. You have succeeded in getting us here. After months of reaching out to us and telling us that you have information regarding an existential threat to humanity, we are here. We are some of the most trusted ambassadors for our respective nations. We hold a great deal of sway with our governments. So, getting us all together is no small feat. There are many existential threats to humanity. So, which one are you here to talk to us about? Climate change? Nuclear war? Famine? Drought? Economic upheaval? Culture wars between the various ideological tribes? Pandemics?"

"Yes," the forty-three-year-old Chadwick Gregory Davenport III stated bluntly as he stood at the head of the table. His black business suit was perfectly fit upon his taught frame and there was not a single drop of sweat upon his forehead as he continued. "Yes. All of that. And then some.

"Ladies and gentlemen, it is with the deepest respect and humility that I thank you all for joining us today. We truly understand the value of your time and we are honored by your presence. I will try to be succinct with my comments. But, again with the deepest respect, if you do not listen to our heeds today, you may be singularly responsible for the destruction of humanity as we know it. As well as the heavens."

Gregory's last comment initiated a round of loud guffawing by the dignitaries. "Oh, we not only have to protect *mankind*, but we must also now protect the *heavens*?" a Middle Eastern dignitary proclaimed sarcastically. "Well, now *this* I must hear! How is it that we can *save mankind* and the *heavens* young man? Please. Just tell us. We will do *whatever* you may need. But please make it fast. We all have dinner engagements."

Gregory looked upon the laughing group with a calm steadiness upon his face before stating, "Yes, I quite understand how this must sound to you all. If you please, just allow me to show you this brief presentation. We would be happy to answer any questions that you may have upon its conclusion. Marcus, would you please dim the lights? Cliff would you please start the show?"

The lights dimmed and a white screen descended from the ceiling. The projector that was placed in the middle of the table lit up and the screen became filled with a rapidly edited array of images of atrocities from the previous century. Images of starving children. Images of mass graves. Images of the victims of murderers. Of rapists. Of pedophiles. Of war crimes. Images of horrendous human experiments. Over and over and over the dignitaries' eyes were bombarded with images of the most grotesque carnage ever created by the human race. Sunken eyes. Terrorized faces. Bruises. Lacerations. Disembodied limbs. Entrails. Corpses. Blood. It was an explosion of morbidity which caused some of the dignitaries to begin to weep. Then suddenly, they were granted a reprieve as the monstrous bombardment mercifully ended. Gregory's relaxed voice could then be heard as a dark red blur replaced the butchery on the screen.

"Ladies and gentlemen. There is one common thread that holds together all the horrendous images that you have just witnessed. And that singular thread is that these atrocities were committed by human beings in name only. They may be biologically 'homo-sapien,' but they are not truly *human*. Because they aren't *humane*. Those that commit these atrocities are *incapable* of being humane because they lack a *soul*. Or, if they *do* possess a soul, it is as black as the darkest of nights.

"Yes, ladies and gentlemen, there truly is *pure evil* that walks amongst us in our world. And what you have just witnessed is but a small fraction of what they have done to us over time. It is but a small fraction of what they *intend* to do to every living person and every enlightened soul that has departed from our Earth. These images do not represent the end. They represent the *beginning*.

The beginning of the suffering and torture and destruction and death. *This* is just the beginning.

"So, what is the end to all of this you may ask? The end for these soulless demonic servants is the toppling of our great democracies, replacing them with brutal dictatorships. The end is the creation of more and more dark souls that they can use and then sacrifice. The end is these sacrificed dark souls being summoned from their Earthly existence to wage war against the enlightened souls who reside peacefully in the heavens. The end is to rule every plane of existence where humanity resides. The end is the complete elimination of both Earth and Enlightenment.

"And that, my most esteemed friends, is the greatest existential threat that we have ever faced. All the threats that you listed are nothing more than tools for them. They will use them all, and then some, in order to breed distrust amongst us. Then hatred. Then violence. Then mass murder until Earth finally succumbs and the battle is engaged with our loved ones in Enlightenment.

"This battle is being overseen and waged by a *true* demon. A demon named Vetis. He is known as the 'Tempter of the Holy' and he creates then recruits human dark souls to build an army to fulfill what he believes is his ultimate destiny. Domination over the Earth is step one. Domination over Enlightenment is step two. Then, nothing will be able to stop his ultimate goal of his barbaric rule over the cosmos."

As Gregory concluded his final sentence, the image on the screen came into focus. It was the image of a devilish-looking beast sitting upon a throne of fire. He wore a sinister smile upon his dark red face and his forehead had protruding horns that twisted upward. His muscular torso had four arms, the scarred hands of which were squeezing blood from a screaming human being. He looked like a demented child that was gleefully torturing his toys. There was an audible gasp from the group as they were transfixed by this most nefarious sight.

"Poppycock!" the British dignitary exclaimed as he hastily got up from his chair. "What insanity! What rubbish! A demon is taking over the world and heavens? It is laughable and this has been an utter waste of our time! Come, my friends. Let us not waste one more moment listening to these…these…heretics!"

"I thought that you might react that way, Mr. Ambassador," Gregory responded calmly. "Marcus, Cliff, would you please bring in the isolation chamber and our special guests?"

"I will not stay for one more moment!" the British dignitary bellowed as he turned around and began his march toward the exit. He was stopped in his tracks as seven red dots converged upon his forehead.

Marcus and Jefferson wheeled in a plexiglass box that was six feet tall and three feet wide. In the center of the box was a metal chair with straps. And they were each carrying metal boxes that were shaking violently.

Gregory began approaching the frozen dignitary with ease as he stated, "I am sorry for this shocking development. I truly am. I want to assure the rest of you that you are completely safe. All that we ask is that you stay until the end of the presentation. Then, you will be allowed to leave completely unharmed. None of you have anything to fear because *your* souls are intact. *You*, on the other hand…"

Gregory's voice trailed off as he glared at the British ambassador with an intense serenity. "*You* do not possess a soul. *You* are a traitor to your mission. *You* are a traitor to your country. *You* are a traitor to your colleagues. And *you* are a traitor to all of humanity. So, won't you please take your seat in our chamber? We have a few questions to ask of you. Or would you prefer to have my friends blow your fucking brains out?"

The British dignitary dropped his hat and began trembling as Gregory led him into the chamber and bound his arms and legs to the metal chair.

"Good," Gregory stated in a satisfied tone. "Now we can begin the *true* presentation. This can go quite easily on you, or we can introduce you to our special guests. All you must do is answer one simple question for all of us. Is what I have just presented true or false?"

The dignitary began stammering as spittle flew from his pasty lips. "I-I have no idea what you are talking about! Release me this instant! I-I-I shall have you executed for this outrage!"

"Ah, the hard way," Gregory replied as he calmly circled the increasingly frightened man. "Very well, then. Marcus. Cliff. Would you please give our esteemed guest something sweet?"

Cliff climbed a small stepstool on the side of the chamber and opened a four-inch door at the top. Marcus handed him a gallon container containing a thick, golden substance. Cliff smiled, unscrewed the lid, and began pouring the substance over the quivering and confused man's head. The heavy stickiness flowed down his face, upon his shoulders and down his torso like oozing lava. Its golden hue glistened in the lights as it slid down his quivering body and pooled ominously upon the plexiglass floor.

"What you have just been covered in," Gregory began explaining, "is honey. Wonderfully sweet honey. In fact, it is some of the finest honey in all the world. It comes from the apiary of our friend and leader who owns an estate just a short drive from here. She is quite proud of her apiary. It was a gift from her father. Her father who was stabbed in the back by one of your demons. And she does love her bees. In fact, she loves *all* living things. Well, except for traitors, bigots and all the other dark souls that prey upon the innocent. She doesn't really care for *them* much. But she *does* love her honey. And she loves *feeding* her honey to her precious pets."

Cliff and Marcus then took off the metal encasing of each box, revealing a cage with four snarling white rats who were anxiously trying to escape their prison.

"Now," Gregory continued as he tried to contain his sadistic grin, "What will it be? Answer time? Or feeding time?"

"Fine! Fine!" the nearly hysterical dignitary screamed out as he struggled with his bindings. "Fine! I'll tell you! Just-just-keep those things away from me! I'll tell you! Yes! It is all true! Our most glorious Vetis is taking over the Earth. And Enlightenment. He is using the truly evil souls of this Earth to twist other people's faith and sense of patriotism into something hateful.

Something violent. He is building an army of these dark souls and once they are done being used upon this Earth, they will be sacrificed, and their dark essence will be used to wage war against the hapless spirits of Enlightenment! They will be called to action by the two most demonic spirits who have ever existed upon this Earth. They are somewhere in the cosmos, searching for each other. And once they find each other they will use their combined will to summon all the Earth-bound dark souls into battle. And then our most Glorious Vetis shall join us *all* in holy domination over those who do not bow at his feet!"

The dignitary's body convulsed violently as he completed his descent into madness and let out non-stop maniacal cackles from his twisted mouth.

The man's insane giggles continued as Gregory turned to the remaining dignitaries. "So, you see that what we have said is true. We represent a group who has been battling these dark forces for some time now. Until recently, we thought that we were just battling traitorous anti-democratic forces in our respective countries. And we have been quite successful, which has resulted in these movements becoming increasingly fragmented and disorganized. But they still exist in large numbers and remain an existential threat. That is because we have now learned that our battle extends into the heavens. We have now learned that it isn't enough to rid the Earth of this vermin. We must destroy their very essence even after their human form has been vanquished. We are working on several fronts. We are taking out as many of the truly evil souls on the Earth as we can. And we are now working on a way to round up the dark spirits that remain here and then destroy them before they can be summoned for their final battle. But this is a task that is too large even for an organization as formidable as ours and we need your assistance. But first, let us show you what we do to those who aspire to oppress us all."

Gregory nodded at Cliff and Marcus who opened small doors at the bottom of the plexiglass tomb. They placed the snarling cages against the openings and released their locks. The hungry beasts lunged at the still cackling dignitary. His deranged laughter changed into agonizing screams as the rats began ravenously chewing on his honey-covered body. The rats' feeding increased to a frenzy as they began tasting the anguished man's blood that was now being mixed with the golden sweetness. The carnivorous creatures tore through his flesh beginning with his legs. They then moved up to his torso. One rat chewed a hole in the tortured man's abdomen, then tore its way through his body until its gore-soaked furry face emerged from his back. Another rat pounced upon the screaming man's face and began gnawing at his flesh. It ripped off his lips and swallowed them in one gluttonous bite. Then, it ate his nose as greedily as a child eating gummy candy. It paused briefly and stared into the dying man's eyes with an inquisitive look upon its bloody, furry face. Its whiskers began twitching playfully as it decided upon its next action. It took one last long look into the man's pleading eyes before deciding what it wanted for dessert.

The man let out one final wretched squeal as what was left of his body went limp. He now resembled a half-carved rack of lamb that had been shaved to make gyros. Cliff and Marcus kneeled beside the cages and made kissing sounds. The rats dutifully turned around, entered their cages, and settled into a satisfied slumber.

The room then darkened as a thick purple smog emerged from the man's carved frame. It cackled at the shocked group as it began to ascend out of the hole in the top of the plexiglass confinement. Its cackling stopped the moment that Cliff and Marcus began spraying it with holy water from harmless-looking squirt guns. The dense purple mist began shrieking and writhing until it dissipated into nothingness.

The dignitaries' faces held looks of horrified satisfaction as Gregory asked, "Okay then. Any questions?"

A female ambassador from Central Asia stood and looked at her colleagues in a respectful silence. She then inquired sincerely, "And just what is it that *we* can do to help in this endeavor?"

Marcus and Cliff each let out a deep sigh of relief and wiped sweat from their brows as Gregory allowed himself to smile for the first time in days.

———

"Oh, for fuck sakes Josie!" Maddy cried out. "This is totally *not cool*! Y'know, I'm really starting to think that you have problem. We need to take you to a shrink or somethin'!"

"What the fuck is wrong with *you*, Mom?" Josie yelled back.

"Rats? You're now keeping fucking *rats* as pets? Gross!" A disgusted Maddy retorted at the top of her voice.

"Oh, hey. Listen Maddy," Marcus slurred from his slouched position on the couch. "They're, like, really cool. They like to watch TV and shit and eat cheese crackers."

"Yeah. And pizza crust. They really like that," Arima chimed in as she loaded her bowl with a fresh hit. "They're really cool. They just like, hang out and shit. They sit really close to our faces when we're smoking and inhale the extra smoke. Then they get really mellow and chew on pizza or cheese or whatever we're having. There's nothing to worry about, sis."

"Wait just a fuckin' minute!" Maddy yelled. "Where the fuck *are* these things?"

"I dunno," Marcus answered calmly. "They're around here somewhere. They don't really like strangers so maybe they're hiding from you."

As if on cue, a large white rat pounced upon Maddy's chest and stared at her with inquisitive pink eyes.

"Get-this-fucking-thing-off-of-me," Maddy ordered with a trembling voice.

Josie let out a deep sigh and rolled her eyes before going over to her mother. She picked the curious rat from Maddy's chest, giggled, and cradled it in her arms like an infant.

Erick just shrugged at his wife as she stared at him in bewilderment. He then said, "Okay, that's not really the point of the story. But kudos to you, Marcus, and your team. What an interesting way to rid the world of a dark soul. And I really enjoyed the traitor's descent into madness as he was being consumed. It's really an interesting analogy. He is a human 'rat' who betrayed his own kind. That is what human rats do. They consume one another. It was really a very creative way to send the message about how rats consume other rats. Bravo to you all."

"Um," Marcus began as his foggy mind searched for a response. "Thanks for that. But I don't think that's why Gregory did that. He just said that he thought it would be cool."

"What the fuck is it with you and your book reports?" Maddy asked her beloved husband with an annoyed tone. "Who gives a *fuck* about imagery and shit? The fucker's dead and that's all that matters. So, are these governments gonna help us or what?"

"Oh yeah, that!" Josie squealed out. "That's the best part! So, the world's democracies have banded together, and they are providing us with intelligence and logistical support. Jessie identifies the truly evil souls in their respective countries through her Beholding ability, and then they help us locate them. We pretty much do the rest. And not only that, but there are several countries that are run by dictators and other fascist scum that have resistance forces that are starting to help too. So not only are we making strides in saving the Earth's democracies, but we're starting to gain footholds in more oppressive countries to set the stage for the people regaining the power over their own destinies. Isn't that great?"

"Well, that's just wonderful sweetie!" Erick beamed. "We are so proud of you! Look at what you've accomplished in the past year! Look at our daughter, Buttacup. Aren't you proud of her?"

"Well, *of course* I'm proud, but..." Maddy's childlike 'hurt' voice trailed off briefly before continuing. "I'm just kind of *wondering* that if Josie could do all of *this*, then what does the group think about *my* time as leader? I mean, its *really cool* and shit, but *I* accomplished a lot too y'know?"

"Of course, you did, my love," Erick responded tenderly as he realized that his beloved wife's fragile ego needed his reassurance in this moment. "Josie *never* would have been able to accomplish *any* of this if *you* had not laid the foundation in *your* time as leader. And, if *you* had been in charge this past year, I'm *sure* that you would have accomplished just as much *if not more.*"

"Yep! That's fuckin' true!" a rejuvenated Maddy arrogantly declared. "No question about it. Josie, you've done great and I'm *totally* proud of you. But your bragging about this shit is getting a little annoying so don't get a big fuckin' head, alright? Now, somebody get the message out that we're going to have a meeting tomorrow night. It's time that the rest of the group find out that I'm back. And *this* time, I'm not playing fucking games! This time I mean *fuckin' business!*"

"When *haven't* you meant..." Erick's voice trailed off as he stared into his wife's intense, green eyes. "Oh, never mind," he concluded as he looked at his daughter and gave her a knowing smirk.

CHAPTER 82

IF I KNEW YOU WERE COMIN' I'D'VE BAKED A CAKE

A hushed anxiety hovered over the meeting room as Murder, Inc's. top brass sat nervously awaiting the arrival of their leader. Darting glances at one another all communicated the same thing. *What is this meeting about? What is the urgency? Why was the message simply 'Meeting tomorrow night in the conference room 8PM SHARP. Your attendance is mandatory. Thank you.'*

The large oak door opened, and Josie's inner circle entered the room and began taking their seats at the head of the long table in the front. Arima, Marcus, Jessie (with LucyFur), Cliff, Kaneko, Jamie, Kayla, and Rachel took their designated places stage left. Lucy, Jennifer, Jules, Jerry, Sam, Henri, Rod, a still weakened Rosa, and Gregory took their designated places stage right.

Josie then entered the room arm-in-arm with her Lionnel. She wore a beaming smile upon her befreckled face as her curly copper locks bounced with each step that she took. Her brightly flowered minidress was hidden from view as her five-foot-four-and-a-half-inch frame was overtaken behind the large wooden podium. Her ever-present and ever-white-clad Adam, Aaron,

Alexa, and Vai stood directly behind her. Their brilliant blue eyes darted constantly as they surveyed the room for signs of trouble.

The large gathering's anxiety increased as they watched Josie wipe a single tear from her effervescent eye before she began speaking. Their anxiety increased further as two black cloaked and hooded figures joined Josie on either side of her.

"Hello, my friends. Thank you all so much for joining us this evening," Josie began. "I am so sorry that it was on such short notice, but what I have to say tonight simply cannot wait. What I have to say tonight is nothing short of a miracle. What I have to say tonight is…"

Josie's attempt at a heartfelt introduction was unceremoniously cut off by the smaller of the black hooded figures muttering impatiently, "Oh, for fuck sakes. This is taking too long."

There was an audible gasp by the entire congregation as the shorter figure threw off her hood and cloak. Maddy's green eyes were glowing with a fiery intensity, and she had a wicked smile upon her youthful-looking face. She realized the importance of this moment. She realized that her words would have to be chosen carefully. She realized that she could not fuck this up. Maddy fucked it up as she exuberantly bellowed out, "Here ye! Here ye! Here ye! That's right, bitches! I'm back!"

Erick sheepishly took off his robe and quietly shook his head in embarrassment as he heard his beloved wife continue her arrogant diatribe.

"Yep, *I'm* back, my loving husband *Erick* is back and now we're all gonna have some fuckin' fun! I can see by the shocked looks on all your faces just how *thrilled* you all are to have me back. And I just want to say, that just like before, I shall rule this group with an iron fist or a velvet glove. The choice is yours. So, how about we just go around the room quick so that everybody can talk about just how *delighted* they are to have me back, hmmmmm?"

"Mother!" Josie yelled out. "What the fuck are you doing?"

Maddy looked at her daughter. The pair could easily have passed for nearly identical sisters. She delicately placed her hand upon Josie's cheek and said sweetly, "It's all okay, sweetie.

Mommy's here now to make everything better. Why don't you just take a seat and I'll take it from here. I think there's a chair open third row from the back. Thank you very much for your cooperation in this matter."

Josie glared at her mother with a seething intensity as she said through gritted teeth, "Mom. I love you. And I love that you are here. But *I* am now the leader of this organization. *I* am the one that will be conducting this meeting. *I* am the one who is in charge here. And *you...you...you*...are the one that will sit your fucking ass down *now*!"

"Well, isn't *this* just a fine howdoyado?" Maddy responded in her 'wounded' voice. "Of all the disrespectful and hurtful things that you could have said to me. To your own mother. I just don't have the words to express how damaged I feel right now."

Erick stood behind his beloved wife and placed his hands upon her petite shoulders. He leaned his face forward so that his disheveled black hair was tickling her right ear. He then whispered to her, "My love. I know how excited you are right now. But this is Josie's organization. So, I'm sorry to say this to you and I realize that there will be a drought in your wearing sexy outfits for a while but shut the fuck up and let's sit down. This is what she was raised to do."

Maddy let out a shocked gasp. She looked around the room at the confused faces. She looked once again into the glowering eyes of her daughter. She sighed deeply and said with as much hubris that she could muster, "Well, *of course* I will take my seat. That was a test fuckers! I just wanted to make sure that you were all as loyal to our Josie as you were to me. *Of course*, it is your group, sweetie. Please continue. We shall just sit beside you and guide you as your consiglieres."

Maddy then leaned into her daughter's ear and whispered, "It's okay that we're still your consiglieres, isn't it?"

Josie's face softened, making her look once again like an innocent child as she whispered back, "It would be my honor. Thank you, Mom. Thank you, Dad. I love you both so much." The congregation began openly crying tears of joy as they witnessed

'The Family of Fury' lovingly embrace for the first time in over a year.

Maddy wiped a tear from her eye then looked at the two people who were seated on either side of Josie. "Arima! Lionnel! Move your fucking asses! *We* sit to the side of our daughter!" Maddy ordered.

"That's really kinda not cool, sis," Arima casually replied as she and Lionnel got up and stood to either side of the Twins. As Maddy was taking her seat, she heard someone comment from the back of the room, "Wow. I have no idea how she's here, but she sure as hell hasn't changed much."

"Hey!" Maddy screamed as her emerald eyes scanned the back of the room for the culprit. "Who said that? I'll put your head on a fuckin' pike!"

Erick placed his arm around his wife's shoulders and coaxed her body down upon her chair as he said, "It's all okay dear. It was meant as a compliment. Everybody adores and respects you here."

"Yeah, well it had *better* have been a compliment," Maddy retorted loudly.

Josie rolled her eyes and chuckled lightly before regaining control over her meeting. "So, I hope you all enjoyed our little production. We thought that a few of you might have doubted that my parents have been brought back to life, so we thought we'd just put on this little show. I mean, could *anyone* doubt that these are my parents after *that* little scene?"

The entire room let out their pent-up laughter and stood in applause. Maddy also stood and began taking exaggerated bows. Erick placed his head in his hands and shook it in disbelief. And Josie let out her largest laugh since before she had found out just who her parents truly were. Her laugh echoed a cherished time of innocence before she knew that her parents were freedom-fighting serial killers. A time before many of her closest friends and family had been slaughtered by the anti-democracy forces. A time when her biggest worry was finding loving forever homes for her beloved stray puppies and kittens. A time before she herself ascended to this throne of gory retribution. A time before she had literal blood on her hands. And her face. And her body.

"Yep, we're really something, aren't we," Josie stated as she concluded her laughter and motioned for people to take their seats once again. "Okay gang. The complete details of my presentation are contained in the packets that are being handed out to you but let me give you a brief update as to what is going on. As you know, Arima can connect with spirits who have not left our plane of existence and bring them into her soul. My mother still has work to do here, so her soul returned to us. She went looking for my father and she found him clinging to the dark spirit of my grandmother. My mother brought my father back here and they entered my Aunt Arima. Yes, my aunt. My mother and Aunt Arima are half-sisters. The evil Pastor fathered both of them. He is being held somewhere in Enlightenment. My grandmother, on the other hand, is unaccounted for. Anyway, Rod and Rosa developed a way to take my parents' souls, place them into another body and re-animate them. So, here they are until they are called back to Enlightenment.

"But that won't be until their work here is done. Their work to fight alongside all of us to finally take down the evil forces of the demon Vetis. We have done a great job of destroying much of the infrastructure and leadership of the *Underground Autocratic Movement*. We have assassinated many of their leaders. But in doing so, we have created more dark souls who will willingly serve Vetis in his battle against Enlightenment. So, what we are doing now is trying to come up with a way to collect as many of those dark souls that remain here and destroy them. We must destroy as many of them as we can before they are summoned to the next plane to engage in battle against Enlightenment. We must weaken their army as much as we can to give the pure souls of Enlightenment a fighting chance for victory. And we must do so before my grandmother has a chance to re-unite with the Pastor. Because it is through *their* union that the dark souls will be summoned and called into battle. It is *their* unholy union that still presents an existential threat to all of humankind. It is *their* unholy union which we must stop. Any questions? Everybody up to speed? Pretty simple, right? Okay, now moving on to this month's assignments! And please don't forget, that with each traitorous bigot dick that you kill, you get a free puppy or kitten. Plus, I'll even throw in a month's worth of food! Okay, when I call your name, please raise your hand."

One of the Assassination Technicians in the back of the room whispered to her colleague, "I really gotta get less efficient at killing people. I've run out of people that I can get to take all the puppies and kittens that I earn." Her colleague simply gave her a solemn nod of understanding.

———

"Okay, you motherfuckin' douchebag," the spirit of Joseph Angelo Argento stated with his customary surliness. "You know the drill. Gimme your fuckin' hands. Or do we need to do this the hard way like we did last week? Or was it last month? Fuck, there's no time up here."

The Pastor's dark spirit emerged from a blackened corner of his conjured cell and approached the barred door. He began weeping tears of black bile in painful anticipation as he hesitantly placed his newly healed hands between the bars. His hands were immediately bound to the cell's bars by thick, green vines.

"Thanks Botanist, or Herbert, or whatever," Joseph stated to a tall, gangly spirit sitting in the corner next to his green wife, Iris, and their adopted daughter whose twelve-year-old mortal body had been raped and murdered by members of a CHARLIE unit in New Orleans.

"May we watch, Uncle Joe?" a pair of giggling little girls' spirits inquired. "Now, girls," their mother, Becky Peterson scolded. "Please leave Joe alone. He has work to do."

"Ah, it's all right!" Joseph gleefully responded. "It's good for them to see what we do to pricks who are pure evil. And I'll tell you what girls! When we're done with this douchebag, we'll go get some ice cream, okay?"

"Yay!" the girls' spirits squealed with delight.

"We would *all* like to watch. Time is running short, Joseph. I can feel it," Blair Aubrey Sommers-Argento said with a delicate urgency to her beloved husband.

"Yeah! Let's get this show on the road!" Patricia Mercy Sommers cried out. "I've got a rehearsal coming up! I've got George Harrison and John Lennon to close the 'Victoryfuckin-palooza' show with "My Sweet Lord" then "Imagine." And *that* shit wasn't easy to pull off! How fuckin' cool is *that* gonna be? I'm nearly cumming just thinking about it!"

"Yes, we *all* want to watch," stated Howard who was surrounded by Arima's spiritual family and friends. Howard had found redemption through assisting Arima following an eternity of deserved hell while imprisoned in a painting. He was now the leader of this ragtag group of spirits who were completely devoted to Arima's safety and happiness. There were Mr. and Mrs. Roper, who assisted Arima in identifying worthy souls that she could then help to find their way into Enlightenment. Their selfless service was rewarded by Arima as she helped them heal their children before they ascended into the heavens as well. There was Arima and Marcus's supervisor from the morgue, Clyde Manfrengensen, who had been one of many mercilessly gunned down by the Pastor's henchmen on what was to be Arima's wedding day. There was the former CHARLIE member, Lillian, whose disgust at their sadistic actions led her to the same tragic fate as their other victims. Arima's mother, Abdalla Azar was also present as was her loving grandmother, Louise Azar. Louise glared into the Pastor's black eyes while holding the spiritual hands of two of his other victims, Marcus's Moms, and Pops. Her voice cracked slightly as she said in a deep voice, "I can *never* get enough of this. I can *never* get enough of watching the torture of the man who murdered my daughter, Abdalla and tried to destroy my granddaughter Arima. I will *never* get enough of this."

"Nor can I," came the uncharacteristically bold voice of Freddie Sommers's spirit. "In fact, Joe, I was wondering if I might have a bit of fun today as well? Oh, I could care less that he fucked my wife. If they weren't such an existential threat, I would wish that they would spend eternity together. These bastards deserve each other. But to take away my true fatherhood of my beloved Madeline. Well, that I shall never forgive."

"Uh, sure," Joseph replied as he surveyed the slight frame of his deceased brother-in-law. "Yeah, maybe you could do his pinkies or something. Come on over."

"Okay, let's get started," Joseph stated with enthusiasm as he showed Freddie where to place his hands on the Pastor's quivering right pinkie.

"I can call all of this off right now," the spirit of Gwen stated calmly to the Pastor's pleading eyes. "I can make all your pain go away. We will stop the torture and just let you spend eternity jailed here. It will be boring, but there will be no more pain. We will not continue to break your hands and body repeatedly after they are healed. All you must do is help us. Just tell us where she is. We know that you can sense her. We know that you know where she will be coming from. All you must do is tell us, so that I can track her. Then, we will summon her daughter to destroy her once and for all. And all of this will be over. For us. For you. Vetis will not be able to use the two of you to summon his Earth-bound dark souls. There will be no war in Enlightenment. And there will be no more war upon the Earth after our mortal friends clean up the rest of the truly evil souls there. Just tell us where she is, and the pain will go away. Forever."

The Pastor let out a maniacal laugh as he tossed his marked head backwards. All the carved symbols of Vetis convulsed upon his dark purple flesh as his sadistic tittering echoed throughout the cavernous inner sanctum of Enlightenment. He stared deeply with his black eyes into the pure-white souls of each of the witnesses that surrounded him before saying sinisterly, "Go ahead. Do your worst. The pain that I experience today will be *nothing* compared to the pain that you all will feel when I am reunited with her. The pain that you will feel when we summon all the dark souls from the Earth. The pain that you will feel as we slaughter you. But you, Joe. You, I'm going to take my time with. I am going to beat you and tear you apart until your soul is in complete submission. And as you lay there wishing for an end to your agony, I am going to make you watch me drink the blood of your beloved niece and my regretted offspring from her shattered skull. I will floss my teeth with what remains of her copper hair, and I will plop her damnable green eyes into a fresh martini and suck it down in joyous triumph! Now get on with it. I have preparations to make."

CHAPTER 83

CANDY EVERYBODY WANTS

"Hey, whatcha doin'?" Erick inquired of his wife as he entered the bedroom draped in a white towel while drying his hair.

Maddy was laid out on the bed wearing her pink shorts and tank top. Her size six bare feet were crossed as she looked up from the book she was reading.

"Oh, I've decided to write a book, so that's what I'm doin,'" she replied casually. "Since you pricks took out the wireless internet, it's difficult for me to get my ideas out there into the world. Plus, I don't know how much time I'll be down here on Earth before I get called back to Enlightenment. So, I decided to become an author so that I can get my cool ideas out into the world while I have the chance."

"Oh, cool. Are you doing some sort of research? Is that why you're reading the book?" Erick inquired.

"No…well…*sorta*," Maddy replied. "I know it *looks* like I'm reading a book right now, but I'm *actually* writing it. I have to read a bunch of *these* before I can write my own."

Erick, noticing the book's cover and title for the first time replied in a lecturing tone, "Why the fuck are you reading a bunch of romance novels? You hate that shit! And why are the covers always the same? It's always some bosomy woman and some shirtless stud, and they are almost always *white* if you haven't noticed. And then they fuck as humans and then become wolves and fuck as wolves or some shit. So, if you're writing a book, why are you reading *that*?"

An exasperated Maddy looked up at her husband and said haughtily, "Ok, listen, mister. You know *nothing* about being an author. This is how you write books. In order to write books, you have to do something called 'writing to market.' First, you figure out what genre is really *hot* right now. And believe me, people *really* like to read about fucking. Then, you read a whole bunch of popular books in that genre, and you read the reviews to figure out what readers like about them. Then, you put all those popular themes, tropes, styles, plot devices, and characteristics of the characters into a formula. And then you can write your own original book! Once I get the formula down, I figure I can crank out about twelve of these fuckers in the next year."

Erick shook his head in bewilderment and said with a hint of sarcasm, "Okay, let me get this straight. So, you read other people's work, take out the popular parts and rip them off. Wow. How artistic of you. Gee, human A.I. much? Why don't you just write what is in your *head*? Why don't you write what is in your *heart*? If all that you are doing is writing based upon a formula of other people's work, then you aren't adding anything to the human experience. You are depriving the reader of your uniqueness. Sure, it's impossible to be *completely* original in everything that is produced, but there's a difference between being *influenced* by other works and intentionally ripping them off. For example, what do you think about the song "Ice, Ice, Baby?"

"Uh, I hate that fuckin' song," Maddy replied bluntly.

"And just why is that?" Erick inquired further.

"Um," Maddy responded, "because the entire main riff was completely ripped off from "Under Pressure" by Bowie and Queen, but…hey…this is different!"

Erick began chuckling as he asked, "Oh, really? How so? How is ripping off the main musical riff in a song any different than ripping off the main themes and styles in a book? Both are the foundation of the work. And if there are tons of people out there doing that, then the marketplace is saturated by regurgitated drivel and artists who are at least *trying* to be original are drowned out. Maybe they're good. Maybe they suck. But they are at least *trying* to be true to who they are as a person and artist and trying new things."

"But...but...," Maddy stammered while attempting to salvage her dignity. "But that is how you make *money* at this shit! You *have* to give the audience what it wants! Otherwise, you'll *never* find a market, and there sure as shit isn't a market for the fucked-up shit that's in *my* head. So, I must produce something that is *tried and true* so that I can have *tons* of people read my work!"

Erick paused for a moment while calculating his response. He realized that his beloved wife was passionate about this. He realized that he needed to measure his words carefully to make his point without bruising Maddy's tender ego. He could not fuck this up. Erick did *not* fuck it up as he replied with a soft sincerity, "First, my love, it really isn't *your* work. It is your interpretation of *somebody else's* work. It is a caricature. It is an impersonation.

"Secondly, why can't something that is not directly stolen from someone else's work be popular? Why *can't* your fucked up shit find a market? I mean if it's any good at all, it will probably get noticed eventually. And if it isn't any good...well... then at least you've provided the world with some fireplace kindling and doorstops.

"And how do you know *exactly* what people want anyway? Why was "Ice, Ice, Baby" a huge hit? Because that riff was already popular. But it *wasn't* popular when Bowie and Queen came up with it. Someone had to come up with it first. People didn't know that they liked that riff until it was invented, and they had the opportunity to hear it. In music, there are only so many notes. So many keys. So many rhythms. None of that is original. But there *are* original ways to combine those notes, keys, and rhythms to create something that nobody has heard before. The same is true in literature. There are only so many original ideas. There are only so many character-types or plots or settings. But there *are* original ways of *presenting* those ideas. And it is that new combination that is creative. It is that new combination that some might consider to be art.

"So, if you are just stealing from other authors then all you are doing is supplying the market with the same stuff over and over and over with a different bare-chested dude and set of tits on the cover. The market is never *challenged* because they are never presented with any challenging *ideas*. All that I'm saying is that you have more to give than that. You have original ideas or at least an original way to present those ideas. I suppose if all that you are seeking is money and attention, then just churn out the same tired stories, plots, and characters. But true art doesn't come off the back of *other* people's work. True art comes from within *you*. Art connects with people emotionally. If you can get someone to shed a tear or burst out laughing at something that you created, then you have contributed to humanity. And contributions to humanity are art. Cheap knockoffs contribute nothing but a mindless passage of time. It just gets the reader a few hours closer to death, with nothing of substance to show for having had the experience. Originality inspires. Even if it's shit, it still inspires. It inspires criticism. It inspires the creator of the work to try to do better. To be better. And, at its best, true art, true originality inspires people to aspire themselves. To aspire that they *too* can be a writer. Or an actor. Or a musician. Or perhaps just a decent person. That type of inspiration comes from within the creator of the work. There is nothing inspirational about ripping off other people. And if people can't appreciate that, then fuck 'em."

"Wow," Maddy replied softly. "You really don't give a *shit* about biting the hand that feeds you, do you?"

"Nope," Erick proudly replied as he cranked the volume on the stereo which began blaring "Radio, Radio" by Elvis Costello. "Now, do ya wanna join us tonight?"

"Uh, maybe. What are you doing?" Maddy asked.

"Well, we found those three date-rapist frat boys that Josie wants us to use to get back into shape and for a little family bonding time. They've rented a cabin in the woods. It's the same cabin that people say had that old demonic book or some shit. Probably just a myth, but who knows after what we've been through. Anyway, Josie and I were going to go up there, put on hockey masks and cut them up with chainsaws. Wanna come?"

"Fuck yeah, I do!" Maddy squealed out. "Y'know, I've gotta hand it to you. You really are good at coming up with original ideas."

———

Three pairs of eyes peered at the run-down cabin from their hiding place in the dense woods. A thick fog had settled around the teetering structure as loud music was heard booming from its interior. They saw flashes of three laughing young men frequently darting from behind the cracked front window as they danced with a young woman who appeared to be unsteady on her feet. Erick then heard a soft, breathy voice behind his left ear.

"Ch-ch-ch-ha-ha-ha.   Ch-ch-ch-ha-ha-ha.   Ch-ch-ch-ha-ha-ha."

"Would you please stop that?" Erick shout-whispered to his wife. "It's annoying as fuck and your breath is tickling my ear!"

"Hey!" Maddy barked back with the same hushed intensity. "I'm trying to set the mood. This little caper is *already* ruined by us having to wear these fucking kitten masks! And where the fuck are the chainsaws that I was promised?"

"I'm sorry," Erick answered in an embarrassed tone. "I don't know what happened to the hockey masks. I looked all over for them. And these masks are the only ones Josie had in her van. I guess we *are* kinda out of practice for this shit."

Josie then responded to her parents in an apologetic whisper, "Um, I don't know what happened to the hockey masks either. I used to keep some in the van, but now they're gone. And I think Jules borrowed the chainsaws a couple of weeks ago. There were some 'chads' that were terrorizing some elderly folks in an apartment complex and it pissed her off, so she and Jerry took them to the basement of LOHAD and…well…you know. It did give the Twins some new parts to play with though and aren't these kitten masks just adorable?"

"I think that they're really cute, sweetie!" Erick replied enthusiastically. He then looked to his left and saw the face of a kitten sadly shaking its head at him.

"Hey! Here comes one now! He's mine!" Josie announced as one of the frat boys staggered down the front wooden steps and made his way to a tree. He leaned his back up against the tall maple, unzipped his pants and let out a satisfied sigh as a stream of pungent urine fell upon the crumpled leaves on this mid-February evening. He chuckled to himself just before feeling a leather strap being wrapped around his mouth. Then he felt increased pressure as the strap began tightening.

His confused screams were muffled by the constricting leather as he desperately attempted to pry the strap from his now-bleeding mouth. The pressure increased. He could feel his teeth begin to crack then snap off. He gagged as his jagged teeth slid down his throat. The pressure increased. He could feel the strap pushing his tongue backwards into his throat, cutting off his windpipe. The pressure increased. He could feel the strap binding the hinges of his jaw. He then felt someone's fingers pinch his nose. He violently writhed against the tree as he gasped for breath. Then, he became still. His corpse hung from the tree by the tight leather strap around his mouth. A pink rose was inserted into the top of his pants before his giggling assailant could be heard skipping through the brush.

"Wow!" Erick declared. "That was pretty cool!"

"Yeah, it was alright, I guess. Kinda amateurish if ya ask me, but whatevs," Maddy dismissively replied. "Hey! They're dragging that girl into the bathroom. We need to get in there before they do something to her that she didn't sign up for!"

"She clean yet?" one of the frat boys inquired as he drunkenly flopped upon a stained mattress. The creaking of the metal springs harmonized with the boy's evil chuckles as he waited for the arrival of his co-conspirators and latest conquest. *It is just so easy.* He arrogantly thought to himself. *Separate them from their pack. Put a little something in their drink. Drag them off somewhere. Then have all the fun you want. These stupid bitches. All they have to do is give it up. But noooooo. They make us work for it. They sit there and tease us with their tight sweaters and short skirts. They're all little sluts. We're just proving it to them. We're just taking what is rightfully ours. Don't they understand that we men have the right to take whatever we want? To have power and control over them? All they have to do is give us what is ours. And if they don't, well, I guess this little bitch is going to find out what happens, heh, heh, heh.*

He laid there smiling to himself in sadistic anticipation and his foot began tapping as "Footloose" by Kenny Loggins came on the radio. His smile turned to shocked terror as he felt the head of an arrow protrude out of the mattress, into the bottom of his neck and out of his trachea. His blood flowed freely down around his neck and began saturating the mattress with a new crimson stain.

He laid there trembling and let out his final gurgles as the third frat boy came bounding into the room and announced, "Here she is! Time to have some fun!" He did not have time to react to the sight of his dead friend as he was immediately struck on the back of his head by a blunt object. The drugged, scantily clad young woman watched her near-assailant crumple to the floor. She cautiously peered over her left shoulder and looked into a pair of brown eyes staring at her from behind a kitten mask. She let out a blood-curdling scream and passed out into the man's arms.

Erick gently laid the young woman on a tattered couch in the living room and tenderly covered her with a blanket. He then grabbed a sleeping bag and stuffed the unconscious rapist into it. He tied a thick chain around the sleeping bag. There was an ominous 'click' as a padlock was clasped shut on the chain, bringing the bound man back to consciousness. Erick unceremoniously dragged the now screaming and struggling rapist down the front steps of the cabin, picked him up and tossed him onto a neatly stacked pile of logs. The frantically struggling man screamed louder as he could feel something wet being poured upon him. His screams intensified as the scent of gasoline hit his olfactory nerves. His screams then transformed into tortured wails as his entire body burst into hellish flames.

"Fuckin' cool!" One of the 'kittens' excitedly yelled out as she began skipping back toward Josie's hippie-power VW bus. "I'll go get the hot dogs and marshmallows! Best fuckin' family vacation ever!"

"Mom!" another 'kitten' shouted out after her. "Don't forget to grab the ketchup!"

"I will *not* grab the ketchup!" the 'kitten' yelled back. "When are you going to grow up? Ketchup on hot dogs is *doing it wrong!*"

———

The giggling 'Family of Fury' came bouncing into their living room while loudly singing "Footloose." Maddy's sweatshirt was covered in mustard and relish. Josie's sweatshirt was covered in ketchup. And Erick's sweatshirt was covered in nothing as he had used a napkin.

They turned on the living room lights and were greeted by the dark figure of a man wearing tattered grey overalls and holding a machete. He was also wearing a hockey mask. Maddy surveyed the eyes of the man behind the mask and instantly recognized him. As did Erick.

"Well, there's one of the masks!" Erick yelled out as the hulking figure began approaching him.

The figure continued his menacing approach as Erick said, "Jason, I let you sucker punch me once, and I deserved it. But I'm tellin' ya *right now*, that I'm coming off of a thrill kill high so that shit's not gonna fly. So, take a step back or your toes will be pointing to the sky."

"Holy Fuck! You're like a Gangsta Rapper baby! That was great!" Maddy yelled out through her chuckles as the approaching form continued to approach them.

As Erick was being mentally self-congratulatory over his rapping "prowess", Maddy stood upright, looked the form in his eyes and said in a demanding voice, "Jason! Maddy is talking to you! Just knock it the fuck off! And why are you alive? We were told you were dead!"

The menacing figure stopped his advance and allowed the machete to fall pathetically to his side. He looked down sadly, revealing a completely bald head and said in a meek voice, "I'm sorry you guys. I just wanted to scare you. I thought I owed you that. I found the hockey masks in Josie's van and thought I'd freak you guys out. I just wanted to see you scared. Scared of *me*. I guess I fucked that up too."

"Hey, hey," Erick gently said as he approached Jason, placed his hand upon his shoulder and led him to the couch. "It's all okay. It's really good to see you. And listen. You really *did* frighten us. It's just that we're kinda used to having weird shit happen to us. We just had our game faces on, but deep inside we were trembling, right dear?"

Maddy looked at her husband, rolled her eyes and said incredulously, "Nope. I knew who this pussy fucker was as soon as I saw him and…"

Her thoughts were cut off by her husband's glaring brown eyes. "Okay, I'm just so used to acting tough. Yup. You got us Jason. We were all *really scared* of you." She then looked at her husband and mouthed to him as she folded her arms defiantly, *Happy now?*

"Really?" Jason said as he looked up at the pair. "Thanks, you guys. That really helps a lot."

Josie then blurted out impatiently, "Okay everybody! Who the fuck is this that's going around impersonating Jason?"

"I'm not *impersonating* Jason," Jason answered sincerely. He then removed his hockey mask and said, "I *am* Jason. Jason Anderson. I was married to Kristy before she went insane or got possessed or whatever and murdered your mother. I am the biological father of Aaron, Adam, and Alexa. I am the adopted father of Vai. And I've lost everything. My family. My job. Even my fucking hair. I crawled into a bottle a number of years ago and Alexa just couldn't take it anymore. I was an embarrassment to her. So, she came here and told you all that I had died. But she's stayed in touch, and she has always told me that when I'm ready to get help with my problem that I should come here. That you all would help me. That my former friends would embrace me again. And that is why I'm here. To ask for your help. I just wanted to get a little taste of revenge first. I know that was stupid but I'm half in the bag right now. I don't make the best decisions when I'm drunk, which is most of my waking hours. So, can you help me get clean and be a father that my children can respect again?"

"Oh, fuck Jason," Maddy answered sweetly with tears forming in her emerald eyes. "Of course, we will help you. We have connections at a really good rehab place. Our friend Jerry was there too. He can take you. You have always been such a sweet man. It was the absolute lowest point of my life when we took your children away. I'm so sorry about what that did to your life. And to Kristy's."

"You didn't take our children away," Jason replied. "They are different. They are special. You didn't take them away. They ran away to be with you. To help you. To help the world. They told me all about it a few days ago when I arrived back in town. Alexa was excited to see me, and the Twins were…well, they just said that they had seen this day coming so they weren't all that surprised. They then showed me their playroom and introduced me to their girlfriends. I've always wanted grandkids, but I pray that those two girls are…um…taking precautions. The four of *them* raising children? That would be trouble, I fear."

A sharp chill ran down Josie's spine as she simply said, "Yeah. That would totally suck. I'd better tell them to double-bag that shit."

CHAPTER 84

—————

JAILBREAK

The spiritual body of Blair Sommers-Argento lay in tatters in a dark purple ooze. Her arms had been ripped from her torso and were lying helplessly in opposite corners of the penitentiary in Enlightenment. One leg had been removed and had been snapped in four different sections. Her other leg was still attached to the torso but was left hanging from glowing white ghostly tendons. The shocked expression on the face of her decapitated head reflected the sudden savagery of the attack. Her pained bright-white soul crouched quivering in the corner as it looked frightfully upon her ravaged, conjured body parts. Blair's soul knew that she was weakened. She knew that she was defeated. She knew that she was helpless. She knew that she was dying for all eternity.

Her soul looked through the thick cloud of mixed purple and white haze and saw a copper, slithery figure. It cackled with glee as its serpentine form conjured spindly arms. Then legs. Then bulbous, sagging breasts upon its chest. Its scaled hood began wrapping around the top of its head until it formed a tight copper bun of hair. It looked at her with glimmering red eyes and cackled mercilessly once again.

Blair Argento recognized this face. This body. This frail-looking, corpse-like monstrosity. This was Maddy's biological mother, now reunited with her biological father. It had been Blair's turn to guard the Pastor. To keep her away from him. To sound the alarm should her presence be detected. She never had the chance as a copper blur suddenly invaded the bright-white incarceration unit and tore her conjured body apart in seconds. Now, all she could do was look upon this hideous form as she released her demonic love from his confinement. All she could do was watch helplessly as the pair embraced. Then laugh maniacally. All she could do was watch as the sadistic pair approached her shaking essence. All she could do was say one final prayer before they extinguished her soul forever.

"Well, it is quite nice to see you my dear," the Pastor stated to his dark-soul mate. "But you could have arrived a bit sooner. I have been brutalized by these…these…forms. Over and over again. They meticulously snapped my bones, one at a time, starting with my fingers. All to get information from me. Information about you. But I never wavered. I never flinched. I knew that you would come for me. I knew that we would be reunited so that we may now survey the number of dark souls that remain upon the Earth. And once there are enough of them created by these self-professed "patriots," we shall consummate our love once again and call them all here. They will be my ultimate congregation. They shall tear each and every enlightened soul that resides here apart. And then, our most glorious Vetis shall arrive to claim his dominion over the cosmos. So, I am quite grateful to see you, my love. But what took you so fucking long?"

"Well," It began in its nasal, condescending tone. "I may have made a bit of a mistake. It was a mistake to take out our little whore's husband first. To allow his spirit to remain upon the Earth to watch over her. To protect her. And when I used Kristy Anderson's body to murder that wretched little bitch, I had not anticipated that his soul would be there. As her confused soul emerged from her body, I lunged at her to extinguish her for all time. But he intercepted me. He flailed at me, wrapped me up in his essence and took me into a corner of the cosmos. Someplace cold and dark. It was actually quite peaceful in a way.

"And I underestimated the power of his love for her. It gave him strength. Through his pure love he clung onto me. Our souls battled each other for what seemed an eternity. Just clinging to one another, trying to absorb one another's energy. Trying to kill the other. He nearly succeeded. But our impetuous daughter found us and ripped me from his death grip. I was so weakened that all that I could do was fly away and hide out. I hid in the Realm of Perdition and our glorious Vetis ordered all the damned, sinful souls there to care for me. To rebuild me. And they did. It took quite some time for my black soul to regain all its strength. It took longer to satisfy Vetis's wishes and brutalize any damned soul who did not bow to my will. I had to prove myself to him. And I did. Many wretched souls were sacrificed at my hands. And my fangs. I conquered it and now that realm is ours. I am now the appointed ruler of the Realm of Perdition. And it is from there that we will stage our final attack.

"Now, I must admit, that was some time ago. I suppose I could have arrived earlier and released you from your personal hell. But I thought you might benefit from having a bit of tortured time to reflect. Time to reflect upon your failure to rape our daughter into submission. Your failure to bring your other daughter, Arima, into our fold. Your failure to escape the clutches of the souls of Enlightenment. Your failure to keep the half-sisters apart. I sincerely hope that you have used that time of reflection wisely. Because one more failure from you will bring swift and brutal retribution from our glorious Vetis. And it will be done by my hands."

The devilish pair then turned their attention to the quivering bright white orb that was Blair's soul in its most pure form.

"Hello, Blair," It began with an insincere sweetness. "So nice to see you once again. Yes, it is quite nice to see my despised sister-in-law in such a state. Can you feel your life being drained from you? Are you scared? Are you frightened to be nothing? Are you frightened to not be able to be here to protect your loved ones?

Are you frightened about what we are going to do to them? Yes, I can see that you are. It fills me with great joy.

"But I am feeling a bit merciful at the moment. Would you like for me to allow your soul to live just long enough to bear witness to the godless atrocities that I am going to commit against your friends, both living and dead? What I am going to do to your beast of a husband? Your freak of a sister? Your little bitch of a daughter?"

It cackled maniacally before continuing. "Yes. I can feel your confusion at that last comment. Your daughter, Madeline. Allow me to explain. The Pastor and I were placed upon the Earth to convert holy souls into unholy ones. And it was through this proselytization that we would form an army. An army first made up of humans, then, upon their death, dark souls. And it was prognosticated that we would do so with a powerful female warrior of our own making at our side.

"So, we prayed and searched for a soul that I could raise and mold as my own. A soul that was capable of inhuman violence and brutality. A soul that held no empathy for her victims. A soul that had unequalled tenacity and delighted in her gory escapades. A soul that could smile at you sweetly one moment and rip out your throat the next without so much as a bat of her eye. A soul that was beyond redemption. And we found one. And she was perfect.

"But *you* stole her from us. For some reason, this soul was attracted to the family Sommers. And since Patty never engaged in activities that would lead to a child and your brother was such a pathetic worm that he would never get laid, her soul was attracted to you. Her soul was attracted to your strength. And to the strength of your vile husband. You became pregnant. You became pregnant with *our soul*! So, the Pastor placed a call so that your Joseph would be dispatched on a bogus service call. He hired two men to then go to your apartment and beat that soul's life out of you. And to ensure that your womb would never pose a threat to us again. You see, bitch. It was *Madeline's* soul that you miscarried on that night. We took her soul from you the same way you had taken her from us. Her soul was taken from you so that it would be once again free to belong to me. To us.

"But the soul was still attracted to your loathsome family. It was quite easy to manipulate and seduce your dullard of a brother and get him to marry me. The Pastor and I poured the blood that we had saved from your miscarriage over each other. And we fucked. We fucked like two beasts in the most rapturous of heat. And Madeline was conceived. And that child's soul was attracted once again to someone named Sommers. Her soul was attracted to me through my marriage to Freddie the Fool. I allowed you to keep her on the weekends. I found it quite delightful that you had to send her back to me every week. I laughed so hard every week that you sent your *own daughter* back to the one person that you most despised. And I thought that I would have the last laugh when I watched *your own daughter* rip you to shreds after she had been fully indoctrinated. But I was mistaken. Your family's influence was much greater than mine or the Pastor's. And she went down a dark path. She still became a brutal killer. But she killed not in the name of selfish domination. She killed in the name of what she felt was justice. I should have murdered that little bitch when she was a toddler. It would have been so easy. Just stick her little copper head into the bath water and hold it until her little gurgles stopped. But I didn't. And so now here we all are.

"Yes, Blair, you stupid bitch. I may have been Madeline's biological parent. But *you and Joseph* are her eternal *spiritual* parents. And it will be *our pleasure* to rip that little whore apart in front of you and force the parts of her body down your fucking throats! And *that* is why I am allowing you to live! I am allowing you to live because ultimately, I am going to *force you to consume your own daughter!*"

The purple and white mist changed into an ominous dark red as a slow clapping sound was heard. A tall, hulking red figure approached as he said, "You think that you've seen a demon? You haven't seen *anything* you motherfuckin' douchebags!"

The glowing red figure of Joseph Argento lunged and struck

the Pastor firmly under his chin, sending his scarred, ghostly form across the space. It looked at him with deep red eyes, screeched and immediately transformed into a fifteen-foot copper serpent with two arms protruding from its side. It wrapped its tail around Joseph's spiritual body and lifted it up to its cavernous mouth.

"Oh my, I bet you're a kinky one, aren't you?" Howard's spirit gleefully exclaimed as he joined the battle, launched himself onto the beast's back and held its mouth open. The venom from its fangs was dripping down upon Joseph's face just before it broke free from Howard's grip and bit down.

There was a shriek of agony from Freddie Sommers as the vile serpent's fangs plunged into his ghostly form and penetrated his very soul. Joseph stared at Freddie's agonized face that was impaled by the two long fangs. It was the face of the man that he had previously found to be pathetic. It was the face of the man that he now held nothing but admiration. It was the face of the man who had just sacrificed himself to save him.

It reared up and violently shook its head in an attempt to dislodge the fallen soul of her husband from its fangs. It loosened its grip on Joseph just enough for him to break free. Joseph fell upon his side. His entire body glowed red from the intense hatred that he had always harbored towards this unholy succubus. He looked at the glowing orb that was his beaten wife's soul. It was just the two of them silently communicating with one another before he stood and grabbed it by its scaly tail. He whipped it around the room in a violent whirl. With each passing It knocked Its head and the lodged body of Freddie into the Pastor over and over until the evil spirits were gasping for soul-affirming breath.

The disheveled serpent-demon fell upon its side and squealed in agony. Joseph began prying open its mouth and two strong green vines emerged from the blood-red fog and wrapped around the fangs. Joseph pulled on the vines with all his spiritual strength until the fangs broke loose, dislodging Freddie's impaled head and causing his body to fly into Joseph's. Joseph lay on his back and stared into the dying eyes of his brother-in-law. A tear fell from his eye as Freddie uttered his last words. "Take care of my sisters, Joseph. And take care of *our* daughter. Tell Madeline that I will always love…"

Pitch black forms emerged from the red fog near the fallen body of the Pastor. The bright white forms of Patty, The Ropers, Lillian, Marcus's Moms and Pops, Herbert, Iris, and Becky Peterson emerged on the opposite side behind Joseph and Howard. The ethereal figures stared at each other with cautious disdain. They glared at one another, daring their opponents to make a move. The pitch-black forms solemnly picked up the bodies of the Pastor and the copper serpent and regressed back into the nothingness to begin their journey to the Realm of Perdition. Just before its scaly tail disappeared, its nasal voice was heard saying, "This is far from over you fools. We will be back. And we will feast upon you."

———

"J-Joseph?" Blair's weak voice inquired as her eyes opened for the first time since the battle. She looked down upon her reconstituted spiritual form and smiled meekly. Her smile broadened as she recognized the grip of the hand that was holding hers.

"Yeah, baby, I'm here," Joseph's gruffly tender voice responded. "You've been out for a while. Who knows how long. There's no time up here. But you're going to be fine. Your body is completely restored, and your spirit is strengthening by the day. You had me scared there for a while, but I knew you'd pull through. You were always the strong one in our family. I'm so sorry about your brother's soul. He's gone forever. But here. I brought you a present."

Joseph laid two fifteen-inch fangs upon her bosom. His beloved wife smiled and let out a pained laugh. "You always did know what to get me," she said through her tentative chuckles.

"But Joseph. You and I both know that this time, teeth aren't enough. Blood isn't enough. Body parts aren't enough. This time, you will not rest until you have brought me the black heart of that fucking bitch. Do you understand?"

"Of course, I understand," Joseph replied with a confident bluntness. "You just tell me what to do, my love. I'll bring home whatever you want for dinner. Just like always."

The pair embraced as they conjured their song in their respective heads. They swayed together to the sweet melody of "Groovy Kind of Love" while looking lovingly into one another's eyes. Blair broke the silence when she whispered into her Joseph's ear, "And I am not the strongest one in our family any longer. Our daughter is."

CHAPTER 85

OUR LOVE WILL CHANGE THE WORLD

"Awwww, fuck," Josie and Maddy said with dread simultaneously just after they had heard the latest high-pitched "Wooooo!" from a pair of ecstatic twin sisters. Fifteen minutes prior, a giggling Rachel and Kayla had entered the room wrapped around their respective beaus, Adam, and Aaron. Rachel and Kayla's expressions were typical of them. They had carefree looks upon their pretty brown faces as they loudly chewed and popped their bubble gum. Vai took one look at the unusually pleased expressions on the faces of her adopted brothers and instinctively knew that something was a-miss.

"Hello, everyone," Adam began followed, as always, by his identical twin brother Aaron. "Yes, greetings. It is quite nice to see you all."

"Uh, yeah, Hi," Josie replied as she was clearing the table of the breakfast dishes. Making their way from the dining room table into the living room of the Parker-Sommers home were Lionnel, Maddy, Erick, Arima, Marcus, Alexa, and Vai. Each one of them felt a strange sensation in the pits of their stomachs as they looked upon the unusually serene quartet.

"What the fuck are *you* four so happy about?" Maddy bellowed out as she plopped onto the couch. "And why are you late? You're *never* late."

"Well," Kayla giggled in response as she looked mischievously at her twin sister. "We're sorry we're late. But we have a good reason to be late."

"Uh, yeah," Rachel interjected. "But we're not just late for the meeting, *tee, hee.* Boys, would you like to explain why we're... um...late?"

"But of course!" Adam responded to his girlfriend. "Yes! We would be delighted!" Aaron added before explaining. "As you know, Rachel and Kayla have introduced us to the most fun game, 'Hide the Sausage.' And we have become quite good at it. We have been practicing for months now."

"Yes, we have," Adam contributed. "We have been practicing night and day. It is the most fun game that we have ever played, but we learned that we could not win using the game pieces that Josie told us to use."

The entire group turned to look at Josie with perplexed looks of revulsion. "Hey!" A defensive Josie yelled. "What are you talking about? I've *never* been involved in helping you with that-er-game!"

"Yes, you have, Josie," Aaron answered. "You told us that we needed to, and I quote, double bag it. But Rachel and Kayla said that we did not need those game pieces and that it was much more fun without the bags over the sausages and that we would never win the game if we did that. So, we stopped double-bagging the sausage several weeks ago."

"Yes!" Adam exclaimed. "And it did not take us long to win the game after that!"

Vai got up from her seat and cautiously walked over to her younger brothers. She took them both by the hand and led them a few feet away from their girlfriends. She looked into their piercing blue eyes and asked softly, "Okay boys. I need you to be quite clear with me. What do you mean you've 'won the game'?"

"Well, of course we will be quite clear," Adam replied followed by Aaron's, "Yes. Quite clear indeed. We won the game by impregnating both Rachel and Kayla."

"That's right!" Rachel yelled out excitedly. "We're knocked up bitches!" Rachel and Kayla then grinned at each other before releasing their customary, high-pitched, "Wooooooo!"

"Awwww, fuck," was all that could be heard following the announcement. Lionnel rushed out of the room to hide his laughter. Erick took his head in his hands and slowly began shaking it. Arima and Marcus loaded a bowl in their pipe, completely unaware of what was going on. There was what seemed to be an eternal silence until Alexa squealed, "You guys are *pregnant*? Yay! I'm going to be an aunt!"

"Well, well, well," Vai began stammering as she searched for the most appropriate words.

"Uh, yeah, you see Alexa-um-well…" Josie attempted to add until her genius-level brain ran out of responses.

"Oh, for fuck sakes! I'll handle this shit!" Maddy yelled out as she bounded up off the couch and marched toward the four glowing parents-to-be. She looked at each of them in their joyful eyes. She could see how delighted they each were at this moment. She knew that she had to be very careful with the words that she chose so as not to offend or hurt any of them. Maddy knew that she could *not* fuck this up.

Maddy fucked it up. "Pregnant? Are you fucking *kidding me*? This is what you're going to do. You're going to wipe those *fucking smirks* off of your faces and listen to me! Pregnant? This is the most *fucked up thing* that you could've done! First off, you're all what, twenty-five, twenty-six? That's waaaaay too fuckin' young to have a family. Um, I think. That's not the main point. Boys! You have *no idea* how to function in this world without our guidance! How the fuck are you going to raise kids? I mean, you call 'fucking' 'Hide the Sausage' for fuck sakes! You think this is a game! Well, let me tell you, raising children is *no game*! No. This is *not* going to happen. We will take Rachel and Kayla to a doctor and we'll, um, y'know, just take care of it. And you are *fucking banned* from playing 'Hide the Sausage' from this point on. You got that?"

"Yes, we understand, Aunt Maddy," Adam replied followed by Aaron's, "Yes. We believe that we understand quite well. We understand that we have been supportive of you and our extended family for our entire lives. We have done everything that you have asked of us. We have celebrated your achievements and we have mourned with you in your grief. We now understand that our support for you will not be reciprocated. We have achieved something that we are quite proud of. We have fallen in love with these two wonderful women. And we are going to have a family with them. We are going to produce something that is beautiful. Something that is important. It is quite hurtful to us to learn that the people that we have loved and supported do not love and support us back. If you do not support what we love and what we are passionate about, then you do not truly love *us*. And it is *that* level of support that *we* must now reciprocate. We wish you all well. It is time for us to take our leave. And we will do so with the women and unborn children that we love."

"Yeah! Fuck you bitch! How *dare* you shit on what was to be the happiest day of our lives!" Kayla screamed into Maddy's face as the quartet angrily made their way to the front door and exited.

"Nice job, Ace," Erick sarcastically stated to his wife. "You'd better apologize to them, and you'd better make it good. Those are four people that I do *not* want to be on the wrong side of. Oh, and while you're thinking up your apology, you might *also* want to be thinking about the wedding arrangements. I think the best way for all of us to apologize is to throw them a kick-ass wedding. And baby shower. Like it or not, people, this shit is happening. And they're right. They have always been with us. Hell, they murdered their *own mother* for us. I think the *least* that we can do is support them in this. Plus, they are going to need us to help raise their kids. Who the hell knows *what* type of hellions they're going to bring into the world. With the four of *them*, the product of *their* love could change the world. I think we might want to be involved in seeing just *how* they change the world."

"Fuck, alright," Maddy replied quietly with rare contrition. "I'll call Pastor Tim and see when we can get these little fuckers hitched. And I'll call them back here and apologize. But I'm not *wrong* am I? This is really going to be *fucked up*, isn't it?"

Erick went over to his wounded, beloved wife and kissed her on the top of her copper strands before saying, "No. You are not wrong. They are the *last* two people on this Earth that should be reproducing. But some people would have said that about us, too. Just look at how *our* love has changed the world." The pair shed a tear and smiled as their gaze fell upon their own daughter's brilliant green eyes.

Maddy called Pastor Tim. Erick could only smirk as he listened to his wife's side of the conversation. "Uh, hey there Pastor Tim. Listen, so the Twins have knocked up the-um-twins and we need to get them hitched. No, I'm *not* fucking joking. Yeah, I know. I have no idea how those little fuckers got laid either. Nope. Not an option. They're hell-bent on having these little bastards. Okay. Tomorrow night, then. Could you maybe get some flowers and shit? I don't know! Just get someone to throw up some wedding shit! I'll pay you back tomorrow night. And, I promise, we will *not* make a mess of your church this time."

Maddy's next call did not go as well. "Hey, guys! Why don't you just get your little asses back over here and..." her sentence was interrupted by the sound of the phone's receiver being slammed down.

The next call was not successful either. "Okay guys, I know you're pissed at me but..." SLAM!

The third time was not the charm. "Alright you four! You're *really* starting to piss me off! Get your asses over here so that I can apologi..." SLAM!

Erick sighed and took the receiver of the harvest gold rotary phone from his wife before saying, "Its okay. I'll call in the big guns."

Following a brief, polite phone call from Gregory, Kayla and

Rachel were sitting on the couch in the Parker-Sommers home. They had their arms folded and were rapidly kicking their crossed legs. Their irritated expressions stared straight up to the ceiling, as they refused to make eye contact with the five-foot-four-and-a-half-inch waif that stood demurely in front of them. Adam and Aaron were sitting next to their girlfriends, holding their delicate tan hands. The colors of the Twin's pale white fingers intertwined with the dark tan fingers of their lovers resembled a vanilla-chocolate ice cream swirl.

"Sooooo," Maddy began cautiously. "What's new? Just jokin'!" Her attempt at humor at this tenuous moment resulted in dead silence.

"Okay, not in the mood for my great jokes, hmmmm? Well, let's just get on with it, shall we?" Maddy began again. "So, I think that I *may* have overreacted just a *little bit*, but if you *think* about it, I was *totally right* in..."

Maddy's attempt at contrition was interrupted by the sound of her husband loudly clearing his throat.

"No. I'm sorry. I *wasn't* right. I was-um-wr...wr...wr...wrong. There. I said it. I *never* should have reacted that way. I was just-um-surprised. And, hey! You know me! I can kinda fly off the handle sometimes. Not my best quality. So, I was-um-wr...wr... oh, fuck it. I wasn't *exactly correct*, okay? Listen. We love you guys. All of you. I'm *so sorry* about what I said and I'm *so sorry* that I ever even thought about harming your unborn bundles of joy. We love you and we love your unborn children. Okay? Please? Adam. Aaron. You know me. You know this shit isn't easy for me. And you know that I wouldn't be saying this shit if I didn't mean it. Please. Just forgive me, okay?"

"Well, it really isn't up to us," Adam replied followed by Aaron. "No. We cannot forgive you unless Rachel and Kayla forgive you. They are a part of us. In fact, the four of us, along with our children will become a family unit. We love you Aunt Maddy, but it is *their* forgiveness that you must seek."

Maddy sheepishly peered from under her copper bangs at the still-annoyed sisters as she slightly puckered her lower lip and softly shuffled her left foot. *Well, this innocence shit used to work with Uncle Joe. And it sure as fuck works on Erick. Let's see if I can't get these bitches to bite, heh, heh, heh,* Maddy thought to herself.

Without looking at her adopted in-law, Kayla asked, "So. Are you truly sorry, or are you just saying that?"

"Yes," Maddy replied in as innocent of a voice that she could manage. "I *truuuuly* mean it. I'm *so, so, so* sorry."

Rachel then inquired, "And there will be no more judgement or interference from you?"

"Oh, *my* no," Maddy once again responded. "This is *your* family. I will *only* get involved if you *ask* me to. I just think that it is *wonderful* that you are all having babies. And it would be *my honor* to babysit whenever you need-um-assuming I'm still on Earth. Otherwise, I volunteer Arima."

"What?" Arima inquired before her Marcus said, "Don't worry about it, baby. I'll help ya. We'll teach these kids about the good things in life, just like we do the rats. Hey. Pass me that bag of chips, wouldja?"

"Plus," Maddy continued, "We are *sooooo* overjoyed and supportive that we would be *honored* if you would allow us to throw you a wedding tomorrow night, followed by a baby shower. And one final thing. If it's okay with you, we're going to take you off the battlefield for a while. We can handle this shit. We want you four to go to our estate and live there with Stellan and Paciano. We want you all to be safe. We want you to stay safe so that you can raise your children, hopefully in a much more peaceful world. Hopefully *your* children will never be needed to fight what *we* are all fighting right now. No. Fuck hopefully. The world that you raise them in *will* be peaceful. It *will* be welcoming. It *will* be supportive. That's just how its going to be or else my name's not Maddy fuckin' Sommers. And that's my name, so that's how it's going to be. That is my personal promise to you and to your children."

Kayla and Rachel dropped their annoyed gaze from the ceiling and looked at one another. They then smiled and yelled

"Woooooo!" before bounding up from the couch and enveloping Maddy in a tight three-way hug.

"Of course, we forgive you, Aunt Maddy!" Rachel exclaimed. "C'mon! Let's Woo to the occasion!"

Maddy looked at her husband with dread before opening her mouth and belting out "Wooooo!"

"I'm never fucking doing that again," she said to a smirking Erick as the pair ascended the staircase, leaving the jovial party to their toasts and wedding plans.

CHAPTER 86

IF I WAS THE PRIEST

"I don't know why *I* wasn't asked to stand up there with them. *I'm* the one that arranged all this shit," Maddy angrily whispered to her husband from her seat in the front pew as she looked at Adam and Aaron standing at the altar with Alexa, Vai and Josie.

"Shhhhh," Erick whispered back as he gently squeezed her hand. "Today is not about you. Or me. Or anyone else but them. Today is about them and their future. Let's just enjoy the moment."

"Yeah, whatever," Maddy replied dismissively. "It wouldn't have killed you to wear something other than jeans, *by the way.*"

"There are very few things that *can* kill me at this point," Erick snapped back. "But wearing uncomfortable pants all fucking day is *certainly* one of them."

The congregation fell into silence, and they all turned to look to the back of Pastor Tim's church as David Bowie's "The Wedding Song" began to play. The song's effortless rhythm matched the cool glides of Rachel and Kayla as they strode arm in arm with their best friends, Arima and Marcus. Their white sequined wedding mini-dresses left very little to the imagination causing the Twins to immediately contemplate the game they would like to play with their wives once the formalities were over.

Rachel and Kayla smiled at their "bridesmaids," Jessie, Cliff, and Jamie and took their places next to their respective husbands-to-be. They held each other's hands and gazed into each other's eyes. Two pairs of fierce cobalt connected with two pairs of majestic hazel. Rosa squirmed in her seat as she felt the outpouring of energy that these unions were generating. And the growing energy from the unborn fetuses.

"Hello friends," Pastor Tim began as his husband Jeremy stood to his side. "Welcome to this most wonderful day. A day where Rachel and Adam *and* Kayla and Aaron shall enter holy matrimony. A day that will serve as the foundation for their future and the future for their blessed children. And perhaps the foundation for the future of us all. I understand that the four of you have vows that you would like to share."

"We sure do!" Rachel cried out before taking the gum out of her mouth, handing it to Jeremy and saying, "Hey, hold onto this for a sec, will ya?"

A surprised Jeremy took his handkerchief out of his pocket and placed the gum into it as he smiled awkwardly and nodded at Rachel. He then presented the handkerchief to Kayla.

"Oh yeah, thanks!" Kayla replied as she took her saliva-coated gum out of her mouth and placed it in the handkerchief next to Kayla's. The well-chewed pieces of gum looked identical. It would be impossible to know which was whose. This was also true of their respective husbands-to-be, so they had their names tattooed on each of the Twin's inner thighs, to avoid any embarrassing, drunken mix-ups. Adam's inner thigh now said 'Kayla's' in an exotic script meaning Aaron's inner thigh naturally now said, 'Rachel's.'

"Okay guys," Kayla began. "I'm just going to do our vows for both Rachel and me, okay? We both worked *really hard* on this, like, for twenty minutes or something, so here it goes. So, here's the deal. We love you guys and shit. You are both so strong and brave and fun and-um-*really* well hung. Plus, you knocked us up, so we want to spend the rest of our lives with you and shit. Cool?"

"Why yes, of course," Adam stated followed by Aaron's, "Yes. That is why we are here isn't it? We are a bit confused by the question."

The entire congregation let out a light chuckle as Rachel motioned for Stellan and Paciano to bring their adopted baby, Zihad, toward them. She took the rings from the infant's left breast suit pocket and gave them to the Twins. "Yeah, cool. Good enough. Just put these on."

"Very well, then," Adam stated followed by Aaron's, "Yes. Of course, we will put them on. Oh brother, aren't they marvelous? They are made entirely of Bloodstone which will help us face our challenges with courage!"

"Uh, yeah," Kayla sheepishly replied. "We actually just thought the name was cool, but glad you like them. Okay, boys. Your turn."

The Twins once again gazed into the eyes of their respective loves before they both said in unison with the exact same tenderly monotonous tone, "Kayla and Rachel. You have made us feel things that we have never felt before. You have made us feel things that we did not know that we *could* feel. We have seen things as children which have now come to pass. But we did not see this. You have been a surprise to us. A quite pleasant surprise. And we are surprised yet again by knowing that we are to be fathers. We are quite excited to think about all the games that we can teach our children. And the games that they will teach us. It will be quite fun. So, won't you please take these rings and be our wives?"

Adam and Aaron then reached into the opposite breast suit pocket of the sleeping Zihad and retrieved two rings. Rachel and Kayla marveled at the bands that were made from ground Amethyst for spiritual protection against evil and Angelite to assist in connecting with spirit guides. Sitting prominently upon the center of each ring were three-karat diamonds, to assist them to be forces for good in the world.

As Rachel and Kayla began crying and placed the rings upon their delicate tan ring fingers, they could feel the presence of their fallen sister, Gwen. They shed a tear and smiled upward. The introspective moment was interrupted when Maddy jumped up and yelled, "Jesus fucking Christ! Look at the *size* of those fuckin' things!"

An unidentified voice from the back of the room was heard shouting, "That's what *she* said!"

The entire congregation burst into laughter before Pastor Tim said with bewilderment, "Okay. Never a dull moment with this group is there? Now, if anybody here objects to these two unions, speak now or forever hold your peace."

Erick gave his wife a preemptive elbow jab in her side which caused Maddy to give him an overly dramatic pained expression as she rubbed her "wounded" ribs.

"Okay then," Pastor Tim continued. "By the power vested in me, it is my pleasure to present to you all Adam and Rachel Anderson *and* Aaron and Kayla Anderson. You may now kiss your brides."

"We would much rather play 'Hide the Sausage,' Pastor Tim," Adam replied. Aaron then said, "Yes. Kissing is nice but 'Hide the Sausage' is much more fun. May we play *that* now?"

"Oh, shut up and kiss us!" Rachel cried out as the twin sisters grabbed their respective husbands and shoved their tongues down their throats. They released their husbands from their lips, looked at the entire congregation and yelled out, "Wooooooooo!"

"Mozel Tov bitches!" Kaneko declared as she popped a cork from a bottle of Dom.

An hour later, as the newlyweds were opening their presents, an exasperated Josie yelled out, "What's with all the fuckin' weapons? This is a *baby shower* not a ninja convention!"

Lionnel wrapped his arm around his love and said to her, "Seriously, baby. With this group, is there really a difference?"

Pastor Tim and Jeremy looked on with delighted faces as they watched their dear friends laugh and joyfully cry with each unwrapped baby blanket, butcher knife, stuffed animal, throwing star, diaper bag, pepper spray, stroller, or battle axe. They burst into laughter as they heard their dear friends Erick and Maddy in the corner.

"Oh my god, this isn't right, Maddy," a near-hyperventilating Erick was saying. "This isn't *nearly* enough stuff. They aren't prepared. Okay, I'm just going to have to get my old list out and go to the big box store and pick up a few items. I mean, they only have *twelve stuffed animals* so far! They need *waaaaay* more than that. Lucy's going to have to move some of her shit from the basement. I'm going to need the room."

"Hey! Mister OCD!" Maddy yelled back. "Knock it the fuck off! These are *their* kids! It's *their* problem. Just chill the fuck out!"

Erick had not heard a word of his wife's protestations as he was mentally counting the number of diapers and baby wipes that were required to be purchased.

The giggling Pastor Tim and Jeremy looked into one another's eyes. They both held the same thought. That they were the luckiest men in the world. They were lucky to have this group of friends. They were lucky to have this church with this congregation. They were lucky to have their strong faith. And most of all, they were lucky to have the true love of one another. They smiled and leaned in for a loving kiss. The pair slightly parted their lips, allowing the delicate touching of their tongues. Jeremy opened his mouth wider. Pastor Tim felt Jeremy's tongue become intermingled with numerous small, slimy, crawling sensations. Pastor Tim opened his eyes and looked directly into the black, dead eyes of his husband. He pulled backwards and saw hundreds of maggots crawling from Jeremy's gaping mouth. He screamed and began spitting out maggots as Jessie cried out, "Oh Jesus! The evil! The pain!" and collapsed upon the floor.

Jeremy's body floated several feet into the air and began cackling sinisterly. "Well, hello everybody. So nice to see you all once again, heh, heh, heh," the Pastor's slithery voice came from Jeremy's mouth. "Oh, it is *sooooo* nice to be able to invade another's body without their permission. At any time. As long as they are unsuspecting. That is the key. That is the power that I now wield thanks to being reunited with my dark-soul mate."

His eyes then darted towards the fast-approaching Arima and Maddy. "Well, hello girls. You wanna bounce upon Daddy's knee? Aren't family reunions nice? Here. Let me provide you with another one."

The Pastor swooped down and grabbed an unsuspecting Jason Anderson by the neck, lifted him from the ground and began chewing his way through his neck until his body collapsed to the floor with a gory thud. The Pastor squealed with maniacal glee as he sucked the blood from Jason's dismembered neck and tossed it haphazardly against the large crucifix that was hanging behind the altar. Blood slowly dripped from the form of the seemingly helpless, crucified Jesus.

"There! Now he can be reunited with his insane wife, Kristy! Now perhaps all their offspring should join them. Then, on to *my* two little disappointments."

"No!" Jessie yelled out before reciting with a dark determination, "Malum tuum dolorem facit. et dolor meus es fortitudo mea (*your evil causes pain. my pain is my strength*)."

Jessie felt her body begin to absorb the intense pain caused by the Pastor's pure evil, strengthening her body ten-fold. She leapt up and grabbed Jeremy's left leg. At the same moment, the platinum blonde, Amazonian Dragenstein came lumbering forward and grabbed his right leg. The pair pulled downward until Jeremy's possessed body was on his knees between them.

"Okay Maddy," a suddenly sober Arima ordered. "Let's finish off our prick father, once and for all. And let's do it together!"

"Uh, yeah, sure," Maddy replied as she lifted two serrated daggers from the pile of baby shower gifts. "But I'm *kinda* the one that gives the orders around here, so I just want to make it clear that your order wasn't official. Okay, doesn't matter right now. We'll straighten that shit up later."

Arima and Maddy began approaching the cackling body of the possessed Jeremy. His body was writhing as he attempted to free himself from the vice-like grips of Dragenstein and Jessie.

Arima and Maddy lifted their knives in unison and began their fateful downward plunge. The knives stopped in mid-air as they heard Pastor Tim cry out, "Stop!"

"Stop! Please! That's my husband! If you kill the demon, you will kill my husband! Please! There must be another way!"

A serenity fell upon Jeremy's face and his eyes returned to their normal mahogany. He looked up at his approaching love and said peacefully, "It's all okay my Timothy. I am lost. I have very little time to speak with you. He is too strong, and he will retake me at any moment. Please, Timothy. Listen to me. Either you kill me, or he will use my body to commit the most horrendous atrocities. I cannot bear that, my love. But it must be *you* that kills me. Otherwise, he will possess my soul. It must be my one true love. It must be my *soul mate*. And it must be done as we kiss. You will understand as you breathe in my dying breath."

Rosa and the other twelve members of the Coven circled the pair of lovers. Rosa said softly into Pastor Tim's ear, "It will be okay Pastor Tim. I have this. I will have his energy. Then I will give his energy to you. And you will be together forever. Please trust me." The Coven clasped one another's' hands and began concentrating. Rosa's body began to tremble and glow in a comforting light blue light.

Pastor Tim got down on his knees in front of his restrained husband as Arima handed him her dagger. He looked longingly into his beloved husband's eyes, leaned forward, and gave him the most tender kiss they had ever shared. Tears began streaming down his face the moment that he felt the stickiness of his beloved's blood flow freely between the fingers of his right hand that was clutching the dagger. The dagger that was now literally penetrating Jeremy's heart. The dagger that was now figuratively penetrating Tim's heart.

Jeremy let out one final breath and a light blue haze emerged from his mouth and effortlessly glided into that of his husband. Timothy was now truly Jeremy's one and only soul mate.

The dark purple scarred smog of the Pastor belched from Jeremy's corpse. He began morbidly cackling before saying, "No need to reach for your Holy water. I know when I'm not wanted. And I knew that it was quite unlikely that I would vanquish you all here today. This was just a warning. Just a little taste of what is to come. Oh, and girls. Daddy is *sooooo* looking forward to bringing you home. Don't worry. You are my daughters. I will take care of you. Yes. I will take care to *rip you to shreds* and consume *every little morsel* of your pathetic existences! But, until then…toodles."

The setting sun's rays beamed through the stained-glass windows creating a kaleidoscopic spotlight on the mournful form of Pastor Tim holding the corpse of his beloved husband. He looked up at the empathetic face of his dear friend Erick and said with a quiet resolve, "I now understand. I now know what I must do. But I will need your help, my friend."

———

The luxury yacht that Kaneko had purchased for this expedition lightly bobbed in the calm waters of the Atlantic Ocean. They had sailed for several days until they reached the destination that Pastor Tim had requested. Jennifer and Lucy were taking a break from piloting the vessel and sunbathing on the deck as they had decided to use this excursion for a much-needed vacation from exploding heads and oozing entrails. Henri sat above deck with his sniper rifle, scanning the horizon for any signs of trouble. Erick, Marcus, and Cliff were the only other crew members that Pastor Tim had allowed to accompany him, much to the chagrin of Maddy.

"Okay, please tell me what the fuck we are doing in the middle of the Bermuda Triangle?" a slightly annoyed and confused Erick asked his dear friend.

"Well, Jeremy told me that this is the location where my powers would be the strongest and easiest to amplify. This place holds many mysteries. And many opportunities."

"Right, right, *Jeremy* told you. C'mon Pastor Tim. I'm sorry for your tragic loss, but you need to realize that he's gone."

"Really?" Pastor Tim indignantly replied. "Really? This coming from *you*? This coming from the man whose ashes *I personally* put into an urn and who is now standing in front of me is questioning whether I have Jeremy's soul in me? That is quite rich, my friend."

"Okay. You have a point. I'm sorry Tim…um…and Jeremy. And I understand that the Bermuda Triangle is a place where weird shit happens. But how does it help *us*? What the fuck are *we* doing here?"

Pastor Tim chuckled slightly before answering. "Well, as you know, I have developed quite the ability to create Holy water. I have felt these abilities grow over the last year or so. And we know that Holy water can vanquish the dark souls forever. And you are all trying to find a way for Arima to be able to collect thousands if not millions of these dark souls into her essence all at once. And if she can do that, she can then transfer them into an inanimate object or substance to be destroyed. So, if you are successful in this, all you need is one big fucking bowl of Holy water that Arima can discharge the dark souls into. And that is what we are doing here. I am going to use the mystical powers of this location to turn every ocean and every other body of water that is connected to the oceans into Holy water."

"Tim, I've seen some crazy shit," Erick responded as Tim was tying a rope around his waist. "Hell, I've *done* some crazy shit. And I know you've gotten *really good* at the whole Holy water thing, but *this* just seems impossible!"

"We shall see, now, won't we?" Pastor Tim stated as he perched his body onto the edge of the yacht, holding a cinder block. He looked back at Erick and said with tears forming, "Goodbye my dear friend. I hope to see you soon."

"Nooooooo!" Erick yelled out as he watched his friend's body plummet into the sea. Cliff and Marcus grabbed Erick by the arms before he could fling himself off the side. "No, man! The fall will kill you!" Cliff yelled at him. "Let's drop a lifeboat and you can look for him from there!"

"Fuck that!" Erick yelled back as he wriggled away from their arms and dove into the ocean.

Erick swam downward desperately searching the murky waters until his lungs painfully screamed for air. He swam back to the surface, breathed deeply, then immediately dove back down. His burning eyes scanned the watery terrain until he saw a soft blue glow coming from a reef. He swam to the light and found the serene face of Pastor Tim, his arms clinging to the cinder block. Erick's tears merged with the salt water as he embraced his deceased friend's body, trying to will him back to life.

He then felt it. He then felt the absolute love that Pastor Tim's soul possessed. The waters became clear as a soft blue mist expanded from Pastor Tim's body outward throughout the waters of the Atlantic. Then the Pacific. And the Indian. And the Antarctic. Into the connected seas, rivers, and tributaries. All over the world, the Earth's waterways were being expunged of the trash and filth that human society had corrupted it with. The seas of the world began to brilliantly shine as their pollutants were dissolved into nothingness. And it was all due to the sincere sacrifice of one faithful man. One man who had faith in a higher power. One man who had faith that that higher power was purely good. One man who had faith in his fellow man and woman. One man who had faith was able to transform the Earth's waterways from being humankinds' toilets into the most magnificent and Holiest of reservoirs. One man who had faith may have single-handedly saved humankind. Because that one man possessed pure faith in humanity.

CHAPTER 87

REBEL GIRL

Wednesday evenings had been the group's ladies' night since Maddy's college days. The lineup had changed over the years, but the wine, appetizers, gossip, and revelry had remained intact, with a few adjustments. In the past few years, there was frequently the addition of the sacrifice of some 'Chad' just for pure amusement. It gave the group a fun activity to bond over and released some of their pent-up stress.

Some of the "sophisticated" men within their group always assumed that the ladies were relieving their stress through tickle and pillow fights in their undergarments, because Erick had told them so. As evidence, he would point to an endless amount of 80's sex/comedy romps as though they were documentaries. They were very wrong in their assumption.

Although undergarments were sometimes employed as a lure for some sadistic fucker, there was definitely no tickling. Or pillows. There could be, however, boiling water poured over a tied down, screaming worm, or acid that burned off his genitals or scalpels that sliced his flesh from his bone. On occasion, there were all three. Maddy was preparing her black duffle for that evening's escapades as her husband walked into their bedroom.

"So," Erick began sheepishly. "I was just *wonderin'*…um…that since I can't go to Pastor Tim's service tonight and hang with him and Jeremy because…um…well I just lost my friends…um…and I *really* don't have anything to do, so…um…*maybe* I could just tag along with you and the other ladies tonight?"

An amused Maddy looked up at her beloved husband as she was packing a pair of vice grips and said bluntly, "Nope. Ladies' night. You know the rules. No dudes invited. We're all upset about our losing Pastor Tim and Jeremy and believe me, we ladies are gonna take out our frustrations in style tonight. Sorry, baby, but you're just gonna have to find some other way to blow off some steam."

"Fine!" a hurt Erick yelled back. "Well maybe I'll just grab the other fellas and take them to a strip club then!"

Maddy burst out laughing at the suggestion. She knew that her husband couldn't stand strip joints. They were just so impersonal and callous to him. The men viewed the women only as sex objects and the women viewed men as nothing more than walking wallets. It was all so transactional and lacked any regard for anyone's humanity. He didn't really have anything against it. He understood that those establishments catered to people's most primal needs, and as long as no one was getting hurt, who was he to judge. But still, he was personally creeped out by the scene and never frequented them unless he was stalking some quarry or had been assigned to watch over the safety of one of the performers.

"Yeah!" Maddy retorted sarcastically through her laughter. "You do that. You go get the *'fellas'* and take them to a strip club. Fellas? Who talks like that? Anywhooo, talk about fish out of fuckin' water. The first time some chick comes up to any of you and offers you a lap dance, you're gonna blush, wet yourself and leave screaming. Especially Cliff. He won't know *what* the fuck to do without Jessie's approval. So, yeah. You do that, stud. Enjoy yourself. I think I have some extra one-dollar bills if you need them. You go and make it fuckin' rain.

"And speaking of Jessie, tonight is a big night for her. Jennifer's flying us all over to London to check out Jessie's new influencer billboards and to take some abused women to shelters where they will get new identities and be transported to someplace safe. As you know, Jess was a pretty successful influencer back before you fuckers took out the wireless internet. She was hawking everything from perfume to personal-er-we'll say massagers. Now, she's using those skills to try to deprogram some of the women who have gotten themselves caught up in the demonic, anti-democratic movement. There are so many women out there who get caught up in some guy, only to find out that he wasn't *at all* what she thought he was. They find out he's misogynistic, sexist, and often mentally or physically abusive. That's the type of evil fuckin' men that are attracted to this movement. Men who think that women are their property and that they are entitled to anything that they want. Just like my first husband. I sure as hell can't cast a stone at 'em. I had a guy brain-fuck me too. I got sucked into that quicksand and couldn't find a way out until he went too far and burned my cherished photo album. That snapped me out of it. And that's what Jess is trying to do. She's trying to reach out to women who are in bad situations and offer them an escape.

"So, she's doing television commercials, billboards, print ads and on-line shit for those few who can get the internet. And her message is so beautifully simple. It's just her perky little face saying, *You are valuable. You are important. Don't let him tell you that you aren't. Don't let him beat you down. Don't let him get you involved with his evil. Call XXX-XXX-XXXX. We can help. You are strong. You can do this. We believe in you.*

"Pretty cool, huh? She's pretty good at this shit and we wanted to be there to watch the first strong women take their first steps toward regaining their independence and dignity."

"Huh," a somewhat surprised Erick replied. "That *is* pretty cool. I just figured that you were all going to hang out at someone's apartment and have pillow fights again."

"Oh, my fucking *God*!" Maddy roared back. "How many times do I have to tell you that we don't *do* that shit? It's just the imagination of creepy old men! That shit doesn't really *happen*!"

Erick began chuckling and embraced his wife as he said softly, "I know. It's just that you're really cute when you're pissed off. Plus, I think that I've got Lionnel, Marcus, and Cliff to actually believe that shit."

At that moment, their daughter's agitated voice was heard from across the hallway. "Oh, my fucking *God*, Lionnel! How many times do I have to tell you that we don't *do* that shit? I don't care *what* my father has told you, that shit *doesn't happen*! Mom! Tell Dad to stop fucking with my boyfriend's head!"

———

The door on the private jet closed quietly and the ladies of Murder, Inc. settled in for what would be a roughly eight-hour flight to London. Jennifer's British accent came over the intercom. "Hello, ladies. Lucy and I would like to welcome you all aboard Freedom Airlines. Freedom from oppression. Freedom from evil. And tonight, freedom from all your cares and worries. I am looking forward to hearing about your exploits in London. Please prepare for takeoff. We're all about to have some fun."

"Yeah, we are," Josie stated as she looked around the room at her female friends and family members. She saw the anticipatory eyes of Jessie, LucyFur, Arima, Sam, Jamie, Alexa, Jules, Kaneko, Dragenstein, Vai, Rosa, and her mother. Their eyes began glowing intensely as she said with a diabolical smirk on her face, "Now, listen up ladies. I have something special in store for us tonight. And we have *my father* to thank for this idea."

Lucy entered the main cabin and strapped herself in as the airplane was beginning its taxi. As she listened to Josie's plan, she flashed an evil little smile as she felt a familiar primal urge. Following Josie's instructions, which were met by a fit of uncontrolled laughter by all the passengers, Lucy looked at the group and said, "Okay everybody. Since we have some time to kill, I wanted to give you all an update as to our progress. From the selfless sacrifice of Pastor Tim and Jeremy, we now have a way to destroy millions of dark souls all at once. All we have to do is have Arima absorb those dark souls, get her over the ocean or a body of water that is connected to the ocean and have her expunge them into the Holy water. They will burn up and be destroyed the moment their evil essence hits the blessed water.

"But how to get thousands of dark souls into Arima at one time? She can only absorb three, maybe four at once if she's really focused, which isn't very often. And no more than one if it's Howard. Everyone refuses to be in Arima if *he's* there. We must increase her ability thousands-fold. And I think that we've come up with a solution. Alexa has been learning at my knee and is now just as good at creating toxins as I am. Maybe better. You are so brilliant, Alexa. We have been working on a new formula along with Rod and Rosa."

"And Herbert, don't forget about him. He's the most important part," Arima interjected. "He's been coming into my soul and tweaking different herbal combinations. And we think that once we get the right recipe down, our concoction's powers can be enhanced by the scientific and spiritual manipulation of its energy by Rod and Rosa. All I will need to do is inhale, and my ability to absorb souls will be incredible! So, Maddy and her army kills them in human form, and I then absorb their dark souls and burn the bastards in the ocean of Holy water. It's gonna be the copperhead's and our father's worst nightmare. It is what they most feared. Two sisters working side by side to vanquish them. It's gonna be a helluva trip. Hey, pass those cookies, wouldja?"

———

"Now, you have fun today, but don't go *too* crazy on me, love," Jennifer lovingly said to Lucy as she was about to depart the plane in London. The pair embraced then engaged in a passionate kiss before Lucy whispered into Jennifer's ear, "You are my rock. You are my anchor that keeps me from floating away in a sea of anger."

"I know," Jennifer playfully responded. "You would be quite

the nutter if it wasn't for me. Now go and have your fun. The plane will be fueled and ready for you when you all return."

As Lucy descended the plane's stairs, she looked back at her waving lover's enticing blue eyes and allowed herself a rare moment of satisfied calm.

The billboard was unveiled, and a smiling Jessie's face beamed down upon the pedestrians of London. It did not fail to garner attention. Jessie noticed that males would stop and stare at her pretty face briefly before walking on. She also noticed that females would stop and take the time to read the message on the billboard. Several wrote down the number.

"Oh, my sweetie!" Jamie exclaimed. "We are all *so proud* of you! Look at what you are doing! Look at what you have *done*! Let's go visit the first women that you have inspired!"

"Yeah, it is pretty cool, I guess," Jessie replied with a hint of arrogance. "I mean, I think there's, like, twenty-four women who we are going to get away from abusive, toxic assholes and be taken to safety. And that's just the start. Plus, I *really* look great on that billboard. Just *look* at all the people who are paying attention to me!"

"Twenty-four, huh?" Maddy interjected as her jealous, green eyes darted at Jessie. "Yeah, that's a really cute number. Nice job. Of course, that's not *nearly* as many as *I* have helped over the years, but…"

Maddy was cut off as her daughter firmly elbowed her in the side and whispered through gritted teeth, "Mother. Shut the fuck up. Today isn't about you."

"Okay, whatevs, bitch," Maddy replied in her "hurt" voice as she once again rubbed her "wounded" ribs.

The thirteen women of Murder, Inc. entered a lavish dormitory-style holding residence. They met with each woman there and listened to every story. They heard horrendous recounts of mental abuse. Physical abuse. Rape. Captivity. Threats to their loved ones. All done to satisfy spineless men's tiny egos and indoctrinate the women into their twisted fantasies of a White, male dominated society. There was one young woman who told the story of her escape from her parents' plan for her to be forced into an insidious religious practice of genital mutilation. They witnessed the women's scars, both physical and emotional.

There were tears. And embraces. And more tears. Until finally, laughter as the women realized that they were going to be alright. Their laughter intensified after they had been invited to watch how the women of Murder, Inc. threw a party.

The bright flood lights came on in the operating theatre. Ten confused and naked men looked up at the stadium seats that circled above them and saw twenty-four enthralled female faces.

"What the fuck is this, bitches?" One of the skin-headed, fully bearded men yelled out. "You'd better let us out of here! You don't know who you're fucking with!"

"Oh, but we do," came Josie's playful voice over the intercom. "We know *exactly* who it is that we're dealing with. And we know *exactly* what it is that you think of *us*. You think of us as your property. As your servants. As your playthings. Now, don't worry. There is nothing to be concerned about. What would ten *big, strong men* have to fear from us *tiny little women*? We are here today to make your fantasies come to life. To give you what you so rightfully deserve. C'mon, boys. You *know* you wanna see an all-girl pillow fight, *right?*"

The operating room doors opened, and thirteen women entered. One was in a wheelchair and whispered and pointed out one of the men to her dark-haired friend before entering. The women were all wearing innocent-looking flannel footie pajamas and not-so-innocent smiles. They were also all carrying inno-cent-looking pillowcases.

"Slaaaaashdaaaaance!" Alexa squealed as Kaneko pushed 'play' on a CD player. As the guitar-driven beats of The Pink Spiders came pulsing through the speakers, the men realized that the pillows were far from innocent and were not filled with feathers.

And they also realized why these violent women were playing a song titled "Little Razorblade."

Jamie was the first to land a blow with her blade-filled pillowcase. The razors protruded through the fabric and sliced the hysterical man's throat, nearly cutting off his swastika tattoo. Arima and Maddy were tag-teaming another screaming man. Arima was slicing through his torso with a whirlwind of blows while Maddy hit the man in his scrotum repeatedly until his slimy testicles tumbled out of his mutilated sack. They knew that he was the father of the girl who had been threatened with genital mutilation and chose him specifically for this special treatment.

Jessie sliced through a man's calves, causing him to land on his knees, then beat him repeatedly on his face until it looked like raw, pre-cooked stir-fry beef. One man was defensively flailing wildly at Alexa who skipped and giggled around him before she took the ends of her pillowcase, wrapped it around his face and violently slid it back and forth until the yelping man succumbed and fell to the floor in a bloody heap.

The platinum blonde Dragentstein looked down at the man nearest her and blew him a gentle kiss before swinging her pillowcase with all her might at the man's neck. The force of the blow decapitated him in one thrust and his head went flying toward the observation deck. A woman jumped up and grabbed the head as it was flying above her. The entire observation group exploded into cheers and bloody high-fives.

Lucy swung her pillowcase, and she heard shattering glass tubes as it made an impact on the man's skull. She began to quiver in ecstasy as she quietly watched the man's face melt off his skull as a result of her new acid.

"Great! Nice job Lucy! Way to put a wet spot in your pajamas! Now we won't be able to return them!" a blood-soaked Maddy jokingly yelled out to her dear friend as she viciously beat another anguished man with a childish enthusiasm.

"That's right, bitches!" Kaneko yelled out as her arms swung her pillowcase repeatedly against a wailing man, "Let's fuck these bastards up!"

Rosa and Vai worked over one of the remaining men on each side of his face. He shrieked in agony as he could feel the sharp blades slicing through his cheeks, nose, ears, and eyeballs. Sam ejected the blades on the feet of her wheelchair and sliced the final man's feet off. He howled in pain as he tumbled to the floor and Jules cauterized the wounds with a blowtorch.

Josie approached the writhing man and said, "Hey, are you guys gonna finish him off or what? I haven't had any fun yet, and I'm in the mood to dance." As Josie lifted her deadly pillowcase above her head, Sam said, "No. Please stop, Josie."

"Why? What the fuck, Sam?" a confused Josie asked as she forlornly lowered her case.

"Well, I have some bad news, everybody," a remorseful Sam replied. "My dear Pogo has passed away. His body just couldn't take the punishment anymore and I'm really upset by it. He made such a wonderful pincushion. And ashtray. And knife-holder. And corkboard. And the hooks I stuck in his back were just perfect for Henri's ties. So, I wanted to keep this one as my new Pogo. That will be all right, won't it?"

"Of course, it's all right! I'm *so sorry* for your loss!" a tearful Josie exclaimed as she wrapped her flannel arms around Sam's slender neck. She then wiped her tears from her eyes and yelled up at the observation seats, "Hey, ladies! Any of you wanna hold this prick down while Jules and Sam cut his limbs off?" There was the thunderous sound of forty-eight stampeding feet eagerly making their way to the operating floor's entrance as an enraptured LucyFur was lapping up blood from around the fallen corpses.

Maddy's blood-soaked form stood in the middle of the carnage with her hands proudly placed upon her hips. She flashed her mischievous smile before saying, "So. Are any of you boys in the mood for a little pillow talk, *hmmmmm*? Hey, do you guys get it? Pillow talk? Why isn't anybody laughing? That was pure fuckin' gold!"

The thirteen giddy women made their way along the darkened tarmac and approached the welcoming stairs of their private plane. Pogo II was squealing in pain as he was being dragged face down behind Sam's wheelchair, leaving a trail of blood on the harsh concrete.

Maddy was the first to enter the cabin and yelled out, "Jennifer! We're back! Let's get this fuckin' bird in the air!" She then felt a heavy liquid splash on her forehead. "What the fuck is this?" she asked as she wiped her forehead and looked at the thick, iron-scented substance on her fingertips. She then looked up and fell into a shocked silence.

"What is it?" Lucy inquired as she pushed her way through her friends to the top step.

"No, Lucy," Maddy pleaded as she placed her hands firmly on Lucy's petite shoulders. "Don't go in there, okay? Just, Just, don't."

A frantic Lucy shoved her friend to the side and stood there with the same shocked silence. Blood was dripping from the walls and ceiling of the plane's main cabin and human body parts were hanging from the backs of seats, tables, and overhead compartments. Arms, legs, internal organs, bones, and skin were strewn everywhere. The heavy stench of the massacre hung in the foreboding silence. Jennifer's semen covered, decapitated head sat on the floor next to the cockpit door. On the door it read, *It's a man's world, bitches.*

"Okay, Lucy," Maddy began in a desperate voice. "Listen. We'll find out who did this and we'll fuck them up, okay?"

"I already know who did this," Lucy replied with an eerily calm determination. "*Men* did this. Get off the plane, Maddy."

"Lucy, dammit, just listen to me, and…"

"Get off the plane, Maddy."

"Lucy, I love you. We all love you. You can't be alone right now, okay?"

"Get off the plane, Maddy."

As the remaining twelve women watched the private jet soar into the sky like a predatory bird, Josie turned to Alexa and said, "Okay Alexa. Just what *else* has she been working on?"

CHAPTER 88

FORTY-FIVE

"Well, here we are," Alexa stated to the group twelve hours later. "Lucy's laboratory in the basement under the bookstore. Here's what she's been working on. He should be about ready."

A feeling of dread was hovering over all the ladies who were now joined by Erick, Marcus, Henri, Cliff, and Gregory as Alexa walked them toward a naked, screaming man in an otherwise empty soundproof glass booth. He was standing in his own waste as he pounded on the glass frantically and screamed at them.

"So, who is *this* then?" Josie cautiously inquired as the man continued his futile pounding and began hurling his feces at the glass.

"I'm not sure," Alexa replied. "Lucy just said he was someone who had it coming. I've learned not to ask too many questions of her. She gets really agitated if I pry too hard about where she gets her test subjects. But she *does* love questions about her inventions. And their *effects*. And she said that this *new* toxin that she has created will make the world safe for women forever. That this toxin will wipe out all the males of our species. Well, except for the ones that we decide to keep locked away and use for stud in order to preserve the human race. Or at least the *females* of the human race. She said that if we failed in this war that this would be the final and definitive solution. She then got this really creepy smile on her face and said, 'Part of me *hopes* we fail. Part of me *hopes* that this will be the final solution.'

"Anyway, she calls this new one, 'Toxin T.' The 'T' stands for 'Testosterone.' It can be distributed in water supplies or can be airborne and is comprised of millions of microscopic spores. Once it is ingested by breathing it in or drinking it by a female, the toxin immediately dies. The high level of estrogen kills it and there are no effects. This would also be true of males who have higher levels of estrogen and lower levels of testosterone than normal. However, once it is ingested by a *male* with *normal* levels of testosterone and estrogen…well…then things get interesting.

"You see, these spores are attracted to higher levels of testosterone. In fact, they thrive on it. So, the spores congregate in the male testes and just…um…kinda hibernate there. For seven days the spores strengthen. And the inflicted male is highly contagious. He has no idea that there's anything wrong. There are no symptoms…yet. For seven days he is walking around infecting other males. Just by breathing near them. Or shaking their hand. At their workplace. Their schools. Their churches. Their grocery stores. Everywhere they go, they are infecting other males. Lucy said that she could take one infected male and put him in a stadium full of unaffected men and that the entire stadium would be infected within twenty minutes. Just by the men passing it from one to another. Seat by seat. Row by row. Section by section. It would spread that quickly. Kinda like when fans do the wave. Only *this* is deadly. After seven days, the spores hatch and…"

Alexa's voice trailed off as she witnessed the encased man fall on his back and begin writhing in pain. The group fell into a shocked silence as they witnessed the man's skin literally crawling. They then gasped as thousands of large black spiders tore their way through the man's skin from his head to his toes. His entire body violently shook as it was covered by the fierce arachnids that were consuming his flesh. After feasting for five minutes, the insidious spiders instantly died, leaving a half-eaten corpse.

"Yep. That's what happens. I *thought* he was about ready to hatch." Alexa stated matter-of-factly. "You see, after seven days, the spores hatch into thousands of creepy, black, carnivorous spiders. They immediately grow to about two inches in diameter, crawl throughout the body and begin eating their way out through the skin. Lucy specifically engineered them to die after five minutes of their hatching because, and I quote, 'Women have enough shit to deal with. We're not dealing with an epidemic of carnivorous spiders too.' This is the sixth and final test subject. I guess the piranhas in Maddy's old office next door are going to be happy tonight. So, this toxin is ready to be deployed. Lucy now has a weapon to virtually eliminate every male on the planet."

"Okay, guys," the ever reasonable and diplomatic Gregory interjected. "Listen, I'm sure Lucy is a little bit...um...off the rails at the moment. And for good reason. She just saw the torn apart body of her murdered love. We would *all* get a bit loopy after something horrible like that. She probably just needs some time to cool off. Maybe take out a few 'Chads.' She'll be okay. I'm sure that she doesn't intend to deploy this. I mean, my God! If she did, then she would kill *all* of *us* as well. We are her friends, and she would never do anything to harm us."

"Yeah, maybe," a suspicious Maddy stated as she walked around the glass encasement and surveyed what little remained of Test Subject Number six. "Tell me Alexa. Did she develop anything to deploy this toxin on a large scale or is she limited to just lab experiments right now?"

"Oh yeah. She could deploy it via waterways or by air on a massive scale. Fly a crop duster over a metropolitan area. Pour the liquid form into the water supply. And she already has the infection route developed. She knows just where to concentrate her efforts to spread it most efficiently. Region to region. Country to country. Continent to Continent. She said that it would take approximately nine months to wipe out eighty-six-point-three percent of the males on the planet. The remaining ones could be rounded up and kept in isolation, away from the toxin. Then, she said, we could use *them* for their seed. And target practice. She also said that it would be a blessing for any good souls who died, because they would get a fast-track to Enlightenment. The dark souls could be destroyed by Arima and others like her over time. And she said that there *would* be others like Arima. And Jessie. And Rosa. That without the heavy hand of men's persecution, women would evolve more quickly, and we could then be the stewards of this Earth as God intended. But you're right Maddy. Without the stuff in *this* room, she can't deploy it on a large scale. Maybe we're all just getting worked up over nothing."

There was a loud 'creak' as a metal door was opened then the soft 'click' of the light switch. The entire group let out an audible gasp before an unnerved Erick said, "Is it okay to get worked up *now*? Because what I'm looking at is a room full of *nothing*."

"Aw, shit," Alexa softly said as tears began to form in her blue eyes. "It's gone. It's all gone. All of it. The canisters of the gas and the aerial distribution system. Gone. All of the cannisters of the liquid toxin. Gone. All she needs is an airplane, which she has, and she could infect the entire world."

"Okay, then," Josie said with unease in her voice. "Step Numero-Uno. We find her. And we put Rod and the rest of the men on that. She may have loved you all once, but we must assume that she's completely distrustful of men right now. And that includes you guys. So, go get Rod and track her movements. She has an airplane that must land somewhere. And we have her infection route. She's very routine-oriented. She will stick to her plan.

"Step Numero-Two-O: When we find her, we will talk with her. We will get her to surrender to us. And if she *won't* come with us, then…"

Josie's statement was cut off by Maddy's mournful voice. "Don't say that, Josie. Don't *ever* say that. She is my best friend. Plus, we don't take out other women. It will be all right. She will listen to me. It *will be* all right. It *has* to be. Sweetie, I love you, but don't you *ever* finish that fucking sentence."

———

"Oh my," Rod's nasal staccato voice was heard saying as he was looking at the data that Erick had requested. "She is much too smart for this. She couldn't have remained hidden from us forever, but this is like she is wanting to be found. She has left us quite the trail of breadcrumbs to follow."

"Not exactly breadcrumbs," Lionnel replied. "But definitely, a trail. A trail of exploding heads. A trail of intestines. A trail of bodies that all lead to…what is this point on the map, Rod?"

"Well, let me see here," Rod answered as he put his pop-bottle lenses up against the screen. "Oh yes. That is the Catskill/Delaware Watershed."

"Uh, huh," Marcus replied before asking with trepidation, "And just what is the significance of *that?*"

"Well, you see," Rod answered. "That is where approximately ninety-five percent of the water comes from for New York City."

Erick, Lionnel, Jerry, Marcus, Cliff, and even Gregory let out a simultaneous "Fuuuuuuuuck."

———

"Why did those two little bitches get themselves knocked up," Maddy incredulously asked her sisterhood as they made their way through the woods surrounding the reservoir. "We could have really used Rachel and Kayla's tracking ability. This place is fucking huge! But *noooooo!* We just *had* to teach the Twins to play 'Hide the Sausage' now didn't we!' *Then* we had to tell them not to double-bag it! Dumbasses! Now we have to squirrel them away at the estate to protect them and their fucking little blessings! Those little fuckers will be blessings all right. Blessing for fucking Satan probably! Whatevs. Jessie, can't you Behold her or something? It's gonna take forever to find her here!"

"I'm sorry Maddy," Jessie answered, "But I can't. I never could with her. Her soul is neither pure good nor pure evil. Her soul is conflicted. Her soul is whatever it is required to be at any given moment. So, no. I'm sorry. I can't and…Oh! Goddamit!"

"Hey, man, what's wrong?" Arima asked her friend.

"Oh, I just broke another nail, *that's all*! How do you expect me to influence women to get out of abusive situations looking like *this*? Plus, I'm *totally* wearing the wrong shoes to stomp through the woods. And look at my blouse! Completely covered in sap! I really think that I should wait back in the bus. I'm just too… um…*important* to be out here rummaging around in the weeds."

"No, we stay together. We will do this together," came Josie's immediate and blunt order. Jessie decided that it was best not to question her leader at this particular moment.

There was a loud *CRACK* twenty yards ahead of them. "Hey, honeys," came Dragenstein's soft, petite voice. "Come this way. I just took this tree out of our way, *tee, hee*."

"It *is* kinda nice to have an Amazonian bulldozer drag queen with us," Maddy whispered to her daughter before tripping and falling face-first into the dense brush.

"What the fuck?" Maddy yelled out as she looked down at her feet and saw the arm of a police officer sticking out of the bushes on the ground. "What's this? Number *seven* that we've found? And all men. The only surviving officer that we have found so far is that lady officer that was gagged and bound to that tree. So, we know three things. Lucy is sticking to our code to not harm women. Lucy is *not* sticking to our code of only taking out men who deserve it. And finally, we are definitely going in the right direction."

The women came out of the wooded area with its sounds of rustling leaves and snapping twigs. Those sounds were replaced by the tranquil lapping of waves upon the shore. Approximately fifty yards from their position stood Lucy who was navigating a remote-controlled boat into the center of the body of water. On top of the boat rested a large metal cannister. And a small black box with a flashing red light.

"Okay guys. You approach her from here. I'm gonna circle around in the woods and try to get close to her. Just keep her talking until I can get there," Maddy instructed before her lithe frame disappeared into the timber.

"Hey Lucy," Josie said casually as she discreetly pulled an arrow from her quiver and placed it into her bow. Lucy looked up and saw Josie's dark green cat suit become increasingly visible as well as the forms of Jules, Dragenstein, Arima, Jessie, Jamie, and Alexa.

"Oh, hey guys," Lucy responded nonchalantly. "Nice to see you. Where's Sam and Maddy? They won't want to miss this."

"Oh, they're just back at the bus keeping the champagne chilled for us. We're all going to celebrate your homecoming," Josie answered calmly. "So…um…whatcha doin'? Should we just go ahead and get on the bus and get the party started? Then we can get down to the business of stopping these damned wars. C'mon. What do ya say?"

"Naw," Lucy answered dismissively. "I think that I'll stay here for a while. And after tonight, you really won't be needed to stop the wars. I'm taking care of it. Now, please just stop approaching or else, okay?"

"Well, sure, Lucy. Whatever you say," Josie replied as she obediently held up her left hand to halt the progression of her troops. "But I'm a bit confused. Or else, what? And what do you mean that you're going to end the wars tonight?"

Lucy let out an exasperated sigh and said, "Or else I hit this little button on this remote. And this little button will make that box on top of that cannister on the boat go boom. And then the liquid contents of that cannister will be spread throughout this reservoir and into New York's water system. Then, *that* water will go into the mouths of the men of New York."

Lucy then began trembling with orgasmic excitement and the cadence of her speech quickened. "And then, and then, do you know what will happen? And then the toxins that are in this water will be in the men of New York. And the men who are *visiting* New York! Yeah! And all the men of New York will die in like, seven to thirty days. And all the men who were *visiting* New York will take *my toxin* back to their homes. And *they* will spread it! Throughout the world, *my toxins* will be spread! And it will kill *all the males*! Yeah, isn't that *cool*? They will all *die*! And they will die *painfully*! They are going to be eaten from the *inside out* by *my* engineered spiders. All over the world men will be *eaten alive*! Isn't that *great*? All I have to do is push *this* little button and we will be *free* from men for *all time*, heh,heh,heh,heh,heh,heh,heh."

Josie lifted her bow and pointed it at Lucy as she said in a relaxed voice, "Lucy. You know we can't let you do that. You know our code. We don't take out innocent people. So please just put the remote down and come with us. Please, Lucy. I don't want to have to do this."

"Do *what*?" Lucy retorted angrily as her face turned from unhinged glee to maniacal intensity. "Just what are *you* going to do Josie, huh? Shoot me? I don't think so. As soon as you let that arrow fly, I'm going to press this button. You're a good shot, but you aren't *that* good. Or that quick. I'm really disappointed in you all. Maddy would understand. I wish she were here to explain it to you. She would understand because she was *mind-fucked* by the *same man* that I was! And she knows *deep down* in her soul that *all* men are that way! They are cruel! They are violent! All they want is power! All they want is to dominate others! To dominate *us*! To beat us! To rape us! To murder our loved ones and tear them limb from limb and leave them strewn about an airplane! That's *men* that did that! Not just a *few* men, either! *All* men did that because *all* men are *capable* of doing that! They destroy *everything* that they touch! They destroy this planet! They destroy our livelihoods! They destroy our bodies! And they destroy our souls! Maddy understands. I *know* that she does."

"Lucy, that isn't *true*!" Josie pleaded. "Not all men are evil! Hell, not even *most* of them are evil. Most are good, kind souls. Like Erick and Marcus and Lionnel and Henri! What about Pastor Tim and Jeremy? Look at how their selfless sacrifice might save our world! That was *men* that did that, Lucy! Now please. Put down the remote and let's just get out of here, okay? Please, Lucy. I don't want to do this."

"Yeah, well, you probably have a point," Lucy answered with a renewed tranquility. "There might be a *few* that are worth saving. Maybe they are the ones that we keep for their seed. And some might be sacrificed. Yeah, I suppose we might have to break a few eggs. But you know what they say about breaking eggs to make an omelet, right? Well, I really *love* fuckin' omelets!"

Lucy's thumb began to press down on the detonator button just as she felt a sharp pain pierce her heart through her back. Then, an arrow penetrated her right wrist, causing her to drop the detonator. Everyone gasped as the detonator tumbled from her grasp and fell to the ground. They briefly stared at it before their eyes darted toward the remote-controlled boat. There was no boom.

Lucy's lifeless body collapsed backward, knocking Maddy to the ground with it. Maddy stared into the dead eyes of her best friend, and she shook her bloody fist at the sky while screaming out to the universe, "Why? *Why* you motherfuckers? Why did I have to kill Lucy? Why did it have to come to this? Why is the world so hateful? Why is the world turning us all into heartless bastards? Why? This is it! This is the end of it all! Because if I can murder my best friend, then there's no hope for *any* of us! This war is over! And we just fucking lost. This truly is the end of it all."

A sobbing Maddy cradled and lightly rocked her dear friend's body as she began singing REM's "Why Not Smile" through her cracking voice. From their time in college, it was the song that they had always sung together during dreadful times. They would hold each other and weep and sing along with Michael's beautiful voice. At the end of the song, they would always look at one another and smile. Then laugh. Then Maddy would say, "Now get the fuck off of me!" And they would hug and laugh again. They had sung this song together countless times through countless tragedies. Maddy knew that this was the final time that she would ever sing this song because Maddy knew there could be no greater tragedy than this.

Arima's body began lightly shaking as her eyes rolled back into her head and her body elevated four feet off the ground. Her pretty ebony face looked directly into Maddy's tearful green eyes. She opened her mouth. And she joined Maddy in singing the rest of the song as she smiled widely.

Upon the song's conclusion, Lucy said through Arima, "Thank you Maddy. You were the only one who could have done this. You were the only one who could have freed me. You were the only one who loved humanity enough to sacrifice your best friend. I'm glad that I died at your hands. I'm glad that I died at the hands of the woman who I love and respect more than all others. It's okay, Maddy. You have nothing to feel guilty about. You had no choice. I gave you no choice. I gave you no choice but to send me to my Jennifer. And now, I will get the fuck off of you. For now. Win this war. I will see you on the battlefield in Enlightenment."

There was a light blue and white streak that emerged from Arima's descending body. It wistfully hovered over the astonished and grieving women for a moment before ascending into the heavens.

"Well, fuck," Maddy stated with resignation. "I guess this *isn't* the end of it all. It fuckin' sucks though. Okay. Let's get her precious body back to the bus. Let's get home. And let's find and destroy the demonic fucks who made me do this!"

CHAPTER 89

OH LORD

"It looks like we both had the same idea," a drowsy Maddy stated as she saw Arima's ass sticking out of her refrigerator.

"Oh, hey, Sis," Arima replied sleepily. "Yeah, I sometimes enjoy a little midnight snack. Or one AM snack. Or three AM snack. What time is it anyway?"

"It's twelve-thirty," Maddy replied as she perched her petite born-again frame up onto the kitchen island and smiled to herself as she watched her sister rummaging through the leftovers. "So, anything in particular that you're looking for? And don't say 'tato chips. Erick is getting *really pissed* at everyone eating his 'tato chips. Except Josie. That little bitch can do whatever she wants around here."

"I dunno," Arima casually responded. "I'm kinda in the mood for something sweet."

"How 'bout some ice cream?" Maddy excitedly replied as her size-six bare feet slapped back down onto the cool linoleum floor and she opened the freezer door. "Here, let me show you something." The freezer light illuminated Maddy's ornery smile as she began removing packages of frozen dinners and vegetables from the bottom shelf and handing them to Arima. "Here. Hold this.

And this. And this. And…ah…here we are. Now, Arima, I have trusted you with a lot of my secrets. But there is *no* secret that is more important than this one. I haven't told *anybody* about this, so you must keep this a secret. Underneath all this frozen healthy shit is where I keep my secret stash of butter-ripple ice cream. Erick doesn't even know about this, okay?"

"Yeah, cool," Arima replied as she handed the frozen vegetables and dinners back to her sister who began carefully placing them back into the freezer.

"Now, if you ever get in here," Maddy began instructing, "it's *very important* that you put everything back *exactly* as it was. Erick is anal-retentive as fuck. He even has an organizational system for frozen food, and he'll notice if anything has been disturbed, okay?"

"Yep. Got it," Arima answered. "So, do we need some bowls or…?"

"Fuck that," Maddy interrupted. "All we need is two spoons and we'll eat it right out of the container. Just as the good lord intended."

The pair of giggling sisters flopped their pajama-clad bottoms onto the white, plush couch cushions in the living room and eagerly opened the brand-new container of ice cream. They giggled a bit louder as their large, silver spoons dug in for their first bite.

"Oh, yeah, that's the stuff," an enraptured Arima sighed as her first taste was dribbling off her lower lip and onto her pajama collar.

"Yeah, this shit's the best!" Maddy exclaimed. "This is the flavor that my Uncle Joe and I would eat together. We would just talk and laugh and eat ice cream. I cherished those moments. Oh, shit! I just realized something!"

"What's that?" Arima inquired as another overflowing spoonful of ice cream was being excavated from its frozen container.

"I just realized that you and I haven't had a chance to really… um…talk. I mean, everything has been so fucking busy and chaotic that we haven't just been able to…um…y'know…" Maddy's voice trailed off as she looked away from Arima's inquisitive face.

"Hey, Sis, what's wrong?" Arima asked.

"Oh, fuckin' nothin'," Maddy chuckled as she wiped tears from her green eyes and embarrassingly looked back at her sister. "I'm just being a big fuckin' pussy. I can tear the fuck out of people. I can run an international hit man syndicate. Or, assassination technician syndicate, or, *whatever* the fuck Josie calls them now. I can cut people up, blow people up, dissolve them in acid, dismember them, make them watch as I feed their flesh to my piranha, and all sorts of other twisted shit. I can walk out of that room, covered in their blood, and never give them another thought. I have absolutely no emotional connection to what I've just done to another human being. None. I'm cold as fucking ice, and I *like* being that way. But when it comes to my friends, and my family, I get…well…sentimental. And it just fuckin' hit me. *I have a sister!*"

Maddy broke down in tears and physically embraced Arima for the first time. Arima hugged Maddy tightly in response and the shoulders of their respective pajama tops became saturated in their joyful tears. They each felt a strange sensation as they held each other. It was as though they had found a missing piece of themselves. Maddy's internal ember seemed to burn with a greater intensity. And Arima's inner-fortitude and ability to connect with souls seemed to be enhanced. They looked at one another, smiled, laughed, and hugged once again. For the first time, the sisters had connected emotionally. They felt their care and love for one another. They felt one another's feminine strength. They instinctively knew that their souls belonged together. And they now knew that their combined forces could never be stopped.

"Oh fuck! The ice cream!" Maddy yelled out as she pulled away from her sister and looked at the crushed and partially melted ice cream container that was between them.

They both looked down at their sugar-coated tops and broke

out into hysterical laughter. "Ah, fuck it," they said in unison as they picked up their spoons and began scooping the melted ice cream from their respective tops and shoveling it into their mouths through their playful giggles. Maddy didn't even mind that four white rats had joined them to help in their clean-up efforts. They then began rapidly hurling a barrage of questions and comments toward one another. The moment one would finish, the other would begin. They had years to catch up on. They had years to make up for. And they were determined to do it all in one evening.

"So, how did you meet Erick?"

"So, how did you meet Marcus?"

"Oh my God! I loved *Cinderella* too!"

"What's your favorite color?"

"What's *your* favorite color?"

"I fuckin' asked you first!"

"Who was your first boyfriend?"

"Okay. You're stranded on a desert island, and you can only take one album with you. What album is it?"

"Really? Springsteen? Me too!"

"When did you first know you could connect with souls?"

"Who are all the people you have helped to Enlightenment?"

"You did *what?* You ate hotdogs off a burning corpse? That's so cool."

"You did *what?* You put his dark soul in tacos, ate him and then killed him by shitting him out? That's gold Arima! Fuckin' gold!"

"Who was the first person you killed?"

"Who was the *second* person you killed?"

"Who was the *third* person you killed?"

(An hour later) "Who was the *fifty-third* person you killed?"

Over two hours had passed, and the exhausted and exhilarated sisters collapsed back onto the seat cushions with feelings of newfound tranquility.

"Hey, sis," Arima stated with regret as she wiped the final remnants of butter-ripple from her chin. "I'm so sorry that you lost your best friend. Especially that way. She was a cool person. I'm sorry she's gone."

"Thanks, Arima," Maddy thoughtfully answered. "Yeah. She *was* cool. Really fucked up but cool. And, as we all now know, she isn't really gone. I mean, she is from *here*, of course, but she isn't *gone, gone*. I mean, I'll see her again when our work down here is done, and we get called back to Enlightenment. Oh, fuck. Part of me wishes that this war just goes on forever. Part of me wishes that I could stay with you and the rest of my loved ones forever. But another part of me wants it to be over. For us to beat the fuck out of these evil pricks once and for all. For us to beat the fuck out of my demonic mother and our demonic father. Then, Erick and I can move on. Back to my loved ones in Enlightenment. I feel so fucking torn. This is why I hate feeling anything."

"Hey," Arima softly answered. "There's no need to feel conflicted. What you are doing...what *we* are doing is right. And the sooner it gets done the more people we can save. We need to get this shit done as fast as possible. And listen. You can always come back into my soul whenever you want. You can visit me and Josie and everyone else whenever you want. I told you before that you have an open invitation to come into my soul. Just... um...call first, okay?"

"Okay," Maddy answered through a new bout of laughter. "Yeah, I don't wanna jump into you while you're getting busy or somethin'! Wow! It's gonna be like I have my own little personal time-share on Earth. Yeah! This could be cool! Best of both worlds! I get eternity in Enlightenment with Erick and my deceased family plus I get to visit my Earth-bound friends and family whenever I want! And the best part is that I can make fun of 'em as they get old, and their tits get all saggy and shit! Especially Sam! That's gonna be classic!"

"Well, we should probably get to bed, Sis," Arima regretfully stated. "Rod has called us all to a big meeting in the morning."

"Yeah, I suppose," Maddy responded with the same tone of regret. She never wanted this moment with her sister to end. She then thought of a way to extend it, if only for a brief time. "But first, there's one thing left to do! I have danced with *everyone* that I've ever cared about. Erick. Uncle Joe. Aunt Blair. Aunt Patty. Josie. Lucy. All my friends and family. I danced with them all. And now, my beautiful sister, I want to dance with you!"

Maddy leapt off the couch and playfully swayed her hips as she sauntered toward the entertainment center. She opened the bottom cabinet and took out a dusty cardboard box that still contained fifty-four records. It was the box of records that Erick had purchased in 2022 from Maddy's store. After all these years, every record remained in that box, in the exact order as when he had brought them home. She chuckled lightly to herself, and a single tear rolled down her slightly befreckled cheek. She looked up at the clock, smiled broadly, and exclaimed, "And I know the *perfect song* to dance to!"

She placed the forty-five on the turntable and lowered the needle. After a few seconds of crackling vinyl, Arima and Maddy were swaying, spinning, jiving, and grooving to Gary US Bonds's R&B classic, "Quarter to Three."

The song ended and the pair burst into laughter as they heard Erick's booming voice from the top of the staircase. "Hey! You two had better not be eating my 'tato chips!"

"This isn't working, Pastor," its nasal voice stated as It peered down at the dancing pair of sisters from Its unholy perch in the Realm of Perdition. "We need to end this now. We need a new strategy. She is stronger than we imagined. They both are. They have bonded and they can now combine their strength. Just as *we* have done. Our Earthbound forces are depleted. They are losing the war there. But with every human that we lose comes a new dark soul to wage war against Enlightenment. The fools are building our cosmic army for us. It is time to collect as many dark souls as we can. As many as we can get to congregate in one place. Men, women, *and* children. Collect them all. You will go to Earth and convince them, Pastor. Manipulate them one final time and convince them to commit the ultimate mortal sacrifice. Convince them to sacrifice themselves and their wives and their children. Convince them to destroy any good souls that might arise from the fallen bodies. Convince them to stand back, stand down and be ready. Ready for when we call them here. We shall do this in reverse. We shall conquer Enlightenment. Then, we shall destroy the good souls *after* they leave the Earth. Once we have conquered Enlightenment, there will be *no* place for the good souls to go. Except their own personal hell of *our* creation!"

———

"It's okay, Rod. I'll explain what's going on," an understanding Rosa stated as she looked upon her profusely sweating friend. She then leaned into his ear and whispered, "But you might want to stop staring at Jessie's chest. I think Cliff is getting pissed."

"Why are *you* so fucking perky this morning?" Erick inquired of his wife quietly. "You and Arima were up half the night."

"Yeah," Maddy responded. "I'm probably still on a sugar high from all the ice cream I ate last night."

"Ice cream? When did we get ice cream?" a confused Erick asked followed by their daughter. "Yeah! When did we get ice cream?"

"Would you two just shut the fuck up!" Maddy whisper shouted. "Rosa's about to start talking. Show some fuckin' respect!" *That was close,* Maddy thought to herself as she flashed her sister a mischievous grin.

"Madam President," Rosa respectfully began as she looked down upon Josie who was sitting to her immediate right next to her parents. Josie gave her mother a brief, haughty look. The ever-diplomatic Maddy rolled her eyes and stuck out her tongue.

"We have some very good news and some news that…well… we are confused by. Jamie has been working with Rod on keeping tabs on the most dangerous Earth-bound dark souls. These are the self-proclaimed militias, skinheads, radical militants, and their ilk. Jamie, could you please present what you and Rod are finding?"

"Yes, of course dear," the thirty-year-old, African American transexual replied as she sauntered her mini-dressed frame up to the podium. Rod's gaze immediately went from the ceiling to Jamie's burgeoning bosom. "The Earthly forces of the Underground Autocratic Movement, also known as the demonic forces of Vetis are quite depleted. Since Gregory, Marcus, and Cliff were able to forge a partnership with the Earth's great democracies, they have been rounded up or killed off by precise military strikes. Some of these strikes have been conducted by various governments and some have been conducted by us. And, due to difficulty in being able to spread their hate-filled propaganda, they are unable to poison the minds of the weak-willed into joining their movement in large numbers as they did twenty years ago. So, the result is that the most radical and violent of their movement are now small in numbers and are clustered in various tribes. And these tribes are on the move. They are all jumping in cars, boats, and planes and heading to a dilapidated, closed resort in Florida. I have heard that it is so run down that even the rats have abandoned it. We estimate that there are approximately 10,000 people that are congregating there. This would be our best chance to wipe them out, once and for all. Then, we would need to deal with their souls. There is a problem, however. These evil men are bringing their families. Their wives and children are being brought along as well. We do not know why. So, Josie wants us to have a formidable force go to Florida and observe what they are doing. Just observe. We do not have any desire to harm the women or children. If there is an opening to take out the men, then we shall do so. But only as long as they aren't using their families as human shields. We shall leave immediately following our meeting here today."

"Thank you, Jamie," Rosa said as she retook her place behind the podium. "Okay, gang. Yes, that is confusing news. We don't know what they're up to. Maybe it's just a good-ol'-boy hootenanny. But we doubt it. They may be planning some sort of offensive. So, we'll watch them and act accordingly.

"Now, for the good news. We have done it. We have found a way to enhance Arima's ability to draw souls into herself, then expel them into the ocean of Holy water. We estimate that she will be able to absorb approximately 1,000 souls at a time."

"Wow. That's really cool," Arima replied in her customary relaxed tone. "But, like, is this gonna hurt?"

"No! That's the best part!" Rosa excitedly answered. "In fact, I think that you will find this very enjoyable. As you know, Herbert, otherwise known as The Botanist, has been entering and taking over your body and doing experiments with us. He has been working with a number of plant and herbal combinations that are designed to interact with your specific DNA. And he has found one that will work. The only drawback is that you're going to have *one hell* of a case of the munchies. He has combined various strains of cannabis with other plants and herbs. I then connected with and enhanced the spiritual energy that these herbs contain while Rod enhanced their effects on the molecular, biological level. And the result is, well, heh, heh, heh. Some *killer* fuckin' weed."

The entire room burst into a fit of laughter as Maddy sat with her arms folded, leaned over to her husband, and said, "What's with all the laughter? It wasn't *that* fuckin' funny."

"Do you wanna try some?" Rosa asked as she looked into Arima's widening eyes. Rosa had her answer.

Rod left the room and came back a few minutes later holding a five-pound bag of the most powerful stank weed known to man. "Um," Rod stammered nervously, "this is all that we have at the moment, but we'll be able to grow more soon. I hope it's enough."

"Y-y-yeah. This'll be great," a nearly hyperventilating Arima responded as Marcus loaded up a bowl for her. The entire group went into the backyard of the unassuming Brooklyn home and Marcus handed his beloved wife the pipe. "Have a nice trip, baby," Marcus lovingly said before giving her a passionate kiss.

Rosa leaned over to Maddy and said, "And since you are her sister, you share her biology. This weed will enhance *your* skills as well. Your tenacity. Your bloodlust. And it will allow you to be psychically connected with your sister. Your bodies will be acting separately, but your *souls* will be in constant communication with one another. You can coordinate your efforts that way. Still think my joke's not funny?"

Maddy smiled widely, hugged Rosa and yelled out, "Funniest fuckin' joke that I've ever heard! Hurry up, Arima. Take a hit! And don't bogart the entire fuckin' bowl! Save some for your older sis! Let's take this shit on a test-flight!"

A second pipe was loaded to ensure that Arima was unable to bogart the entire fucking bowl. The sisters looked at one another and took a long drag. As they exhaled the smoke, they both said, "Whooooaaaa!" and began giggling.

Arima floated into the sky. "Oh man, the colors," she said in a trippy voice. "So many colors. I'm going to 1,000 feet over the ocean. Stay in touch with me, Maddy."

"Will do, over and out!" Maddy responded as she was unsure as to whether she was still in the back yard or the communications director on a bomber.

"Are you okay?" a concerned Erick asked his wife.

"Oh, man, I'm more than okay." Maddy responded through her intoxicated giggles. "I just wanna fuck some motherfuckers up. I think that I'll start with that prick neighbor who always mows his lawn at six in the morning. Then that old fucker with that fuckin' yippie dog. I hate that fuckin' dog. Then…"

"Mother!" Josie interrupted. "Get it the fuck together! Control your impulses. Being high is *not* an excuse for random murders! Although you do have a point about the mowing guy. He *is* kind of a prick. But, no! He is a good soul. Annoying, yes, but still a good soul."

"Yeah, okay. Whatevs," Maddy replied in a lilted voice. "Let me just see what's going on with Arima. Soul Sister! This is Lil' Redhead! Do you copy? Over and out!"

"Yeah, I hear you," Arima responded to Maddy's soul. "But what's with the names?"

"Those are our cool code names that I just came up with. Pretty cool, huh? Over and out!"

"Yeah, that's pretty cool, I guess. Wow, Maddy. I wish you

could see what *I'm* seeing. I'm floating high above the ocean, and I can literally *feel* Pastor Tim and Jeremy's spirits here. I can feel their love. They are so peaceful. And they are hungry. They are ready to feed on dark souls."

"That's really cool Soul Sister! Tell Pastor Tim and Jeremy that we love them. And please use my cool code name. Over and out!"

"I just told them, Madd…I mean Lil' Redhead. They said they love us too. I'm opening my soul now Maddy. I'm opening it up wider than it has ever been. Oh Lord, I feel so strong. So powerful. And I can feel them, Maddy. I can feel the dark souls coming to me. They are attracted to my soul."

At that moment, hundreds of dark souls which had been confined upon the Earthly plane came from all directions. There were hundreds of mystical purple streaks of dense fog converging upon Arima's body. They cackled with glee as they approached and entered Arima's soul. Then, the cackles turned to ungodly screams.

"I have hundreds of them in me, Maddy! Hundreds! I'm closing my soul now. They thought that they were attacking me. They thought that they could destroy me! But once they entered my soul, they realized that it was a trap! I can easily overpower and control them all! All they can do is try to struggle to break free. But they can't! Not unless I allow them too. And I think that I'll accommodate them right now."

Arima re-opened her soul, parted her lips and hundreds of streaks of dense smog were regurgitated out of her gaping mouth. The force of Arima's expulsion caused them to plummet into the ocean. The dark souls screeched in burning agony as the blessed ocean water tore apart their very essence. Small pieces of their being were being burned away and were immediately eaten by the aquatic wildlife. The oceans bubbled violently as the white-hot hatred of the dark souls were extinguished by the coolness of the universe's love. And Arima laughed. She laughed at the image of hundreds of sinister beings' faces being frozen in horrendous torment before letting out their final insidious gasp. The dark smog cleared from the water leaving it a shimmering blue. The ocean was nearly perfectly still, and the fair-weather puffs of clouds reflected off the water. As did the image of a bright purple aura in the shape of a thirty-year-old Jamaican American heroine.

"Oh, Lord, Maddy! That was incredible!" Arima yelled out. "I just killed off like six or seven *hundred* of those bastards. All at once. I just puked them right out of me! And I know that I can do more. I'm not done yet! I'm opening my soul again. Come to momma you bastards!"

"Um, that's really great there, Soul Sister, and a little bit gross, but I really don't want to have to keep reminding you to use my cool code name, alright? Over and out!"

An hour and countless vanquished dark souls later, Arima and Maddy were running down the street together towards the nearest grocery store.

Erick turned to his daughter and said, "You wanna go get a pizza someplace? I get the feeling that we aren't safe around them with food tonight. And do you have any cash? Your mother and aunt are gonna max out the credit cards."

———

There was a loud squawk of feedback on the PA system, then a light buzz. Then the arrogant voice of the Pastor. "Greetings my blessed ones," the Pastor began. His adopted pale face wore a devilish smirk. He had chosen a devastatingly handsome forty-something priest to inhabit. He reveled in the ability to run his fingers through the soft, blond locks of his latest victim. His tone six-foot-four body was adorned in a purple gown and his shadow towered over his congregation in the courtyard and beyond into a vast clearing. His victim's eyes had once been a soft blue. They were now as black and cold as the heart that pumped unholy bile throughout the body.

"Yes, greetings my most holy friends. My most *patriotic* brothers and sisters. Thank you all for heeding my call. Thank you for joining me on this most momentous occasion. I am here today to tell you all that…we have won. Yes, my friends. We have won. It may not seem like it to you. It may seem as though the unholy forces of wokeness and inclusion have beaten us back. But they have not. All the news reports about our brothers being slaughtered are all lies. *We* are the victors! *We* have taken the Earth! *We* have taken the Earth from those who would deny us our rightful place! Our rightful place of dominion over the women. Over the sexual deviants. Over the dark skinned. Our rightful dominion over all the Earth's resources! Over the animals! Over the plant life! Over the oil, gold, and jewels! It is all ours! It is all *yours*! Your God-given right of dominion over *anything* that you want has been granted by our most glorious Lord!"

Tearful cheers and applause exploded from the thousands of naïve male congregants as the women and children remained in a protective, brainwashed hush. The men began chanting, "It is ours! It is ours! It is ours!" The inner circle of Murder, Inc. could only watch with trepidation as they wondered what the ending of this scene would be.

"Let's just go down there and start tearing these fuckers up!" Maddy exclaimed.

"Shaddup. You're still high," came her husband's immediate response.

"Wow," Maddy replied in a stunned tone. "*That* was a rather *blunt* response. Get it? Blunt? 'Cause of smoking pot? Get it? Why aren't you people laughing? That was pure fuckin' gold!"

"Not as gold as mine, I guess," came Rosa's catty reply.

"Would you people please be quiet?" Josie ordered. "I'm trying to hear this!"

The members of Murder, Inc. fell into an obedient silence as did the mesmerized congregation a quarter of a mile away.

"Yes, my friends, it is ours. It is *yours*," the Pastor began again as his tender ego was being pumped up by the effectiveness of his lies and manipulation upon his willfully ignorant followers. "And it is all due to *your* sacrifice. For years, *you* have been waging war against those that profess to be good and kind. They profess to care about everybody! But did they care about *you*? Did they care that *you* were preordained to rule over them? No, they did not. They just kept putting so-called human beings into positions of power over *you*! Did they care when *you* fell ill? No, they did not. They just tried to inject a vaccine of government microchips into *you*. Did they care when *you* lost your job? No, they did not. They gave *your* job to some unqualified so-called minority. They gave *your* job to someone who they said was a victim of something that *you* played no part in! Then, they made *you* feel guilty about it! They made *you* feel guilty about *your* White heritage! They made *you* feel guilty about being born the way that *you* were! They are *not* the victims! *We* are the victims! *You* are the victims! But not any longer, my brothers! For tonight, *not only* have we taken over the Earth, but *tonight* we shall begin our glorious march to the heavens! Tonight, we shall begin our journey to rule not just the Earth but *all the cosmos*! *You* have been chosen by our glorious Lord for this mission, my brothers! Join me now! Join me in this final battle to *take back* your God-given dominion over *everything*! Raise your guns into the air! Yes! Raise them high my brothers! Let me see the sun's beautiful rays *gleam* on their right- eous barrels! Now place your guns against the temples of your loved ones! Yes! Let them *feel* the cleansing strength of your steel! Now, pull the trigger and baptize them in your endless love!"

Thousands of gunshots were heard just before Jessie's anguished voice cried out, "Jesus fucking Christ! The pain! The evil! The pure *evil*! Oh, Lord! They're slaughtering their own children!"

Chapter 90

Attack of the Ghost Riders

"Why daddy?" the eight-year-old, blond-haired tyke inquired as his brilliant blue eyes stared up into the gleefully deranged eyes of his father.

"Because, son," the father said back in a trance-like tone, "This is how our lord shows us his love." *BLAM*!

The father looked down at his fallen son lying in his own brains and began cackling maniacally before placing the revolver to his own temple. *BLAM*!

A confused white and blue streak hovered over his own corpse and watched as his father killed himself. He then watched as a black smog emerged from his father's body, looked at him with flaming red eyes and swooped toward him. He begged his father's dark soul to stop as his essence was being choked out of him. Then, his blue and white streak dissipated into nothingness and the boy was gone forever.

The frantic members of Murder, Inc. watched the same scene play out over and over across the complex. *BLAM*! *BLAM*! Heeeee,heeeee,heeeeee, No! Please stop daddy! Please sto..."

"Oh fuck! They're not just killing their children! They're murdering their *souls* as well!" Josie screamed out. "Mom! Arima!

Take a hit! Arima! Float above the complex and draw as many of those children's souls into you as you can! Mom! You, Jules, and Jessie get on the ATV's and try to attract the cult members to you. Rosa! Try to manipulate the energy of the dark souls and hold them up for as long as you can! Dragenstein! Cliff! Marcus! Dad! Get on your ATV's and try to get as many living women and children as you can to safety. Henri and Sam! Stay here and take out any fucker that tries to get to us! And Lionnel. Stay here with me and pray. We'll take care of the wounded as best we can. Now go!"

"We didn't exactly put it up to a *vote*, so I'm not sure those are *official* orders," Maddy lamented quietly as she and Arima took long drags off their pipes. "Whooooaaaa!" they said simultaneously as Arima lifted into the sky and Maddy rushed to her ATV. "Oh well, who gives a fuck. I need to kill some motherfuckin' douchebags!"

Arima hovered fifty feet off the ground and opened her soul as wide as she was able. "Hey, um, kids," she said in a hazy cadence. "Like, um, come here, ok? You'll be safe here. Come on." Her soul was bombarded by hundreds of panic-stricken blue and white streaks. Once they were inside of Arima, she could feel them cowering with each other and weeping with despair.

"Let me try something!" Jules barked out as she and the others were speeding their ATV's toward the vile resort of the weak-willed. The vein in her forehead began pulsing from her extreme level of concentration until a large clowder of feral small cats, bobcats, and panthers came running into the clearing and began zooming around from one man to the next. Smaller cats would lunge at a man's face and bite and claw him as they had dreamed of doing to toilet tissue and shoes. The larger cats bit their legs off and began eating them.

"I told them to try not to kill them!" Jules yelled at her friends. "Just take them down. If we kill them, then we'll have more dark souls to deal with!"

"Yeah! Great point, Jules!" Jessie replied before saying to herself, "Malum tuum dolorem facit. et dolor meus es fortitudo mea." Jessie felt her physical strength grow ten-fold. She zipped from one man to another in her ATV, pulling their arms from their sockets in one motion as she passed by them.

Who the fuck put them *in charge of our little group?* Maddy thought to herself as she sliced men's legs off with a broadsword as she passed them. Each time her black vinyl cat-suit was splattered with a new man's blood, she would giggle and shout out *WHACK*! Her drug-addled mind flashed back to one of Erick's 'pussy' songs. She laughed out loud and began singing Neil Sedaka's "Laughter in the Rain" as loudly as she could as she drove around swinging her bloodied sword at the bearded cult members.

Dragenstein leaped off her ATV and began violently mowing men down as though she were an all-pro pulling guard. A group of quivering men surrounded her and raised their guns. She smiled at them demurely and took off her white, chiffon dress revealing a stitched together perfectly formed muscular female. She giggled lightly, and said breathily, "I always *wanted* to be a ballerina, *tee, hee*." She blew them a kiss then began spinning rapidly. Her engorged, steely penis looked like the whirling blade of a helicopter as it effortlessly sliced through the men's abdomens. The men screamed in agony as they felt their intestines unravel and plop onto the ground.

Cliff, Marcus, and Erick picked up screaming children and placed them onto the back of their respective ATV's. They rushed them to Lionnel and Josie who would immediately begin attending to their blood-covered bodies and their traumatized psyches. The three men would then drive once more into the heart of the carnage looking for surviving women and children.

Rosa concentrated on the energy of the dark souls. She focused on overstimulating their demented minds, causing them to be distracted and flail around in the air in confusion. But there were simply too many of them and her Coven was not there to draw strength from as they had been assigned to watch over Rachel and Kayla at the estate. After five minutes of intense manipulation of the dark souls' energy, Rosa collapsed from exhaustion at Lionnel's feet.

Arima saw the dark souls become released from Rosa's influence. She smiled to herself as she said, "Hey guys. Um, do you want your kids' souls? Just follow me." She drifted away from the land and over the Atlantic Ocean. "Okay, kids. We're going to have some fun now, okay? I'm going to take you swimming." Arima re-opened her soul and sent the hundreds of blue and white streaks into the salty water where they were immediately embraced by the love of Pastor Tim and Jeremy. The ashen souls squealed with delight as they followed the blue and white streaks of their murdered children into the inviting cool blue waves. The squeals changed from delight into anguish as soon as their dark essences hit the water and were painfully extinguished by the universe's love. "Thank you, Arima," hundreds of children said as their souls ascended from the now-tranquil water and floated into the heavens.

"Not a fuckin' time to get sentimental, Soul Sister! Over and out!" Arima heard Maddy's voice scream at her. "C'mon! Let's go say 'hi' to daddy! Over and out!"

The Pastor's blackened eyes contained an uncharacteristic gleam as he watched his two daughters approach him. Arima floated closer as Maddy's ATV cruised just beneath her. He began giggling when they finally were standing directly in front of him. They glared at him with burning hatred and readied themselves for battle.

"Oh, my darling daughters," the Pastor's slithery voice said as he peeled his new body away from his dark essence revealing a scarred, dark purple mass of smog and leaving a discarded bloody carcass on the granite floor. "Now is not the time, my dears. But just be patient. It will soon be your time. Very, *very* soon, heh, heh, heh."

His spiritual body began shifting and growing until it was in the form of a fifteen-foot part-man, part black mamba. His long, forked tongue darted out of his serpentine mouth and licked the faces of both of his offspring. He then released a sadistic laugh and disappeared into the darkest portion of the late afternoon sky.

"Uh, what the fuck was that, Soul Sister? Over and out!" a confused Maddy asked.

"Um, hey, Sis," Arima replied. "I'm standing right next to you so; I don't really think we need the cool code names or the 'over and out' at the moment. And I have no idea what the hell just happened. All that I know is that I need another hit so that I can start collecting the remaining dark souls and throw them in the ocean."

"Uh, what remaining dark souls?" Maddy asked as she watched several thousand streaks of dark smog following the same path as the serpentine Pastor into the cosmos.

"No!" Arima uncharacteristically cried out. "It isn't possible! They can't leave the Earth! They can't move on to Enlightenment or any other plane of existence! Not without me! What the hell is going on?"

"Well, Arima," a befuddled Maddy replied. "I don't know. All I know is that I just saw those fuckers leave the Earth. We did the best that we could. Let's just get with the rest of our gang and regroup and figure out what the fuck to do now. And let's do it fast. I'm fuckin' starvin'.'"

———

The representatives of Murder, Inc. looked down upon the devastation. There were thousands of men, women, and children's corpses rotting in the triple-digit Florida heat on this darkening mid-February evening.

Josie stood before her cherished friends and family and quietly tried to shake the violent images from her head and compose herself. They all had heightened anticipation as they awaited their instructions. "Hey. Are you okay?" Erick asked his beloved daughter as he placed his arm around her slender shoulders.

"Aw, fuck, Dad," Josie answered tearfully. "So much carnage.

So much death. So much despair. And *why?* For *what?* For *power?* Prestige? Money? To pump up small egos? *Why?* What is *fucking wrong* with these people?

"I remember a time not so long ago when I saw everything as rainbows and butterflies and unicorns. I saw everything and everybody as having good in them. A time when I couldn't even *conceive* of the concept of pure evil. I was so stupid. So naïve. Just like so many others who were too busy checking their fucking 'likes' or swiping left or playing stupid video games or watching their fucking sports. They were too busy to see what was happening right before their eyes. They were too busy to see that millions of people were becoming brainwashed into a movement of pure evil. Hell, they fucking attacked our capitol on live TV and hardly anyone batted an eye.

"Well now, I have seen it. And so have the apathetic lemmings, many of whom have fallen victim to this. Over and over and over again I have seen it. I have seen innocent people get ripped apart. Thousands of them. For no other reason than the feelings of entitlement of a few ignorant, knuckle-dragging fucks! That's what this all boils down to. The election rigging. The threats. The physical intimidation. The attempted over-throw of our elected governments. The treatment of anyone other than people like them as less than human. The complete lack of regard or respect for their fellow man, woman, and child. They don't care about *anything* but themselves! They want what they want when they want it, and they don't give a *fuck* about how they get it. They don't care if they have to lie, steal, cheat or even murder! They just don't *fucking care!* It is all about *them!*

"And isn't a fucking mental illness either. God, how I hate that! Have you ever noticed that if a Black man shoots innocent people, he's a 'thug'?" And when it's someone from the middle east, they're a terrorist? But when it's a *White* motherfucker, they're always 'mentally ill'! Bullshit! Hatred of other people just because of who they are isn't a mental illness! It is *bigotry!* And bigotry is pure *evil!* Which makes these *fucking bigots* pure evil!

We have just seen it! They are so *fucking evil* that they would murder their own *families* just to get what they want!

"And all that they want is to feel important. To feel noticed. To feel cared about. That's what they want. But when you combine those very natural human desires with unhinged hatred and bigotry, then you get evil. And when you get enough of them, you get an evil movement. That is what Vetis and his demonic pawns have exploited. His pawns in the government and business and churches and the media. They have been working in concert to exploit these people. And they have turned people's reasonable desires into pure evil. They have turned their sense of *patriotism* into pure evil. They have turned their *faith in a higher power* into pure evil. They say that Vetis is known as 'The Tempter of the Holy'. Well, he sure as fuck is. So, this is what we are left with. Thousands of bodies, many of them completely innocent. Okay, fuck this. Let's get a status report. Lionnel, what are the numbers as best as you can calculate?"

Lionnel wiped his brow and approached his beloved girl-friend. He kissed her lightly upon her mauve lips before beginning.

"Okay, these are pretty rough numbers, but here it goes. There were approximately 10,000 people here today. Now, the good news is that most of these deplorable men have succeeded in driving their wives and children away from them. Probably another thing that they're pissed about. They're so toxic, that they can't get laid. Anyway, that means that about 8,000 of the people here were men. There were about five hundred women and about one thousand children."

"Okay," Josie stated. "So, what's left?"

"Well, again these are pretty raw numbers," Lionnel began again. "But it looks about like this. There are about eight hundred men that are still alive down there. Barely, but still alive. They were partially eaten by the cats or dismembered one way or another by our forces."

"Henri, Marcus, Cliff. You know what to do," Josie ordered. The three men picked up their rifles and Holy water guns and made their way back down to the killing fields. The entire group paused to listen to eight hundred popping sounds followed by shrieks of agony as each of the surviving men were shot in the head and their dark souls were extinguished by being saturated by the Holy water. Cliff said a silent prayer to his God and asked for forgiveness each time he pulled his trigger.

The three men returned and Lionnel continued. "Okay. Well, *now* there are *zero* surviving men. It looks as though Arima was able to lure about four thousand dark souls into the ocean. That means that around three thousand escaped to…um…well, wherever the hell they went.

Most of the women took their own lives as well. The ones that were indoctrinated into the cult are among the dark soul count. Those that weren't escaped into Enlightenment."

"So, how many survived?" Josie asked cautiously.

"Well," Lionnel paused before answering. "Seven."

"Seven?" Josie cried out. "Only *seven*? Oh, Jesus! How about the kids?"

"Okay," Lionnel began again. "Better numbers there. Of the thousand children, around four hundred were murdered for all time. Their bodies *and* their souls. Around six hundred were able to get to Enlightenment. And, well, we have twenty-three kids here who are alive. Some are in pretty bad shape, but they all should make it."

There was an astonished silence that hovered around the group. They simply stared at one another in a shocked stupor. No one, not even Maddy, could find any words at this sullen moment. The silence was finally broken when Maddy turned her head towards the brilliant setting sun and said, "What's that Uncle Joe? You mean right now? But it's Josie's eighteenth birthday in a few days. No, I understand. Just…just…give us a few minutes, okay?"

CHAPTER 91

GO NOW

Come to me, Pastor, Its nasal voice was heard just before his dramatic serpentine transformation. *Come to me now before they destroy all of our beloved children. Come to me now before your daughters can do any more damage. Come to me now!*

The half-man, half-mamba spiritual form of the Pastor rose from the balcony, squealed in delight, and ascended to the darkest part of the Realm of Perdition where he found his awaiting dark-soul mate. They hissed at each other then became entwined in one another's scaley bodies. They squirmed and writhed against one another in heated ecstasy as It screamed out, "Yes, Pastor! Yes! Impregnate me! Together we can bring our demonic children from the Earth! Together we can bring them here! Together we can ready them for battle! Yes! Don't stop! I can feel them coming to me! They are entering my being! Thousands of our beautiful children are squirming within me! Yes! Yes! Yes!"

Following one final orgasmic scream, It opened itself and thousands of black snakes with copperheads emerged from her amidst a torrent of cosmic blood and demonic afterbirth. The pair held each other with morbid tenderness and giggled briefly before It said, "Now. Just one more earthly order. We must eliminate the one *true threat* to our glorious Vetis. None of *them* can destroy him. But those children can. We must have them killed before they are born."

———

The members of Murder, Inc. could only stare at each other with somber disbelief until Maddy looked at the beautiful sunset of bright orange, yellow and red. In its elegant rays she saw two forms emerge, cast in a vibrant white light.

"I'm so sorry to tell you this Buttacup," Uncle Joe began. "But it's time for you to go now. It's time for you to join us. Your work on Earth is done. It is time for both you and Erick to join the battle here."

"What's that Uncle Joe? You mean right now?" Maddy responded to her beloved Uncle.

"Yeah, fuck," Joseph answered regretfully. "Right now. We have preparations to make. It's gonna be a fuckin' bloodbath up here."

"But it's Josie's eighteenth birthday in a few days," Maddy pleaded.

"We understand that dear," Aunt Blair stated. "But the battle has now shifted from the Earth to Enlightenment. You are needed here. It is time for you to join us. It is time for you and Erick to come home, my dearest.

"No, I understand. Just…just…give us a few minutes, okay?" Maddy answered as she turned away from the forms of her cherished aunt and uncle and back towards her friends and family. Her eyes locked upon each one in turn. When her brilliant green eyes met those of her daughter, she began sobbing uncontrollably.

"I-I-I'm so sorry, sweetie. But we have to go now," Maddy's remorseful voice cried out.

"What do you mean?" Erick shouted. "No fuckin' way! Not yet! Not now! I am *not* missing my daughter's eighteenth birthday! Not happening! You just tell whoever just told you that to back the fuck off! Just a few days! That's all we need. Then…then we'll go."

"I'm sorry baby," Maddy answered as she embraced her husband. "It doesn't work like that. They need us and they need us now. We have to say our good-byes. I fucking hate this too. But we have to. We have no choice."

Erick wiped the torrent of tears from his eyes and gave his wife a smile of resignation. The pair turned toward the group and embraced each one. Sam. Jules. Jessie. Cliff. Marcus. Jamie. Rosa. Dragenstein. Henri. Lionnel. They squeezed each one as though they were pleading for them to be their anchor. Their bodies were pleading for them to never let them go.

Maddy approached her sister and hugged her tightly. She whispered into her ear, "I would rather have just a short time with my sister than to never have had a sister at all. I love you, Arima. I'll stay in touch. Please. Watch over them. Watch over them all. Watch over my daughter." Her voice then lowered to a barely audible level as she concluded with, "*You* are the one who must lead them now. I now know that it isn't just Josie's legacy to lead them from this point on. It is both yours *and* Josie's."

Josie stood expressionless as her parents' mortal bodies approached her for the final time.

"No. This can't be happening. I can't lose you again. Please. Talk to them. Stay with me. Please. Mom. Dad. I need you. Please don't leave me."

The pair embraced their sobbing daughter as Erick said, "No. You don't need us any longer. You are an adult. You are a genius. You are the best of the both of us. You will make us proud just like you have from the very day that you were born. The first time that I held you, I looked into those gorgeous green eyes and knew that you were special. Not because you were our daughter. But because you were Josie fucking Parker. You don't belong to us. You belong to the entire world. And you were brought into this world for greatness."

"Listen to your father, sweetie," Maddy added. "He's right. You are better than me. You are better than him. You are better because of the inherent compassion that you have for other people. Your father and I don't really have that. We have a sense of justice which has led us to try to protect the downtrodden. The picked-on. The bullied. The persecuted. But we don't really have compassion for them. You do. You have our sense of justice combined with a deep and genuine caring for others. And that makes you stronger than either of us. Never lose that. I know this world is fucked up. I know that true evil will never be completely extinguished. There will always be evil people and evil movements to wage war against. Greedy, self-centered people will always exist. But you understand that there is much more good in this world than evil. You've known it since you were a child. You saw goodness in your friends and teachers and stray animals. You saw goodness in everything that truly possessed it. That is special. *You* are special. I'm sorry sweetie, but we have to go now. There is a final chapter to be written and we've been called to play our part."

"But, but," Josie began stammering. "How will I know if you're going to be alright? How will I know if you've won? How will I know if you've survived?"

Maddy looked deeply into the eyes of her nearly eighteen-year-old daughter and smiled before saying, "You will know. The entire Earth will know. Your Aunt Patty has one hell of a victory concert planned. Once the music starts, you will know that it's over. And you will know that your mother and father are singing along with the angels. And you will know that we will be watching over you for all eternity. Plus, Arima said that I can use her soul as a time share, so we'll visit, okay? Goodbye my most beautiful daughter. My most *brilliant* daughter. We are so proud of you. You are our greatest accomplishment."

Josie collapsed upon her knees and screamed in anguish at the universe as her parents' bodies transformed into dust. As she was clutching her parents' empty clothes, she heard two birds singing in the distance. She wiped her tears from her eyes and winked at them as they flew away.

"Aw, fuck this shit! Let's get back home and regroup. We need to figure what, if anything, we can do at this point," Josie ordered as her five-foot-four-and a half-inch frame stood upright once again.

"Um, hey Neice Josie?" Arima stated. "Um, I think I know what we're supposed to do. I just heard from your mom. We gotta get to the estate."

———

Maddy's soul rushed up and hugged her Uncle Joe. Joe extended his hand to shake Erick's who was standing there with his arms folded and a look of disgust on his face.

"What the fuck's wrong with you?" Joseph bellowed out.

"Oh, he's just really pissed that we're going to miss Josie's birthday so he, um, isn't talking to you right now." An embarrassed Maddy explained.

"Listen, Erick," Joseph said as tenderly as his gruff voice would allow. "Listen. I understand. She is a special girl, your daughter. But I don't make the rules around here. I get my orders from up on high, then it's our job to bring folks back. I was just following orders."

"Maddy," Erick stated in a haughty, lilted tone. "Would you please tell your uncle that I understand that but I'm still not speaking with him at the moment."

"Oh, for fucks sake!" Joseph yelled out as his beloved wife Blair was attempting to conceal her amusement. "Listen pal! You're kinda being a douchebag right now! So just forgive me, alright? And if you don't, well, then *fuck you!*"

"Maddy," Erick began once again in the same belittling tone. "Would you please tell your uncle that use of profanity isn't really helping anything at this moment and that I'm a bit offended by his use of such vulgar language."

"Alright you two, that will be quite enough," Blair interjected with a calm bluntness. "We have far bigger things to worry about and we haven't time for this petty family squabbling. I will not stand to have a feud between Maddy's father and the man she loves. Now, both of you apologize and shake hands."

"M-my father?" a confused Maddy asked. "Why did you refer to him as that, Aunt Blair?"

"Oh, my dearest," Blair answered sweetly as she placed her hands upon Maddy's petite shoulders. "That's right. You don't know. My brother, Freddie may have been the father who raised you. And the vile Pastor and the Copperhead may have been the ones who were your biological parents on Earth. But my darling, *we* are your spiritual parents. Your soul was attracted to *our* family. And it was *your* soul that I was pregnant with when I miscarried. A miscarriage that was orchestrated by your biological parents so that she could become pregnant and carry and raise your soul. They tried to steal you from us. You see, my dearest, Joseph and I are your *spiritual* parents. You were always destined to be with us. And now you are. For all time. And we couldn't be happier."

"Well, *that's* fuckin' weird," Maddy exclaimed. "But what the fuck *else* is new? At least *this* is a *good* weird and not a fucked up weird. So, do I call you guys Mom and Dad now, or what?"

"Naw!" Joseph replied as he wiped a spiritual tear from his eye. "That's too fuckin' awkward. Let's keep it the way it has always been. Our souls being connected means everything. Titles don't mean shit."

"Well, in that case," Maddy replied as she flashed her ornery grin, "Uncle Joe! Apologize to my husband and shake his hand! And Erick, you do the same! I'm with Aunt Blair! I'm not gonna have the two most important men in my life arguing. Now, fuckin' do it!"

Erick and Joseph looked at one another with an awkward suspicion. They extended their arms and lightly shook each other's hand while softly muttering, "Sorry." They then immediately folded their arms and looked away from one another.

"Well, *that* was fuckin' pathetic!" Maddy bellowed out angrily. "What the fuck was *that*? I'm telling you; I'm really starting to get..."

Maddy was cut off as she felt someone pinch her conjured ass and whisper into her ear, "Well, *hello*. So nice to see you again, my little red-haired toy. Are you finally ready to have some fun with me?" Howard lasciviously said as he conjured a strap-on dildo around Maddy's pelvis.

Howard then fell to the floor from the force of Erick and Joseph's fists landing on his jaw. The in-laws looked at each other, began laughing and embraced.

"I'm so sorry, Joe. I overreacted," Erick said.

"No, no," Joseph answered. "*I'm* the one that should apologize to *you*. You've been through a lot, and I could've handled that much better."

"No, no," Erick began again before being cut off by Maddy.

"Yeah, yeah, great. You're best of friends now. Can we just move on *please*? I don't know what's worse. Watching you two be pissed at each other or watching this fuckin' pukey love fest. And Howard! Why the fuck are *you* here?"

"Well," Howard replied with disgust as he rose from the misty floor, rubbing his chin, "I don't believe that I'll answer that until I receive an apology for this rude treatment!"

"Apology?" Erick roared back. "I'll give you a fuckin' apology! I'll give you an apology up your ghostly ass!"

"Well, now we're talkin'" Howard answered flirtatiously. "I've never really swung that way, but hey, any port in a storm, right?"

Howard then found himself once again on the floor following Maddy's fist landing firmly on his jaw.

"I'm telling Arima about this!" Howard yelled out as though he were a five-year-old.

"Yeah, you do that. You tell my *sister* on me," Maddy answered back just before sticking her tongue out at him. "Now, just tell us. Why the fuck are you here?"

"Oh, very well," a defeated Howard responded. "I am here to give you all some very important news. And to make our battle plans. Joe, I know you and I haven't always seen…um…eye to eye, but we need to work in tandem. They are planning their attack. It is originating from the Realm of Perdition. It will be the Pastor and his Copperheaded bitch along with a whole *shitload* of dark souls that that wretched creature has just given birth to. I propose to usher my forces against their demonic offspring. And while I am doing that, you and your family will destroy the Pastor and the Copperhead. None of the rest of us can do it. They can only be destroyed by someone who has a personal connection to them. Like, a daughter. So, my little redheaded spitfire, that is why you had to return now. You are the only one who can destroy them both. The rest of you can wound them. Weaken them. But my lovely little temptress here must be the one to put the final dagger in them. Agreed?"

"Yes, that sounds like a plan," Blair answered. "But Howard, all you will have to do is hold off their army. You won't be required to destroy them all. Just hold them off until Maddy can cut the heads off these vile serpents. Then, like all little snakes, they will go crawling back under their rocks once they have seen their leaders felled. They will lose their will to fight, because they really have no convictions about what they are fighting for. They are mindless pawns. So, Howard, you just keep them away from Enlightenment. We'll take care of the rest. And I am going to feed on the black heart of that bitch once and for all. Then, we'll see about taking out Vetis."

"Well, that's a problem and the other reason I'm here," Howard answered. "Vetis is powerful. He is too powerful even for all the blessed souls in Enlightenment. We could combine all our forces and *never* completely defeat him. Which means he is a threat to us for eternity. But there are four *new* souls who are about to come into the world that can."

Before Howard could finish his explanation, a frantic Patty burst into the area. "Hey, fuckers, what's going on?"

"Well, my dear sister," Blair began explaining. "We are in the middle of a planning session and Howard here was about to explain how Vetis can be defeated. So, as you can see, we are a bit busy here."

"*You're* busy?" Patty yelled back. "Do you know what the fuck I'm *dealing with* right now? I *finally* got the final lineup for 'Victoryfuckinpalooza' posted and do you know what happened? All these dead artists came up to me and started cussing me out because *they're* not in the lineup! So, I had to explain to them that the *asshole* who is writing this shit didn't want to speculate on when someone might pass away, so if an artist isn't dead by the time he wrote this shit in 2023, then they can't be in the lineup! Then, I had all these hip-hop cats come up to me and demand representation. So, I had to explain to *them* that this asshole author isn't well-versed in hip-hop, so he didn't include them either. But, he has quite a few Rhythm and Blues artists to represent one of the foundational musical forms of hip-hop. But did *that* make anyone happy? *Fuck no*! They *still* blame me! They're blaming me and getting all up in *my* ass instead of the *dickhead* sitting in the Midwest typing up this shit. So, excuse me for interrupting your little gabfest, but I've got stress of my own! Oh, fuck it! I gotta go make sure the light and sound crews are ready to go for whenever you pricks get off your asses and win this fuckin' war! C'mon Jacklyn, let's get the fuck out of here!"

———

"Um, hey Neice Josie?" Arima stated. "Um, I think I know what we're supposed to do. I just heard from your mom. We gotta get to the estate."

"Why? What's going on?" Josie immediately asked.

"Okay, let me try to remember everything your mom told me. She was talking really fast. Then she kept saying 'over and out,' so then I thought she was done talking but then she just kept talking. Okay. I think that I remember. They think that they can defeat the demonic souls, but they can't defeat Vetis. He's too powerful. And they're worried that he's just going to keep coming back over and over until he finally wins. But the universe has created four new souls. Four souls whose combined power can vanquish Vetis forever. And those four souls are about to be born. They will be the children of Rachel and Kayla."

"Rachel and Kayla?" a confused Josie asked. "What do you

mean? They're each only having *one* child. Rachel is having a little girl and Kayla is having a little boy."

"Uh, yeah, that's what we all thought," Arima replied. "But I guess they disguised themselves within one another for protection. And now that they're about to be born, they have split. Rachel is having *twin* girls. And Kayla is having *twin* boys. So, the Twins and the twins are each having twins. Wow. That's actually pretty cool, if you think about it. They're each having a bonus kid that they didn't plan on. It kinda reminds me of this one time when I ordered a twenty-piece chicken nugget, but when I got home, they had put *twenty-six* chicken nuggets in the box. Man, that was one of the happiest days of my life. They even gave me extra dippin' sauce. It was so cool."

"Aunt Arima!" Josie cried out to get the conversation back on track. "So, what are you telling us?"

"What was I talking about again?" Arima asked of herself before continuing. "Oh yeah. So, these four babies have the combined power to take out Vetis. The problem is the demons know this. They are sending their remaining Earthly demonic forces to the estate to murder the babies before they are born. So, my point is that we really need to get up to estate. And that if there's time that we should stop for some chicken nuggets. Y'know. If there's time."

CHAPTER 92

PURPLE RAIN

February 14, 2042. Valentine's Day. Josie was sitting outside her estate in Upper State New York watching the impending storm clouds roll in with Stellan and Paciano. They were listening to a radio broadcaster who was saying, *An unbelievable event seems to be happening all over the world. There are dark storm clouds that are forming over the entire planet. Every populated region is preparing for torrential rains and strong winds. We don't know whether this is a Biblical event or not, but I, for one, have got my arc ready, ha,ha. This segment is being brought to you by Sandler's Tire Service. A Tire for you and a tire for me. Buying new tires ensures your safety. Now, to Kip Kippering with today's sports scores.*

"Yep, laugh it up, motherfucker. You have *no idea* what type of show that you're in for," Josie dryly said to the disembodied voice. "The world's governments do, though. Gregory and Kaneko are at the United Nations right now telling them about the cosmic battle that is about to be waged. And here we are, celebrating my birthday by protecting our friends once again. Protecting them in the one place that was supposed to represent peace. This place was to be my parents' retirement home and our family's getaway home of serenity. But that's not how it will turn out. Just like every other place on the Earth, this place isn't going to be about peace. It will be tainted by bloodshed and war."

"I do not agree with you, my young friend," Stellan stated reflectively as he placed his brawny, silver-haired arm around her green vinyl-clad shoulder. "I do not agree with you at all. Yes, there will be a battle here tonight. But that battle will be waged in the *name* of peace. It will be waged to welcome four new souls into our world. Four new souls who have the power to ensure a lasting peace. This place is the *epitome* of peace. And I, for one, am proud to call it my home."

"As am I, lover," Paciano contributed as he fed his nearly two-year old, Zihad, some string beans. "I am proud to call this *my* home as well. I am proud to have worked for your parents. I am proud of our friendship with Arima and all the others from New Orleans. And I am proud to know you, Josie. I am proud to have a friend that commands such respect. A friend who is so caring. A friend who I know always has the backs of others. I am proud of you. *We* are proud of you. And we are ready to march into battle with you alongside the others."

Josie gave the married couple a long tearful embrace before saying, "Thanks guys. That means a lot to me. But I hope that you won't be going into any battle. The forces of Vetis will soon be here. Rod just sent his final recon report. They are the last truly demonic souls remaining that represent our four societal pillars. They will come together, within their respective tribes, each from a different direction. We have the assassination technicians in trees in the surrounding woods who will take out as many as they can as they approach. But there will be too many of them. Vetis's representatives within the clergy will come from the west. That is where Rosa and her Coven will meet them. His remaining pawns from the propogandist media will come from the east and will be met by Marcus, Jamie and Dragenstein. His remaining forces from what is left of the White Nationalist political party will come from the north. That is where Sam, Jerry, Jules, and her big cats will engage them in battle. And finally, his remaining forces from the business community will come from the south where they will be met by Jessie, Cliff, and Henri.

"Arima will take a hit from her killer weed and absorb their dark souls as soon as they emerge from their fallen bodies. She will then send them into the nearby pond that was blessed by Pastor Tim. I will stay at the house and protect it as best I can. If it looks like the house is going to be breached, I need you two to carry Kayla and Rachel upon your backs to the stable. Regardless, you two will assist Lionnel in the birth of the Quad. Adam, Aaron, Vai, and Alexa will be their family's last defense. I fear that it will not be an enjoyable game for those dear boys, tonight. But, no matter what, we must ensure that those infants are born, and we must ensure that they survive. You two will see to that. If it gets too…um…hairy, heh, heh. I truly didn't mean that as a joke guys. Anyway, if it gets too dangerous and the babies are born you will take them with you and Zihad. You will get away to someplace safe and never look back. You will keep them and protect them until such time as they are prepared to engage Vetis. Understand?"

"Yes, we understand perfectly," Stellan replied. "But it won't come to that. We will not need to retreat and hide with these children because you are going to be victorious on this evening or else *your* name isn't Josephine Patricia Sommers Parker. And that, my dearie, is your name. So that is just how it's going to fucking be."

The three friends burst into nervous laughter and embraced one last time. There was a flash of deep red lightning from just above them and the storm clouds turned deep crimson. Then, the rain began. A torrential rainfall of blood began to soak the Earth as the battle for Enlightenment had been engaged. Josie's pretty face was awash in blood as she looked directly up into the warring storm clouds. "Well, here we go. I love you Mom and Dad. Kick their motherfuckin' ass."

———

Maddy and Erick were nervously awaiting the warning siren. Erick paced around their conjured perfect replica of their home in Brooklyn. "Okay," Maddy stated in an effort to calm herself and her anxious husband. "Let's kill some time before we kill my bitch mother and dickhead father. How 'bout a couple rounds of real movie name to porn movie name?"

"Maddy, I'm really not in the mood at the moment," Erick answered before Maddy blurted out, "*Star Wars!*"

"Star Whores!" Erick enthusiastically responded. Maddy could only smirk as her sly manipulation put a beaming smile upon her beloved husband's face. "Okay, okay, let me see here," the easily distracted Erick retorted. "How 'bout *Dolores Claiborne.*"

"Oh, fuckin' easy!" Maddy screamed out laughing. "Clitoris Claiborne! Okay, try this one. *Field of Dreams.*"

"Well, that's a fuckin' softball," Erick scoffed. "Field of Creams! If you build it they will cum!, heh, heh, heh!"

The siren began blaring throughout the entirety of Enlightenment. Millions of blessed souls began conjuring a large white wall around their tiny portion of the vast cosmos. Howard began mobilizing his troops and stood waiting just inside their mystical fortress. He was wearing nothing but a smile and a strap on sword. Standing beside him were all the souls that Arima had helped during her time in New Orleans. The Ropers. Lillian. Herbert and Iris. Becky Peterson and her two daughters. Rachel and Kayla's sister, Gwen. Clyde Manfrengensen. Marcus's Moms and Pops. And Arima's mother Abdalla and her grandmother Louise.

Leading another contingent of warriors on the far side of the wall were the glowing spirits of Lucy Vang, Jason Anderson, and Kristy Anderson. The reunited friends held hands and smiled at one another as they waited for the onslaught to begin. They all stood in front of their amassed army of brilliant blue and white souls. They stood and stared intensely as they heard pounding at the bright white brick walls. They readied themselves as slight cracks began forming from the intense pressure of the demonic souls who were demanding to enter. The cracks grew into fissures and then, all hell broke loose.

Millions of fiendish, human sized black serpents with copper heads slithered rapidly into the awaiting warriors. Everywhere that one could see were flashes of serpents' fangs into jugulars and slashing conjured metal swords. The moment a vile serpent or a blessed soul were injured, their wound would immediately heal. Arms would grow back. Heads were replaced. Intestines would be sucked back into their caverns and the conjured body would be restored. Millions of bites and gashes resulted in nothing more than an eternal stalemate.

"Oh well, fuck!" Howard bellowed out as he was thrusting his sword/penis into a serpent's belly. "We can't kill them! And they can't kill us! All we can do is wound each other. Blair was right! We just need to hold them back so that Joe's forces can kill the leaders of this wretched movement. We need to hold them back so that they are unable to help them. Just keep slashing mother-fuckers! Just hold them!"

Howard looked down at his feet and saw the white clouds that they were standing on turn jet black. They then turned into a dark red liquid. And all the spiritual blood that was being shed was being absorbed into the clouds of the cosmos until the sheer weight of the crimson, iron-scented substance tumbled out of the heavens and began drenching the entirety of the Earth.

———

Arima passionately kissed her loving husband, lit her pipe, and inhaled deeply. "Whoooaaa!" she dreamily said as her ebony body began floating above the estate. Her purple hibiscus adorned dress was immediately saturated with bloodfall and began violently whipping around as the winds suddenly went from calm to tropical storm strength. She heard light popping sounds from the surrounding woods. Her body began glowing until it was encased in a purple aura as she opened her soul and began welcoming the newly departed dark entities. She smiled to

herself as the demonic spirits were attracted into her and immediately bound. All they could do was struggle as they awaited
their final, tortuous fate.

Multiple "holy" men carrying guns emerged from the woods
and began marching toward the main house of the estate. They
stopped in their tracks, smiled at one another, and raised their
rifles as they encountered thirteen handholding, black robed
women standing between them and their quarry.

"Now sisters," Rosa began speaking softly. "Let us now show
these abhorrent men what happens to those who betray their
faith. What happens to those who betray their congregations.
What happens to those who choose to gaze longingly for evil.
What happens to those who betray humanity. Concentrate sisters
and send your energy to me. Concentrate on the saltiest
substance that you can think of. Yes! I can feel your energy
flowing into me!"

Rosa's eyes turned pure white as she stared at the bemused
men and said, "Now, motherfuckers! *Now* is your time to meet
your lot in life! And death!"

Confused expressions were replaced by screams of agony as
the men's rifles fell harmlessly to the ground. Their extremities
were being turned into salt beginning at their fingers and toes.
The screams grew in intensity as the transformation spread up
their arms and legs and into their torsos. Their final shrieks
could be heard as their salty bodies were immediately melted
away by the torrent of bloody rainfall and their smoggy, purple
souls were absorbed into a glowing figure floating above the
house.

On the east side of the estate, Marcus, Jamie, and Dragenstein
could hear the perfect broadcast-ready male voices chanting 'Kill
the kids! Kill the kids! Kill the kids!' The men had spent their
careers in the service of Vetis's unpatriotic, inhumane movement.
They had spent endless hours, days, weeks, months, and years
knowingly spreading lies and propaganda to indoctrinate the
self-centered, weak-willed and willfully ignorant masses into
their hate-fueled army. Now, all they could do is chant one final

insipid, three-syllable phrase as they rushed toward the main house. All that they were able to do is chant from their frothing mouths. And die.

There was a high-pitched giggle before Dragenstein rushed into the throng of men and began haphazardly ripping their limbs from their bodies. Tortured screams could be heard as Marcus and Jamie joined the battle. Marcus slashed through the men's pudgy torsos with a long machete as Jamie whipped her legs up and around her body in a frenzy. With each swipe of her long, chocolate legs, the jagged heels of her stilettos sliced through yet another set of misused vocal cords.

"There's too many of them!" Marcus yelled out. "There are several over there that are getting away! I'll call Josie on my walkie!" Josie! Josie! We got most of ours, but there are about four that are running toward the house. We can't get to them in time! Get the girls out of there!"

The White Christian Nationalist movement of Vetis was mostly awash in testosterone. It was a movement by ruling white men to ensure the eternal dominion of white men. Their political careers had been advanced by an unholy alliance with demonic members of the world's clergy, media, and business leaders. They had been able to sit in their plush offices and block any attempt at humane laws designed to assist the needy. The minorities. The downtrodden. They wrapped themselves in the language of freedom, law enforcement and democracy while passing laws to censor free speech, halt the funding for any legitimate litigation of their brothers, and rig election systems. The business leaders were always available with open checkbooks. The clergy were always available to bastardize the words of Jesus Christ. And the propogandists were always available for their nightly brainwashing of the masses. All these politicians needed to do was sit back and pass the laws that would ensure their eternal dominion over others both on Earth and at the feet of Vetis. They were nothing more than pawns that had been promised everlasting power. And money. And sex. They basked in the glow of Vetis's movement on Earth while never acknowledging that Vetis held no loyalty to them. They were simply pawns. This was what these men were. And a few ignorant, power-hungry women.

Emerging from the woods in front of their more cautious male counterparts were two female Governors from Midwest states, a congresswoman from Colorado and another from Georgia. They wore evil little smiles on their deplorable, cartoonishly-made-up, and withered faces as they marched over the neatly groomed lawn toward the main house. The smiles faded as a grey, fluffy housecat sprang from a tree limb and began clawing out the eyes of one of the female governors as efficiently as a hawk.

LucyFur licked the blood from her whiskers then leapt upon the other female governor. Her razor claws tore through her collagen-injected lips before moving down and viciously chewing through her neck until it became disembodied and fell to the ground as helpless as a garden gnome.

The congresswoman from Georgia turned green as a lion being ridden by a beautiful African American woman pounced upon her and ripped her grating voice-box out of her throat in one bite. Sam chuckled to herself as she watched her paralyzed legs being sprayed with the blood of a traitor.

Before the congresswoman from Colorado could raise her sidearm, a cougar ripped her from her frequently visited vagina all the way through her body and face until its claws had snapped her geeky black glasses in half.

Jules and Jerry came bounding in on the backs of Bengal tigers accompanied by a pair of panthers. The ferocious creatures leapt from man to man, ripping their arms from their torsos and their internal organs from the bodies, leaving them laying on the ground screaming in a pool of their own blood mixed with the celestial blood that was mournfully falling from the heavens.

Two dark figures were seen scurrying toward the house as Jules yelled into her walkie, "Josie! Two got away! Get the girls out of there!"

"What the hell do we need to do this shit for?" a demonic gun manufacturer stated angrily as he watched several of his colleagues' brains get blown out by bullets from the trees. "We're getting picked off one by one! And by my own fucking guns!"

"Just keep running!" a disgraced so-called business "visionary" yelled back. "There are too many of us! They can't get us all! We have to get to that house! We have to kill those fucking babies before they are born! And I don't *mind* if a few of us get killed! Even more of that gifted baby blood for me! Then I will be powerful enough to restore the wireless internet and dominate the messages that are spread throughout the world! The people will know only what I *allow* them to know!"

The pair were gasping heavily as they exited the woods and looked toward their target. They laughed and high-fived as they saw no forces of resistance. Their arrogant guffawing stopped when they heard a female voice from behind them say, "Malum tuum dolorem facit. et dolor meus es fortitudo mea." Their silence then turned to painful screeches as a former high school football star smashed their heads together. They fell to their knees and their confused expressions looked up at a life-size glamour doll. Her shimmering blonde hair flew in a tangle of bloodied gold around her perfectly made-up face. She smiled at them and extended her hands.

"Do you like my nails?" Jessie inquired sweetly. "I had them made up just for you. I know how you sexist bastards like your women to always look like your little trophies, so I wanted to make sure to look special for you. Because I am the last woman that you will ever leer at again!"

An impressed Cliff looked on as he observed his wife's strength. His Jessie could be self-absorbed. She could be selfish. She could be arrogant. But she could also be self-determined. Caring. Merciful. Psychologically strong. And, in this moment, physically strong. Because Jessie West was not one-dimensional. Jessie West was not a stereotype. Jessie West was a woman who refused to be type-cast into a role for the amusement of men. Jessie West was a complete woman. And not one to be fucked with.

Cliff burst into uncontrollable laughter as he watched his love take her perfectly manicured nails and bury them into the jugu-lars of each of the squirming men. She then lifted them up by their necks. Blood was pouring down her hands to her elbows as she raised the men over her head and simply held them there. Their bodies were writhing in pain as they gasped for air from their shattered windpipes. And Jessie just held them there. She held them there and thought about how so many of her sisters throughout the ages had been held in submission. She thought about all the women who had been stifled, suppressed, abused, and oppressed. She thought about all the women whose voices had been drowned out. Whose dreams had been shattered. Whose very souls had been smothered. And she persistently held them there. She held them there until the squirming stopped. She lowered her arms and tossed the limp bodies to the side as she watched their polluted essence rise and immediately become absorbed by her elevated dear friend.

Henri emerged from the woods carrying his sniper rifle over his shoulder wearing a broad smile. "Oh my," he said to the pair. "I'm now sorry that I didn't leave a few more for you. I can never get enough of watching a strong woman in action."

"You got that right," Jessie replied before looking down at her hands and yelling out, "Goddammit Cliff! As soon as this is over, you're taking me to the salon! I've broken three nails!"

Josie put down her walkie and shouted up the stairs, "Okay everybody! We have seven of these pricks coming at us. We're not taking any chances! Stellan and Paciano! Get Rachel and Kayla on your backs and get them out to the stable! Lionnel! Go bring those babies into the world. And the rest of you guard that fucking stable as though your lives depend on it. Because it does. Now, go!"

"No, Josie," Adam stated flatly followed by his twin brother, Aaron. "No. We cannot leave you. We have been your protectors since you were born. That is why we are here. It is the game that we were brought into the world to play. And we shall continue playing until we are no longer able."

"Oh, my lovely boys," a tearful Josie replied. "You are both just so beautiful. But that is *not* why you are here. You are here to bring these new souls into the world. You are here to raise them and love them and prepare them for their future. To prepare them for their destiny. Your loyalty belongs to them and your wives. Now go. Go protect your families. Go be the nurturing protectors that all men are supposed to be."

Stellan scurried down the stairs carrying a screaming Kayla upon his back followed by Paciano and Rachel. "Fuck!" Stellan yelled out. "I think her water just broke! And all over my lovely designer shirt!"

Vai and Alexa opened the back door of the house and waved them towards the nearby stables. Adam and Aaron took one last long look upon their Josie. "Thank you, Josie," Adam said followed by Aaron's, "Yes. Thank you. Thank you for being our friend. Thank you for guiding us. And thank you for your sacrifice. You are sacrificing your safety so that we may bring our children into the world. I do not know if we will see you again. We have not seen this ending. But we have seen your compassion. And we have seen your strength. You are stronger than your father. You are stronger than your mother. Because you are Josie. You do not belong to them. You do not belong to us. You belong to the world. We love you, Josie."

"I-I love you too!" Josie blurted out as she wiped tears from her emerald green eyes. "Now get the fuck out of here, okay?"

The Twins all-white suits turned instantly to murky red as they left the house and walked out into the violent blood storm. Josie's dread-filled heart sank as she lifted her bow towards the front door. One final tear fell to the floor as she stoically awaited her fate. Alone.

———

"Where *are* those motherfuckin' cowards? Mommy? Daddy? Where aaaare yoooou? Your baby girl has a fuckin' surprise for you!" Maddy screamed out as she saw Howard's bright blue and white forces clash with copper headed, black bodied serpents on the periphery of Enlightenment. She stood at the ready holding a conjured serrated broadsword. At the end of the handle, there was a plastic male doll hanging by its neck. Her loving husband stood in his customary place directly beside her, ready to support her in any way that she needed, including murder. Directly behind her stood her Uncle Joe and Aunt Blair. They all secretly wondered if their combined might would be enough to defeat the greatest existential threat that humanity had ever known.

"C'mon bitch!" Maddy called out once again. "Are ya afraid of lil' ol' me? C'mon! Are you a *big pussy* that can't take someone on without being surrounded by your posse? Your fuckin' troops are a bit preoccupied at the moment, so you may as well come on out. We've been preparing for this since the day I came out of your musty fucking cunt, so let's do this shit! There's no one around to help you now!"

"I don't need anybody's help to slaughter you, you little whore," Its cold, nasal voice was heard as It slinked up from the misty floor. Its body was entirely serpentine, with large copper scales. It had two human arms jutting out from Its chest. Its face was surrounded by a copper, scaley hood. And Maddy could not help but notice that Its face was, for the first time in Its existence, more youthful and almost pretty.

"What the fuck Mom!" Maddy yelled out. "They got some sort of health spa in Perdition Land or whatever the fuck it's called?"

"You might call it that, you little slut." It replied haughtily. "You have no idea what the power of our glorious Vetis can bestow upon you. I have been able to suck the life force out of millions of dark souls. I have absorbed their power. Their energy. Their evil. Their beauty. I am the most powerful being in the cosmos! You and your little family stand no chance against me now. But I'm in a generous mood. Come to me, my daughter. Come and wage war by my side. Together we can rule the cosmos at the feet of Vetis. It is time for you to come home, my daughter. It is your destiny. Do this, and I will spare the rest of your family."

"Uh, well, I gotta admit that evil shit gave you quite the makeover. And I do love my family and I don't want to see them destroyed. But, how about my friends and family on Earth? What are you gonna do for them?"

"Oh, very well," It replied in an unconvincing, sweet tone. "Your precious sister, Arima, your beloved daughter, Josie and all the rest will be spared. There is an attack happening as we speak on your estate. Our forces will destroy them all on Earth and then we will permanently destroy their souls once they enter Enlightenment. Come to me now, my daughter, and I will call off the attack and spare them as well."

Its glowing red eyes glared in quiet anticipation as Maddy turned around to her family. She and Erick flashed a quick wink at one another as their eyes briefly met. She then stared into the face of her beloved Uncle Joe. She stared at the first man who had truly cared for her. He was her guide. He was her anchor. He was her hero. They looked at one another's knowing faces and silently communicated before Maddy said, "Gee, I just don't know. What do you guys think? I mean, on the one hand, I really want to kill my bitch mother. But on the other hand, I don't want anybody I love to be harmed. Gee, it's just so confusing. I feel so torn. But I guess I know what I must do. I'm not saying that it will be easy, but this is what I must do now. I'm sorry, everybody. Please forgive me."

Maddy turned to face her mother, lowered her sword, and bowed her head in reverence. "I have my answer, mother. It was really a struggle to figure it out, but I know now what I must do. Yes. I will join you." She then burst into laughter and yelled out, "Just fuckin' with ya! I'm gonna kill you muthufuckaaaa!"

Maddy leapt at the fifteen-foot serpentine figure of her mother and was immediately slapped back into the white mist on the floor by the long, black tail of a snake. "Well, my dear, I believe we have our answer," The Pastor's voice stated out of the mouth of a giant Black Mamba.

"Indeed," It answered calmly. "You know what to do. Destroy them."

The Pastor opened its jaws and struck out at Joseph while hitting Blair away with his tail. Just before his venomous fangs could impale Joseph, Erick leapt upon his head and held his jaws open. Joseph reached into the serpent's mouth and ripped out it's forked tongue causing the Pastor to rear it's scaley head back in pain. Erick looked deep into one of the Pastor's pitch-black eyes and drove a dagger into it. Erick was immediately covered in a black, sticky bile substance. "Oh, fuckin' gross! I've got demon eye cum all over me!" he yelled out as he retrieved his dagger and thrust it into the other eye, causing another geyser of demonic ejaculate.

The Pastor was whipping his body around in a frenzied attempt to free itself from Erick and Joseph, who was holding his mouth open with one hand while pulling a venom-coated fang out with his other. The Pastor let out one final high-pitched shriek as Maddy jumped on his head and sat astride him just behind her husband. The Pastor felt Maddy's broadsword penetrate the top of his skull and plunge all the way through his lower jaw. His painful squeals continued as Maddy pushed her husband off and then used the jagged edges of her blade to saw through the Pastor's head, severing it in two. The lifeless and spiritless form plopped into the white mist that was now mixed with unholy black bile.

"Well, *that* wasn't so hard!" Maddy excitedly exclaimed. "One fucker down, one to go! See Daddy? You always wanted to find out if your little girl gave good head. Did you like it, Daddy? Did you like how your little girl gave you head? Hey! Why isn't anybody laughing? That was gold! Pure fuckin' gol..."

Maddy's exclamation was cut off as It lunged down with It's jaw wide open and swallowed her daughter in one bite. Erick, Joseph, and Blair stood with their mouths agape as they watched the spiritual bulge of their fallen loved one slowly slide down the copper serpentine frame.

The moment that Maddy was encased by Its sadistic form, she felt the intense pain from Its demonic acid that was beginning to eat away at her essence. She could feel tiny pieces of herself being stripped away and being digested by the vile entity that had consumed her. Images of her life began flashing through her weakening mind. Her weekend dance and junk food parties with her beloved aunts and uncle. Her meeting her first true love. The retribution of the man who had raised her. The birth of her most precious daughter. The bonding with her newfound sister. She shed tears that were quickly absorbed by the pure evil that she was inside and knew that this was finally the end. Maddy knew that she had failed.

She then heard a familiar voice speak to her soul. "Um, hey, Sis. Or, um, I'm sorry. I mean Lil' Readhead? Whatcha doin?"

"I think I'm dying Arima," Maddy's soul meekly answered.

"No, you're not," Arima hazily replied. "Here. Just take my hand. Use my strength to fortify yours. And let's end this. Together. This was what they most feared from us. Because not only can *you* enter *my* soul at any time, but *I* can also enter *yours*. We are two souls that can become one. And once that happens, we can combine our strength. We can do *anything* together. So, stop your whining and let's get this over with. I've got the worst case of munchies right now. Hey, I just thought of somethin'. When I get here, I can conjure anything that I want right? So, like, I can conjure up an order of twenty chicken nuggets but there will be twenty-six chicken nuggets! That's gonna be so cool."

"Yes, what a fitting ending," It said snidely as it could feel It's daughter being digested into Its ungodly being. "The mother eating it's young. It is so perfect. And now you can see that all is lost for you. That little bitch was the only one who could truly destroy me. And now, I shall consume her and shit her out of me, just as she did on my grave. It is just so satisfying to have the last laugh. It is just so…"

Its arrogant diatribe was cut off as It violently flailed Its head back and hissed in agony. Maddy's broadsword came jutting out of Its copper sternum and viciously sawed its way down to Its tail. Maddy's head crowned from between the gash, covered in dark red and green ooze. She forced her head through the opening while saying to Arima's soul, "Thanks Soul Sister! I love you! See you soon! Over and out!" She crawled out of the fallen wicked serpentine body of her mother, opened her emerald green eyes, looked around with innocent amazement and let out a high pitched cry.

"What the fuck are you doing?" Erick asked his wife.

Maddy looked up at him, flashed her mischievous grin and said gleefully, "It's performance art! Since you fuckers don't get my great humor, I thought I'd use this opportunity to re-enact my birth from this fucking bitch. Pretty cool, huh? I'm even covered in goo and shit. Did anybody record this? This would be a total hit on the internet! Oh, right. Hardly anybody gets that anymore. That sucks."

Maddy looked down upon her pathetic mother's form transforming from a powerful, demonic serpent back into the withered hag from Its time on Earth. She listened to Its dying rasps and said sweetly, "Are you happy now Mommy? You always wanted me to be born again, so there ya go. Sorry about the inverse C-Section thing. Y'know, I always wondered what this moment would be like. I even had a long speech planned as I stood over your dying, bitch ass. But you know what? You're no different than all the other 'Chads' that I've taken out. You're just another piece of sadistic, narcissistic trash. And you aren't worth my fuckin' time. C'mon Uncle Joe. Let's conjure up some ice cream."

"In just a moment, Buttacup," Joseph responded. "I have a promise to keep." He strode over to the gasping form of his despised sister-in-law, reached into her chest and ripped out her barely beating, black heart. He silently walked over to his beloved wife and presented his trophy to her. Blair Sommers-Argento took his gift, smiled at him with eternal love and voraciously bit into the unholy, still-beating organ.

"Jesus Christ, Aunt Blair!" Maddy screamed out. "Gross! You coulda at least *cooked It* first!"

It laid in the white, black, red, and green mist and let out one final gasp. The entirety of Enlightenment began shaking as the millions of cowardly, demonic serpents turned away from their battle and slithered back to the Realm of Perdition. There was an explosion of brilliant purple lightning and the entirety of the cosmos turned to a majestic lavender.

From a far corner of Enlightenment came Patty's booming voice. "Wow! That was fuckin' cool Mads! Okay, Prince! Get your fuckin' ass on the stage! We've got a party to throw! And Jerry Lee, don't give me that fuckin' look!"

———

The front door exploded into splinters and seven men came rushing inside. Josie launched three arrows in quick succession into the foreheads of three of the assailants. Their dark souls immediately emerged and began swirling around her as the other four men prepared their attack.

"Arima!" Josie cried out as she ran into the adjacent living room. "Arima! Get these fuckers off of me! Where are you?" *Ah, fuck it, I'll just do it myself,* she thought to herself as she fought her way through the black smog, pulled her knife and slashed the throat of another man. The blood from the gash violently splashed on the family portrait that was hanging over the fireplace. Josie was keeping her promise that she had made to her mother two years prior. Josie was painting the walls of the estate with their blood. She picked up an axe next to the fireplace and viciously swung her petite arms, decapitating two approaching attackers with one swing. Blood erupted from the necks of the fallen men before their bodies succumbed to their final fate. Six evil souls were now swirling around her as the final intruder made his escape. The Congressman from Ohio wrestled his way off the floor and hastily made his way to the back exit.

Josie was flailing her axe in futility at the disembodied spirits as they cackled and swirled around her. Their morbid forms were then suddenly sucked away from her and out the front door. She allowed herself to catch her breath and wear a slight smile as she heard a voice from above the house say, "Hey, um, Niece Josie? Sorry about that. I had to go help your mom, I mean, Lil' Redhead, um, no, I mean, your mom for a minute. I'm just gonna take them to the holy pond. I'll be right back. I'll meet you in the stables. Hey, do you guys keep any 'tato chips or anything in the stables? Oh well, it doesn't matter. Now, what was I doing? Oh, yeah. I'll be right back."

Josie ran out the back door and found the final living demonic soul on Earth, being confronted by Alexa, Vai, and the Twins.

As the blood rained down upon them, Adam said, "you will not harm our children." "No, you won't," Aaron added. "And you are too late. All but one has been born. You can hear their cries. They are cries of innocence. They are cries of dignity. They are the cries of justice. And they are the cries of revenge. They will grow up and exact revenge upon you and all like you. The evil doers who use hate to fulfill their own wishes. The evil doers who find joy in torturing the downtrodden. You are soulless. You are demonic. And our four children shall defeat you all. We wish we had more time to play with you, but we have our family to attend to."

Adam and Aaron slowly approached the shaking man who fell to his knees and began pleading for mercy. Blood was dripping from their light blond, long strands as they looked down upon the pathetic creature that coward beneath them. They looked at one another, kicked the man over and proceeded to stomp on the man's head repeatedly with their previously all-white boots. Adam and Aaron rarely showed emotion. They did not play their games out of anger. Or hatred. They played their games out of necessity. They played their games to ensure the safety of others and to allow the downtrodden to blossom into whatever it was that they were destined to be. To allow the innocent to thrive. To allow the patriotic to lead. And to allow all genuinely kind souls to love.

This was a rare occasion of unbridled anger. As the Twins stomped on the man's face repeatedly, they shouted out, "Die! Die! Die! Die! No one threatens those that we love! No one threatens our wives! And *no one* threatens our beloved children! Go to hell *motherfucker!*"

Josie went running up to the pair, shook them and said, "Hey,

hey guys. It's okay. It's over. He's dead. And I just saw Arima take his soul away. It's all over. You can stop now."

Adam looked down at the putty-like glob of flesh that was once an intact face and said in his normal, controlled tone, "Josie, did we use the term 'motherfucker' correctly?"

Josie burst into laughter and embraced the pair. The wind began picking up and there was a horrendous shriek that was heard from beyond the clouds. The roof of the stable was blown off, sending shards of wooden planks and shingles flying for miles. Josie, Adam, Aaron, Vai, and Alexa rushed into the stable and found Kayla holding her two twin children to her bosom as Lionnel was handing Rachel her newly born second child to protect. Standing over Rachel, Kayla, and their children were four Shetland ponies. They had widened their legs and stood astride over the mothers who were desperately holding their newborns. The ponies were unflinching against the onslaught of the blood hurricane as they instinctively used their undersized frames to provide shelter for the squirming infants.

"C'mon! Let's get you guys back in the house!" Josie ordered. Arima arrived just in time to be handed Kayla's baby boy. Josie then picked up one of Rachel's baby girls and wrapped her in a blue baby blanket. Adam and Aaron tenderly lifted their infant son and daughter and placed them inside of their jackets. Stellan and Paciano rushed over to the new mothers and began assisting their weary and sore frames to their feet. Trees across the estate were bowed over as the wind and bloody rainfall increased. There were flashes of copper lightning erupting all over the sky. Josie was clutching the baby girl and was nearly blown over by a final gust of wind when she saw an explosion of purple lightning. The red clouds transformed into a lush lavender and the torrential rain of blood turned to a warm purple shower.

Everyone stood in the gentle rainfall and looked upward to the sky as the lavender clouds brightened the entire Earth. "Oh my God! It's over! We've won!" an exuberant Josie shouted out as she heard Prince strum the amplified opening cords of "Purple

Rain." Josie, Arima, Adam, and Aaron lifted the children in the air, laughed and began twirling them in the cleansing purple rain.

All over the Earth, people came out from their tattered shelters and looked up to the sky. They listened to the music and watched the brilliant light show in the clouds as they held hands and swayed. They watched the blood of angels and demons being washed away by the warm rainfall. They wept as they now understood that humanity had just been saved from itself. And they understood that it was now *their* duty to ensure that humanity would persevere.

Josie and Arima listened to each song that was being heard throughout the world and danced. And smiled. And embraced. And wept. And laughed. In the Purple Reign.

EPILOGUE 1

"Well, that was disappointing," Vetis stated with a tone of resignation. "Centuries of hard work down the drain. Ah well. It *was* entertaining, heh, heh, heh." He sat there on his throne of fire in his designated hell within the cosmos. His bright red body was covered in the shifting shadows of the millions of damned souls that he had manipulated into his servitude. His four hands were squeezing human brains that he was using to relieve his tension. The brains were not his only tension relief, however.

He looked down at the orange bulbous man's head that was bobbing from between his legs. The man's sweaty rolls of fat shook and oozed in multiple directions as his head continued its rapid vertical frenzy.

"Well, I suppose it's for the best," Vetis continued. "We'll just chalk this up as a practice run. There are so many other worlds to conquer. And we will have another shot at Enlightenment. If there's one thing that I have, it is time." Vetis then smiled broadly as yet another sadistic plan was being hatched. "Yes! Time! Of course! I am *not* done with the Earth! I can start over! I can go back in time and find fresh new souls to convert. And while these forces of so-called 'good' are spending decades battling the forces that were just defeated, they will be unaware that there is a whole *new* movement being born! A parallel movement! And this time, we will have enough forces to overpower them once and for all! And then, Enlightenment. Yes. Hey! Did anybody take this down? This shit's important!"

"O-o-of course, m-my lord," a condemned soul responded. "You will go back in time to find others to corrupt. They will, in turn, corrupt millions of others. And the two movements will run parallel to one another and overpower the forces of right-eousness. It is a brilliant plan, my lord."

"Of course, it fucking is, I thought of it," Vetis dismissively replied before saying softly to himself, "as long as we don't get any trouble from those damned meddling kids." He then lifted the head of the orange man by his thinning blond hair, looked him in his tearful eyes, smiled and said, "You know, you really fucked up everything you touched on Earth, but I've gotta hand it to you. Credit where credit is due. You really can suck cock. Now get back to work."

EPILOGUE 2

The twins of the twins and the Twins were dubbed 'The Junior Quad,' and settled into their home at the estate. There were two boys and two girls, and they looked identical. Each had pure white hair and perfect, light caramel skin with the faint outline of a lightning bolt embedded into each of their tender faces. Each also had one eye that was brown and one that was blue.

Rachel and Adam named their twin daughters Sigourney and Euna. Kayla and Aaron's twin sons were named Kane and Thanatos. The children contently cooed throughout their first night in the world. The next morning, everyone noticed that they had grown substantially and were well on their way to teething. It was as though they had aged one full year overnight. Which held true on the second morning as they were now ready to be potty trained and were beginning to walk. It was determined on the third day that they had aged three years.

The puzzled parents were frantic to find an answer. "Oh my God!" Kayla screamed out on the morning of day four. "If this continues, they won't live more than three months!"

Rod was called in to work with Lionnel on various tests and Rosa was called in to tap into the children's energy. Every time she concentrated and connected her energy to theirs, she was violently overloaded and passed out, which made the children giggle.

On day five, the Junior Quad were five years old and were able to read, write and speak. Although, they only spoke as a group. Every time the children had something to say it was quadrophonic. On day ten, they were ten years old, and becoming quite mischievous. They would play games with bones that they would find in the yard of the defeated marauders and laugh when they watched violent images on the television. They also delighted in riding the Shetland ponies that had served as their protectors on the evening of their birth.

On day fifteen they were…still ten years old. The Junior Quad approached their concerned parents and explained it to them simultaneously through their four seemingly innocent voices. "Hello, mothers. Hello, fathers. We know that you are confused and worried, but there really isn't a reason to be. We have aged to ten years old, and we will remain that age for all of eternity. Unless someone strikes us down, which will be quite impossible. We are connected. We are four separate bodies connected by one soul. We think alike and speak alike. We understand what our destiny is. We have seen it. There is no reason for you to worry. All you must do is love us. And give us ice cream."

"Very well, then." Adam stated followed by Aaron. "Yes, that seems quite plausible. Oh, what fun games that we will play with our forever ten-year-olds. And yes, ice cream does sound appropriate at a time such as this."

The Twins looked down upon the displeased faces of their wives and noticed them angrily kicking their crossed legs.

"What is wrong Kayla?" Aaron asked followed by Adam's, "Yes. What is wrong Rachel?"

"Well," Rachel began in an exasperated tone. "We're thrilled to have kids and to raise them and everything, but at *some* point, we figured they'd go off to college and shit."

"Yes," Kayla added. "We obviously love them, but at what point do they go off on their own?"

The sisters were answered by four sweet voices coming from the four corners of the room. "You do not have to worry about that mothers. We can look after ourselves. We will stay with you for as long as we are needed here. But once we sense that we are needed elsewhere, we shall go. You really do not have to worry. We will be fine." The foursome then began giggling and running around the room as they were playing 'tag' with dismembered hands.

"Okay, you know what?" Rachel stated. "This is some weird shit, and we haven't been out in ages, and we need a goddam drink. So, you boys change into a clean white suit. We'll ask Arima and Josie to baby…um…child sit. Let's go out, okay?"

"Why yes," Adam enthusiastically responded. "Of course, we can go out and get you drinks!"

"Oh, my yes!" Aaron added. "You may drink as much as you would like. You always ask to play 'Hide the Sausage' when you drink alcohol. Oh, what a fun night of games we will have!"

Kayla shook her head slowly at the Twins and said, "Listen boys. We just pumped two kids out of us two weeks ago. 'Hide the Sausage' just isn't in the cards at the moment, okay?"

"Oh, alright then," a slightly disappointed Aaron replied. "But sometimes you play 'Hide the Sausage' with your mouth. Could we play that way?"

"Yeah, probably," a resigned Rachel responded before looking at her sister. They then both smiled widely and yelled out "Wooooooooo!"

———

"Oh, my fucking *God*! These kids make a fuckin' *mess*!" Josie yelled downstairs to Arima. "I know they're really smart and shit, but they'd better learn to put their fuckin' dirty clothes in a hamper. My dad always said that if the laundry isn't in the hamper, then it isn't getting done! That's why mom rarely had clean clothes to wear. She always left her shit lying all over the place. And why are their clothes covered in blood?"

Josie answered her own question when she saw a lifeless arm sticking out from underneath one of the bunkbeds. "Well," a bemused Josie voiced to herself, "I guess we know what happened to that creepy mailman. Oh well. And why are those ponies sleeping up here with them now? And where *are* the ponies? Hey, Arima! Are the ponies down there?"

"Um, no," Arima casually responded. "Hey. The pizza's here. Do ya want some? It's really good."

"Of course, I want some!" Josie angrily replied as she picked up yet another soiled shirt and threw it in the hamper. "And don't bogart it all! Save me some!"

"Uh, yeah, okay," Arima sheepishly answered. "Yeah, there's still a couple pieces left. It's really good."

"What do you mean *a couple pieces* left?" Josie yelled out as she stomped down the stairs with her sweaty, curly copper hair bouncing. "Have the JQ eaten yet? Hey, where are they?"

"Um, I dunno," Arima replied as she was attempting to discreetly place a half-eaten slice back into the cardboard box. "I thought they were upstairs with you."

"Well, fuck," Josie stated as she felt her anxiety rising. "No ponies, no JQ. Okay. No need to worry. They probably just went out for a ride. No need to worry. I'm sure they'll turn up."

An hour later, a frantic Josie greeted Rosa and Jessie at the door. "Oh my God you guys. Thanks for coming. We've looked everywhere. We have no idea where the JQ are. They couldn't have gotten far, but those ponies are pretty fast. Please, can you help us find them? Can you like Behold their souls or track their energy or something?"

"Sure, easy," Jessie replied as she placed LucyFur on the couch next to her. "Here, Rosa. Take my hand. Tap into my energy and enhance my ability to Behold them. I wanna get this done fast. There's an episode of *Seinfeld* coming on and Cliff always gets turned on by that show for some reason."

Jessie and Rosa held hands and began lightly trembling. After five minutes of concentrated effort, Jessie let go of Rosa's sweaty hand and said softly, "Aw, shit."

"What?" Josie yelled out. "What's wrong? Did you find them?"

"Yeah, we found them, alright," Jessie replied in an annoyed tone. "It looks like I'm gonna miss out on my weekly *Seinfeld* fuck."

"Well, where *are* they?" Josie desperately asked.

"Yeah," Jessie responded as Rosa was holding her shaking head in her hands unsure of whether to laugh or cry. "The question isn't *where* they are. The question is *when* they are. The little bastards can travel through time."

TO BE CONCLUDED IN "TWINFINITY: HANGING CHADS BOOK V"

Song Reference List

The author would like to thank the countless musical artists that have enhanced his entire life. In particular, the author would like to give a heartfelt thank you to the following artists for enhancing the experience of both writing and reading this book.

Cheap Trick- "Hello There"
Beastie Boys- "Sabotage"
Haley Mills- "Let's Get Together"
Bruce Springsteen- "Ghosts"
REM- "Feeling Gravity's Pull"
David Bowie- "Life on Mars"
Pink Floyd- "Hey You"
Jerry Lee Lewis- "Great Balls of Fire"
Love and Rockets- "So Alive"
Rob Zombie- "Living Dead Girl"
AC/DC- "Moneytalks"
XTC- "Dear God"
Rollins Band- "Liar"
Bob Dylan- "The Times They are A-Changin'"
My Life With the Thrill Kill Kult- "Sex on Wheelz"

White Stripes- "I Think I Smell a Rat"
Eileen Barton- "If I Knew You Were Comin' I'd've Baked a Cake"
George Harrison- "My Sweet Lord"
John Lennon- "Imagine"
10,000 Maniacs- "Candy Everybody Wants"
David Bowie & Queen- "Under Pressure"
Elvis Costello- "Radio, Radio"
Kenny Loggins- "Footloose"
Thin Lizzy- "Jailbreak"
Alice Cooper- "Our Love Will Change the World"
Bruce Springsteen- "If I Was the Priest"
David Bowie- "The Wedding Song"
Bikini Kill- "Rebel Girl"
The Pink Spiders- "Little Razorblade"
Dickie- "Forty-Five"
REM- "Why Not Smile" (Reprise)
Brian Jonestown Massacre- "Oh Lord"
Gary US Bonds- "Quarter to Three"
The Raveonettes- "Attack of the Ghostriders"
Neil Sedaka- "Laughter in the Rain"
Bessie Banks- "Go Now"
Prince- "Purple Rain"

PATTYPAZOOLA AKA VICTORYFUCKINPALOOZA

"Oh fuck!" Patty exclaimed as she witnessed the death of the Copperhead at the hands of her daughter from behind Stage One of 'Victoryfuckinpalooza.' "Maddy just ripped that cold-ass bitch in two! Fuck yeah, Mads! Prince, you got what you wanted. You wanted to set the tone for this thing. Well, you got it sweetheart. Get that tight little ass out on that stage and make some motherfuckers cry."

ACT I
Prince- "Purple Rain"
Jerry Lee Lewis- "Great Balls of Fire"

Jimi Hendrix- "All Along the Watchtower"
Freddie Mercury (Queen)- "We are the Champions"
Sam Moore & Dave Prater (Sam & Dave)- "Hold On, I'm Coming"
Joe Strummer (The Clash)- "Know Your Rights"
Ricky Nelson- "Garden Party"
 Lux Interior (The Cramps)- "Surfin' Dead"
Marvin Gaye- "What's Goin' On"
Karen Carpenter (The Carpenters)- "Top of the World"
Tom Petty- "The Waiting"

Patty rushed up to the dressing room door and anxiously knocked on it. "Okay James. Tom's just finishing up on Stage Two, then we'll have a ten-minute break, then you're on Stage One. Make 'em feel it. Make 'em feel the love and triumph. Make their heartbreak go someplace loving. Just like Boston Garden 1968. Make the Earth fuckin' stand up and take notice."

ACT II
James Brown- "I Got You (I Feel Good)"
Tony Williams, David Lynch, Herb Reed, Paul Robi, Zola Taylor (The Platters)- "Smoke Gets in Your Eyes"
Dusty Hill (ZZ Top)- "Tush"
Bill Haley- "See You Later Alligator"
Kurt Cobain (Nirvana)- "Smells Like Teen Spirit"
Stevie Ray Vaughn- "Crossfire"
Dusty Springfield- "Son of a Preacher Man"
David Cassidy- "I Think I Love You"
Whitney Houston- "I Wanna Dance With Somebody"
Sid Vicious (Sex Pistols)- "My Way"
Elvis Presley- "Good Rockin' Tonight"
Little Richard- "Rip It Up"

"Yeah, yeah, I know! I heard ya the first thousand times!" Patty yelled out to Richard Penniman. "I know, I know. You're the *real* king of rock and roll and you ain't openin' for nobody. I got it. And you got the closer in this set. Great job. Now hit the showers.

Okay, where the fuck is Johnny? Oh, there you are. Didn't see you standing there in the shadows all dressed in black and shit. You ready? They are gonna freak the fuck out when you open by introducing yourself!"

ACT III
Johnny Cash- "Folsom Prison Blues"
Otis Redding- "Try a Little Tenderness"
Nilsson- "Without You"
Ritchie Valens- "Come on Let's Go"
Eddie Cochran- "C'mon Everybody"
Robbie Robertson (The Band)- "The Weight"
Ronnie Spector w/ Clarence Clemons & Danny Federici (E Street Band)- "Say Goodbye to Hollywood"
Robin & Maurice Gibb (The Bee Gees)- "Nights on Broadway"
Andy Gibb- "Shadow Dancing"
George Michael- "Faith"
Eddie Van Halen (Van Halen)- "Eruption/You Really Got Me"

"What the fuck are you guys wearing?" Patty yelled out to Johnny, Dee Dee, and Joey. "What's with the pastel leisure suits? I don't fuckin' *care* if you're trying to change your image! Get the fuck back in there and put on your ripped jeans and leather jackets! Jesus Christ! This is a fuckin' rock concert not The Flamingo!"

ACT IV
Joey, Johnny, & Dee Dee Ramone (The Ramones)- "Rock and Roll Radio"
George Jones- "White Lightnin'"
Carl Perkins- "Blue Suede Shoes"
Gene Vincent- "Be Bop a Lula"
Del Shannon- "Runaway"
Johnny Moore, Charlie Thomas, Rudy Lewis, Gene Pearson, Johnny Terry, Jimmy Lewis (The Drifters)- "Under the Boardwalk"
Sinead O'Connor- "Nothing Compares 2 U"

Tony Davis & Cliff Hall (The Spinners)- "Then Came You"
Michael Nesmith, Peter Tork, Davy Jones (The Monkees)- "Listen To the Band"
Chuck Berry- "Reelin' and a Rockin'"
Ruth Brown- "This Little Girl's Gone Rockin'"
Nina Simone- "Mississippi Goddam"

"Howard!" Patty screamed as she opened the dressing room door to make sure the next act was ready. "What the fuck are *you* doing in here? She's the 'Queen of Soul', not the queen of pegging! Get the fuck out of here! I'm so sorry about that Aretha. That little fucker has no respect."

ACT V
Aretha Franklin- "Respect"
Kim Shattuck (The Muffs)- "The Kids in America"
Janis Joplin- "Cry Baby"
Roy Orbison- "Crying"
John Phillips, Cass Elliott, Denny Doherty (The Mamas & The Papas)- "I Saw Her Again Last Night"
Patsy Cline- "Crazy"
Rick Ocasek & Benjamin Orr (The Cars)- "Magic"
Merle Haggard- "I Think I'll Just Sit Here and Drink"
John Lee Hooker- "Boom Boom"
Sam Cooke- "Cupid"
Karl & Dennis Wilson (the Beach Boys)- "Good Vibrations"
Christine McVie (Fleetwood Mac)- "Don't Stop"
Lemmy (Motorhead)- "Ace of Spades"
Bon Scott & Malcolm Young (AC/DC)- "Dirty Deeds Done Dirt Cheap"

"Oh, yeah, Jacklyn. This is the final set. Our last dance tonight," Patty said softy to her eternal wife. "But not our final dance. I'm gonna dance with you for all eternity. And I'm gonna love looking down at my Josie's smiling face as she dances with her Lionnel when "My Girl Josephine" comes on. And Joe and Blair dancing to their song. And all of Joe's friends and family singing along with Bob. Then the closing six songs. It wasn't easy to get them to agree to this, but everyone agreed that Buddy had to close the show. They all said that it just felt right. I did it, Jacklyn. I put on 'Victoryfuckinpalooza.' And *this* shit is just the beginning."

ACT VI
Donna Summer- "Last Dance"
Don & Phil Everly (The Everly Brothers)- "All I Have to do is Dream"
Bob Marley- "Three Little Birds"
Wayne Fontana & The Mindbenders - "A Groovy Kind of Love"
Fats Domino- "My Girl Josephine"
Lou Reed- "White Light / White Heat"
Marc Bolan (T. Rex)- "Cosmic Dancer"
David Bowie- "Life on Mars"
George Harrison- "My Sweet Lord"
John Lennon- "Imagine"
Buddy Holly- "Not Fade Away"